Heavenly Hirani's
School
of
Laughing Yoga

Heavenly Hirani's
School
of
Laughing Yoga

by

SARAH-KATE LYNCH

2015
New Street Communications, LLC
Wickford, RI

newstreetcommunications.com

First Edition published 2014 by Random House, New Zealand.
United States Edition published 2015
by New Street Communications, LLC
Wickford, RI
newstreetcommunications.com

For Barry Robison and Mark Robins,
who got me to Mumbai, then let me have all the fun while they did
all the work.
Spec-TAC-u-LAR!

Be truthful, gentle and fearless.
M. K. Gandhi

Chapter One

Annie knew that her mother's marbles were loose, but had never suspected that one day they would all fly out of the bag at the same time, bouncing into far-flung corners, never to be gathered together again.

That awful morning Eleanor Martyn had presented herself down at the local corner shop in her dressing gown, asking if she could please have a chocolate milkshake, which they had not sold for fifty years. On being told this, Eleanor removed the dressing gown and, naked but for the fuzzy pink bear-claw slippers Annie had given her for Christmas as a joke, wandered along the aisles searching for a suitable alternative.

A neighbor recognized her and called Annie at home, but when she got to the store her mother seemed not to know who Annie was and, worse, seemed not to like the cut of her jib.

A shop assistant had draped the dressing gown back around Eleanor's shoulders, but the shock of seeing her graceful, elegant mother sitting on a plastic chair beside the bread stand with her sagging breasts exposed was one from which Annie doubted she would ever recover. They'd been close, always, but she hadn't seen her mother naked for decades even though she'd lived with Annie and her husband, Hugh, for almost ten years. In fact, now Daisy and Ben had gone off to university in other cities, it was mostly just Annie and her mother at home.

They'd played cards only the day before, and her mother had been fine, Annie was sure of it. Tired, perhaps, and she'd cheated — which was a new development — but fine. Oh, she had forgotten to do her hair, her lips were dry, and she was missing an earring, but there had more often than not been something missing in recent times. Or not matching. Her mother had gone out the month before wearing two different shoes. She'd mislaid three of her four handbags. She'd lost interest in doing jigsaw puzzles.

Annie had thought so little of it yesterday! And now, here Eleanor was; naked and angry — the anger more upsetting than anything — refusing to get dressed, kicking off the bear claws and grabbing at cans of baked beans, which she didn't even like. They didn't like her either, slipping out of her grasp and rolling along the linoleum, one of them hitting her foot before Annie could intervene, splitting her thin skin like a tomato.

That broke Annie's heart. How could such delicate skin ever hope to hold together every wonderful thing that made up her mother? How had it never occurred to her before that Eleanor needed more protection than an organ, so tired after eighty-three years of expert containment, could offer?

The Eleanor she knew seemed to escape into the ether through that brutal slice.

In the days to follow, her gentle loving mother was replaced by a frightened old woman who fought tooth and nail with Annie, with Hugh, with the doctors and even with the police who found her wandering around the neighborhood in the early hours of the morning a week after the corner-shop incident.

'You have to accept the new reality,' the specialist they had been referred to told Annie, patting her hand.

Annie nodded politely, but inside she was howling at the absurdity of the very concept. New reality? Who came up with these things? She wanted to box his ears. What meaningless twaddle.

But by the end of the following month, the twaddle was no longer meaningless. Annie's life had changed forever, her reality was new, and her mother was living at a twenty-four-hour care facility twenty minutes' drive from her house.

'But she might get better,' Annie argued with the specialist when he recommended the move. 'It's been so quick. I can't believe that this is it.'

'In almost one hundred per cent of cases, it does not get better,' he said, adding, perhaps to ease the blow although he didn't seem that sort of a person, 'but in the unlikely event of an improvement, we can revisit Eleanor's domestic situation.'

'Has that ever happened? That someone's gone home?'

'Not to my knowledge.'

Twice in the week before the move Eleanor had slapped Annie in the face, once scratching her from her eye all the way down her cheek. Her mother had never struck anyone as long as she lived, so far as Annie knew. Yet without her in the house Annie panicked. It was bad enough that her children had left home; now she was abandoned by her own darling mother. She spent much of the next month either in tears or baking Eleanor's favorite lemon cake, Daisy's chocolate brownie, and Ben's beloved Anzac biscuits. She loved the way the house smelled, but chucked everything in the trash as soon as it came out of the oven without even tasting it.

Her home — which she had so loved when it was busy with comings and goings — fell silent; three rooms now empty were haunted by memories of chat and clatter and sleepovers and drama and sympathy and love, always love.

Now, all that was left was Hugh, of course, and Bertie, Annie's dog, a wily terrier of mixed origin, a faded redhead who doted on her and she him. Bertie had loved Eleanor, too, and would often be found sleeping on her feet as she sat in her favorite chair in the sunny corner of the living room, but he seemed unmoved by her disappearance. He simply found another spot on the small rug in front of the fireplace in which to snooze in the sun when nothing more interesting was happening, his stump of a tail still wagging maniacally whenever Annie so much as looked at him.

She envied him his adaptability. It didn't seem at all callous coming from a woolly little beast who still cuddled the same sock he'd found balled up under the sofa when he was a puppy.

And then, just weeks after she lost her mother to a depressing room in a dementia ward, Bertie disappeared, too.

Annie had given him his usual breakfast of tuna and rice (ridiculous, she knew, but she could swear he smiled when she got the can of fish out of the pantry) and let him outside into the backyard as she did every morning. By lunchtime he had not come back. By dinnertime she had scoured the neighborhood, rung the vet, the pound, the local radio station and anyone else she could think of, to no avail.

When Hugh got home from work they set off again, separately, calling Bertie's name and knocking on the doors of his favorite neighbors, checking the local park, the school a few blocks away, the now-awful corner shop, the petrol station . . . but of their wily terrier there was not a single trace.

The loss of a dog should not derail a person quite so momentously, Annie knew that, but that did not stop it happening.

She could deal with the children moving away and not needing her, not even keeping in touch, she could deal with her mother moving and not even knowing who she was when she went to visit. She might cry a lot, and be developing an addiction to eating creamed butter and sugar from the bowl, but she could deal with it. She could even deal with a husband who worked long hours, often travelled, and seemed detached, at best, when he was home.

But she could not deal with Bertie's nose not being at the edge of the bed every morning waiting for her to wake up and let him out of the house. She could not deal with him not skittering beneath her feet in the kitchen. She could not bear to see his leash hanging with the children's old raincoats and scarves from the pegs by the back door. She could not stomach the thought of walking down the street without him barking at the birds, or peeing on Mrs Wheeler's letterbox or straining to get even a glimpse of the cat that had once lived across the road but moved three years ago.

Every day for two weeks she called the radio station to advertise Bertie's loss until one day the receptionist kindly suggested she stop. Still, Annie printed up posters and taped them to lampposts, even offering a $500 reward. But the phone number tabs at the bottom of each poster remained intact.

Annie did not remain intact. Her reality was new but she was having trouble accepting it. She still made the bed, tidied the garden and emptied the dishwasher, but she started deliberately mixing the forks with the spoons and knives in the drawer. She stopped reading the foodie section in the newspaper. She gave up going to her weekly girls' Pilates class, and cancelled her appointment with the bitchy hairdresser who charged a fortune for highlights but had the best gossip. When her favorite lipstick got worn to a nub, she started using an old one that she'd earlier discarded because she didn't really like the color. She took to wearing the same clothes two days in a row. And during her daily visits to her mother she just sat quietly next to her, staring out the window, watching Dr Phil or Oprah or The Biggest Loser, with the sound down, no longer patiently explaining who she was, no more trying to recapture the bond she had shared with this kind, remarkable woman for all her life.

She tried not to take it personally when Eleanor seemed frightened of her or, worse, uninterested, preferring the company of the woman in the next room, who had a baby grandson.

'It's not you, it's the disease,' a sweet-faced enrolled nurse told Annie, reading her expression one afternoon.

'But it is me,' Annie wanted to say. How much more personal could it get?

When Eleanor died after just three months in the home,

Annie was stunned. She'd barely had the chance to accept her mother's mind had been swept away to some foreign place when her small, familiar, sweet-scented body had been carried there, too, courtesy of pneumonia.

'It's too soon,' she wept when she got the call. She had not even been there, holding her mother's hand. She'd been at home, watching mindless infomercials on late-night television, wishing that Daisy would call as she had promised. Hugh was away so she'd had peanut butter with raspberry jam on toast for dinner, cheated on the crossword, wept briefly for Bertie, cleaned her teeth, hopped into bed and flicked on the TV.

So routine! If she'd known that day would be Eleanor's last, she would have stayed with her. She should have stayed with her anyway. She'd died alone, her hand clutching the sheet, not the warm flesh of someone who loved her.

They said pneumonia was common, that a lot of the residents got it. They were old and weak, their immune systems were giving up the ghost.

And now her mother was one. And Annie had not been there to ease her exit.

'You could think of it as a happy release,' said the same nurse when she got to the hospital, the shell of her mother impersonating the real thing, lying tiny and empty against the stark white bed linen. 'Some of them live for years and years, you know, and it's very difficult for the family — but your mother was ready to go.'

Annie wanted to re-arrange the features on her sweet, annoying face. Her mother had not been released: she had been catapulted. And she wasn't one of 'them', she was someone else, someone special, someone very deeply loved. As for being ready to go, Eleanor hadn't known where she was, or when, so any choices being made were certainly not being made by her.

The Eleanor that Annie knew would never just have let go, not of her anyway. She wasn't a cheap kite in a brisk northerly — she was her mother's only daughter. A love like that was snatched, wrenched, stolen away — it was not let go. Such a loving, long, uncomplicated story theirs, finished so abruptly; the last neat, healing chapters never to be written.

In the days surrounding the funeral, she felt Bertie's absence like a physical wound. Her arms ached to hold him; she longed to bury her face in his wiry coat, to laugh at his unrequited love affair with the microwave oven. She kept the beloved sock from his puppydom in her handbag, reaching in to squeeze it when no one was around.

The one bright spot was the children coming home. Ben looked unfamiliar and solemn, wearing a suit she'd never seen before and a tight, closed look on his face that she recognized as grown-up grief. Did he have to look so much older every time she saw him? Did nothing stand still? Did reality have to shift every which way?

Daisy at least remained relatively unchanged, sobbing dramatically all through the service and clinging to Annie later that night, inconsolable that her recent plans to come and visit her grandmother had derailed every time.

'She wouldn't have known you anyway, sweetie,' Annie reassured her. 'She wouldn't have known either way. It wasn't her.' It wasn't until she and Hugh had dropped the kids off at the airport for their separate flights back to their different lives, Daisy still red-eyed and emotional, Ben stiff and silent, that Annie realized ??neither of them had asked where Bertie was. She had been crying, at the time, but with that thought her tears dried and knotted in her chest, her throat, behind her eyes, refusing to be shed.

In the days afterward, she moved automatically, in a fog she felt would never lift. She wondered if she would fall into madness or alcoholism like her mother's sister, Vera, who had died of cirrhosis of the liver when Annie was in her twenties, and who had broken her mother's heart for years before with her lies and false promises and endless sob stories.

But Annie didn't much care for drinking these days. She no longer had any vices to fall back on. The kids had teased her about it for years: Mrs Goody Two-Shoes.

If only they knew! Before she grew up and had them, she'd done her time on the wild side. Her first boyfriend had been a musician, into smoking dope and having sex in back alleys and scummy back rooms — not that he'd been very good at it. She'd even dropped acid with him once, although she hadn't cared for the hallucinations. She would rather stay up all night drinking wine with her girlfriends in those days, careening down to the shore in the early dawn to watch the sun come up. She'd been Queen of the Margarita Makers for a while in her early twenties. Tequila was briefly her thing. Not that the kids knew any of this, or would believe her if she told them.

The kids.

She'd thought, somehow, that everything would one day go back to being the way it had been before they went away, with them in and out, busy as bees, but always coming home. But Daisy and Ben now both thought of other places as 'home'. They didn't want to move back, or even check in; they were too busy leading their rich young lives.

And Annie didn't begrudge them that — not at all. She was pleased that she and Hugh had grown two such independent, successful, content young people.

Or she had been.

Now 'pleased' seemed a stretch — everything did. She couldn't quite reach anything, feel anything.

And when Daisy had rung a week after the funeral, not to find out how Annie was coping but to ask if she could have Eleanor's cameo brooch, Annie had fought the urge to hang up. She hadn't been angry, she'd just wanted Daisy to shut up and go away.

This made her feel so sick with guilt that she couldn't eat for two days.

'I think you're depressed,' her friend Rhona said when she dropped in one

afternoon and caught Annie curled up on the sofa, staring into space, a magazine still in its plastic wrapper beside her, her coffee cold on the side table.

'I'm not,' said Annie. 'Depressed? No, honestly. I'm just . . . Well, a lot has happened. All of it awful. So I'm not depressed. I'm just . . . nothing, really. I'm fine.'

'What does Hugh say?'

'About what?'

'About this,' Rhona said, waving her hand at the couch.

'About you.'

'There's nothing to say,' said Annie. And even if there had been,

Hugh wouldn't say it. Hugh wasn't like that, she thought, with a bitterness that surprised her. He was a good husband, a great father, a solid man, a solid person, but he wasn't the type to ask if she was all right, or even notice that she might not be. He never had been.

Then again, she had never not been all right.

'But he must be worried about you,' Rhona said. 'I know I am. It feels like you're disappearing. What can I do?' She looked at her watch. Rhona had four children, three of them still at school, and her husband had decided the previous year that he liked his dental hygienist more than any of them.

Rhona did not have time to worry about Annie.

'Don't go fretting on my account,' Annie said. 'I'll be fine. I'll get another dog. A hamster. A crayfish. Whatever. You know. You go and kiss your darlings for me. Honestly, I'm good.'

But she was not good. She did not want another dog. She wanted Bertie. She really, really wanted Bertie.

And she wanted her kids to move back home, even if that wasn't what they called it anymore, and even if they were silent and selfish when they got there.

She wanted her mother to come back and hold her hand and tell her everything was going to be all right.

And she wanted her husband to— — She didn't know what she wanted from Hugh. It seemed churlish to complain about him when he never really put a foot wrong.

He was not abusive, or angry, or unfaithful, or spiteful, or lazy. He was just like one of those empty rooms upstairs; more alive in the past than in the present. And really was that even so very bad?

Everything would be different, she reasoned, if only she hadn't lost Bertie.

You must accept your new reality, she thought, looking in the hall mirror after Rhona had gone, wondering when the rings under her eyes had got so black, when the frown lines on her forehead had become the most noticeable thing on her face, when everything about her had turned so . . . beige.

Light brown hair, light brown eyes, light brown sweater — her old favorite, a splurge from Comme des Garçons for a boring birthday a few years before, which was only just managing to hang onto its shape, a bit like her. She'd always been a woman on the cusp of beauty rather than right in the middle of it. She needed sharp lines to capture what she had and define it. With tailored clothes, a decent hairstyle and bright lipstick, Annie Jordan sizzled, but without them she faded into the background. What had she been thinking, buying such an expensive piece of exquisite cashmere in fawn? She wouldn't even make it onto a paint chart seeming this drab, let alone be given a glamorous title like Winter Dune or Mystic Pumice.

Her new reality was that Rhona was right; she was disappearing.

Chapter Two

When Hugh came home from work that night, he kissed her on the cheek as he always did, poured himself a whisky and sat at the table, which she had set for their evening meal: a pasta dish that she'd bought from the supermarket and defrosted.

Her lethargy was spreading, infecting the things she used to have energy for, to care about, like her cooking. All her married life she'd been a dedicated home cook. She didn't do fancy, but her babies had eaten vegetables she'd grown and puréed, she'd baked her own organic bread, made all her own cakes and biscuits, put up preserves in the autumn and quince paste in the summer, turned out gallons of tomato relish, strawberry jam, stocks, pie fillings, soups, casseroles and more.

She could still see Daisy's first school lunch — a ham and cheese sandwich wrapped in greaseproof paper tied with string, a cut-up apple, a box of raisins and a chocolate cupcake, low on cake, high on icing, just the way Daisy liked them. Knowing that Daisy was carrying that with her — something Annie had all but made from scratch — had made it easier to send her precious firstborn off for her first day in the big wide world.

And Daisy had put up a fuss, clinging to Annie's legs at the school gates, but only because drama came so naturally to her. The moment she saw her kindergarten friend Tessa skipping into the playground, she was off, smiling and waving before the tears could even dry on her cheeks.

She could remember Ben's first lunch a year later, too.

He'd never liked ham, so just plain old cheese for him. He was always such a serious little boy with his father's dark good looks and black eyes but his own sharp humor; there had never been any blurred edges on Ben. He was definite about everything, right down to the matching lengths on his shoelaces. He had marched off into the vast canyon of the playground and never once looked back.

That was her Ben — always moving forwards.

Through the high-school years Annie had continued to make her children the most beautiful meals, whether they turned up for them or not — hearty cottage pies, French cassoulets, spicy fish stews — moving through Daisy's diet fads as effortlessly as a summer breeze. She'd cracked low GI, low carb, high protein, managed the two-day fast, the Israeli army diet, the liver- cleansing regime, and she'd done it all without starving the rest of the family.

What's more she'd done it with pleasure, even if she didn't think Daisy needed to lose weight. She loved her daughter's rounded form, the delicious flesh in her arms and her rear end. Daisy was perfect just the way she was,

but Annie would do anything to make her happy, so if she wanted leek broth for three days in a row but then said she'd die if she didn't have a chocolate chip and macadamia nut cookie fresh out of the oven, Annie would delight in providing both. Although in truth she was more of a chocolate chip and macadamia nut cookie person. In those days she waited until they were perfectly baked and ate them.

And now here she was not only buying a store-brand arrabiata, but not even bothering to hide the packaging, even though she was pretty sure that Hugh wouldn't know the difference between a defrosted arrabiata and one that she had painstakingly peeled garlic, blanched tomatoes and made her own pasta ribbons for. Nor would he notice that her basil, which usually bloomed enthusiastically in a pot outside the kitchen door, had recently shriveled up and died, along with the mint and coriander she'd had flourishing out there for years.

She plucked some limp spinach out of a plastic bag in the refrigerator and plopped some on each plate, roughly chopping a single tomato that she spread between the two, then adding a bit of Paul Newman ranch, the first commercial dressing she had bought since she was a university student herself.

Not bothering to garnish it any further, she put Hugh's plate in front of him, then sat down. Actually, basil aside, the meal looked pretty much the same as the ones she had put all that effort into. What had been the point, all those years, in going the extra mile?

'Looks delicious, thank you,' Hugh said, helping himself to a mouthful. He ate politely, the way he did everything. 'How was your day?'

She thought about telling him what Rhona had said, about thinking she was depressed, and that Rhona wanted to know what he thought.

But Annie wasn't depressed. So why bother asking Hugh if he thought she was? What difference would it make? 'I called the pound again,' she said. 'Twice, actually, because the usual manager has been away but now he's back.'

'Annie, sweetheart, it's been almost three months.'

'Yes, but if he'd been hurt, or lost, and someone found him, that could take a while, couldn't it?'

Hugh had stopped eating.

'Or if he had amnesia . . . ' It sounded so stupid when she said it out loud. But that's what she'd been thinking all afternoon. If people could get amnesia, then surely dogs could, too.

She'd tried to stop thinking about Bertie and start thinking about something else, but nothing took. She had idly considered updating the curtains in the front room, but that was the sort of thing she would normally talk about with her mother. They'd look at magazines together for ideas, go shopping for fabric, then Eleanor would get out her sewing machine and run them up, because Annie was a good cook but a woeful seamstress. She'd sewn her own finger to a pillowcase when she was fourteen and had not been near a sharp needle since. And who cared about the curtains now anyway? She could probably hang old pantyhose from the railing and Hugh wouldn't notice.

'Anyway,' she said, forcing herself to sound brighter, 'the manager at the pound said he would let me know if he heard anything or obviously if Bertie turned up. He has the photos and he sounded very nice so I guess I just felt better after talking to him.'

That wasn't true. The manager had been very sympathetic as she cried helplessly down the phone, but had sounded doubtful about the amnesia, about the chance of Bertie coming back. He talked to her as if she'd had a stroke.

'Have you got someone there?' he'd asked, and she wondered if he meant a nurse, of the psychiatric type. And no, anyway, she did not have anyone there so that just made the crying worse.

Hugh still wasn't eating his pasta.

He was staring at his plate, as though trying to decide what to say next.

Not for the first time Annie was surprised, when she looked at him, to notice that he had aged. Not that he was doing it blandly, like she was, but just that he was doing it at all. His hair was now completely silver, as was the stubble that dusted his square jaw, his olive skin, like glitter. He still went running most days, so he had escaped the middle-age spread that so many other men his age wore so proudly, or disguised with low-riding pants or hitched up ones, and he had perfect eyesight, so he did not wear glasses.

He really is very good-looking, she thought, as though he were a stranger she was seeing for the first time.

He looked up and saw her staring at him, and such an unfamiliar, unreadable expression crossed his face that she felt a flutter of alarm. Then he leaned over and put his hand on her arm, which was poised to push another tube of rigatoni around her plate.

She looked down at his stranger's hand, taken aback for reasons that really ought not to exist. Did he not even touch her anymore? Not even on the arm? Or did they not look at each other anymore? She felt as though she was floating in space, separated from everything she should know.

She thought of the last time they'd made love. Their sex life might lack the fireworks of their early days, but they still had one. She'd felt so close to him after her mother died, she'd wanted to crawl inside him some nights, suck all the warmth out of him, the strength, the reliability. She'd been able to forget her sadness in bed, with him, in the dark.

But it was hardly passionate. They were like two old slippers ending up together because one was left and one was right.

'I have something for you,' he said, getting up and going to his briefcase, which was sitting in its usual spot next to the sideboard. He pulled out an envelope and handed it to her.

Her first thought was that it was divorce papers.

Her second thought was that she shouldn't have had the first thought.

Her third thought was that if it was divorce papers she didn't know how she felt about that but she probably should.

She took the envelope. Of course it wasn't going to be divorce papers. Hugh was silent, but he wasn't that silent. And anyway, divorce papers probably didn't even exist anymore. They were probably delivered online. Or Tweeted.

It was more likely a voucher for a massage, which she didn't want. Or deeds to the beach house they'd talked about buying for years, which she also no longer wanted. Or even a letter saying Hugh's rich uncle in Canada whom he'd never met had died and left him all his money. But she didn't want that either. She wouldn't say no to it, but she didn't particularly want it.

She opened the envelope and pulled out what was inside.

It was an itinerary, with her name at the top, for a trip to Mumbai. 'Mumbai?' Annie was stunned. 'In India?'

Annie had backpacked — somewhat reluctantly it had to be said — around Europe after college, but she had never been that keen on flying. And even if she had been, India topped the long list of places she definitely never wanted to go. Ever.

'I have to go there again for work,' Hugh said. 'Week after next. And I thought you might like to come, too.'

Why? She'd never expressed the slightest interest in joining him on any of his previous trips. He was an agricultural engineer. His business trips were all about banana-picking machines and combine harvesters.

Besides she had to stay home and — —

Annie folded the itinerary, put it back in the envelope, laid it on the table and patted it as though she would return to it later. She picked up her fork and started to poke at the same limp piece of rigatoni.

It might look the same, but how Hugh could not taste that this meal was inferior she couldn't fathom. But then he'd just bought her — bought her — tickets to one of the biggest, smelliest cities in one of the world's poorest, filthiest countries.

'How's your meal?' she asked.

'Very good, thank you, as always,' he answered, which just went to show he knew more about manners than he knew about cooking.

But when he finished, he pushed his plate away, looked at the envelope on the table, and said, quietly, with a desperation that hit her like a punch to the stomach: 'Please,

Annie. Please.'

He got up, took his plate to the kitchen sink, rinsed it and put it in the dishwasher, the same as ever.

Chapter Three

Annie woke early the next morning, and instead of getting out of bed straight away, as was her routine, she turned over and watched her husband sleep.

He looked sad, she thought. Even in his sleep, relaxed, breathing regularly and peacefully, he looked sad.

She hadn't noticed that before either — just as she hadn't noticed he looked like an older man. Or maybe he hadn't looked sad before. Or maybe she really had stopped looking at him.

He had beautiful eyelashes. They weren't sad at all: curved thick and black, they looked more like fringed smiles on his cheeks. It was his mouth, perhaps, that was giving him a melancholy appearance. When he was awake his mouth was straight in something less than a smile but definitely not a grimace — a totally non-committal expression, when she thought about it.

But in sleep, relaxed, the corners were turned ever so slightly down. And perhaps his eyebrows were crumpled in a way that gravity disguised when he was upright.

If her husband was practising in his waking hours just to be non-committal, then Houston, we have a problem, Annie thought.

Space. That was it: that was the problem. Not the sky sort of space but the empty sort here on Earth. In the house. In her. In Hugh. Too much space.

They'd had a solid marriage, she was sure she was right about that, better than most, until it had turned into whatever it was now. Not a bad thing, but hardly even a thing at all. Still, it was uncomplicated — at least that was one way of looking at it, which she hadn't really done very often but was doing now, because of all the space.

She'd loved Hugh from the first moment she met him, although the feeling then had been so small she hadn't put it down to love. Not in that precise moment. It was more like she had suddenly come upon a vast foreign sea and, unable to resist the water, had dipped her toe in but could not immediately tell if it was hot or cold.

A week after meeting him she knew that it was love — the water was perfect — and that she would not be surprised if they ended up getting married.

He had always been and remained a little buttoned-up, which she came to know was because his father had abandoned him and his mother when he was very young and he'd spent most of his childhood at boarding school or with his elderly grandparents. He'd also told her right at the beginning that he didn't talk much but that didn't mean he wasn't a thinker.

She liked that he knew this about himself, and that he also knew that it needed saying. And she liked that, although he was quiet, he didn't lack confidence. He was more sure of himself than just about anyone else she knew, and he was more sure of her than she was.

They were both only children, though neither was particularly needy. Annie certainly didn't require a man who talked about his feelings and was constantly asking about hers. They were more matter-of-fact than that.

And although Hugh was serious, so was she in many ways; but that didn't mean they didn't have fun. For a start, they were hot for each other, as the kids would say now. ('It's always the quiet ones,' Eleanor had teased her back at the beginning of the romance.)

In those early days they made out everywhere — she'd caught that bug (and luckily only that) from the stoner musician — so she and Hugh were at it like rabbits; in the back of the car, at the beach, once in his mother's kitchen when she was upstairs, twice in the restroom at their favorite bar. Whenever and wherever they got the chance, they were tearing each other's clothes off, desperate for skin, for heat, for fire.

They had fun with their clothes on, too; skiing in the winter, surfing lessons in the summer, going to rock concerts and to see live bands in seedy pubs, throwing pot-luck dinner parties, and then the children came along and Annie could not have been happier.

She left her job in HR at the city's biggest bank without so much as a backwards glance, so keen was she to start her family. She'd fallen into HR anyway, and had little interest in knowing more or getting further where banking was concerned. Now she couldn't believe she had let herself fall into and out of a career. She'd wanted to be a tight-rope walker when she was a little girl, and as a teen had written to RADA in London to find out about drama school auditions. What had happened? Even after graduation she had aspired to work for one of the sexy start-ups in the upper echelons of the finance world. Next minute she was a stay-at-home mom.

And she and Hugh had been so close when Daisy came along, and, not long after, Ben: the three of them and then the four. One perfect modern family wrapped up in a bow and sealed with a million kisses.

Then, when her mother grew frail and started talking about moving somewhere where an eye could be kept on her, Hugh had welcomed her into their house without a murmur of anything even approaching disapproval.

If Annie wanted it, he approved. That had been the story of their marriage. It would be on his headstone, Annie thought. What was the matter with her that it felt like a bad thing?

His happy eyelids fluttered in his sleep, but the rest of his face stayed sad.

They'd had their problems, just like anyone. They'd stretched themselves too far when they first bought the house, Hugh had hurt his back in a minor car accident, Ben had been wrongly, briefly, diagnosed with a terrible childhood illness — but these all seemed pedestrian challenges in retrospect, now that they were well survived.

And there'd been a third baby, miscarried at twelve weeks, just as they were about to announce the impending arrival of their 'little autumn leaf'.

Hugh had initially not wanted a third child, saying they had two perfectly healthy ones already, but because Annie wanted it, he had approved, and eventually it all but came to be. She resented him, for a while, after the baby was lost, even though the fault had not been his, had not been anybody's, as every man and his dog kept telling her, moony eyes glowing with sympathy.

And Hugh had been as heartbroken as she was, white-faced and pinched with grief and worry, so she could not hold onto her bitterness. She was too tired, and too busy with the older two.

Ben had seemed relatively unaffected, as one would perhaps expect in a six-year-old, but Daisy had been seven and going through a strange period, perhaps brought on by her mother's pregnancy. They had stupidly told the children about the baby just days before the miscarriage, so she was understandably confused, then tearful, and at times so anxious that Annie thought they might need to seek professional help for her.

It was Rhona who, aghast at the very idea of 'paying a shrink to counsel a Muppet', suggested that instead they get a puppy.

And so Annie had found Bertie (number one), who had tumbled into their family and made them all laugh with his adorable face, his wicked sense of humor, his trick of bouncing up and down on the spot when he saw them.

Had it been a stupid idea, to cheer up a slightly dented family with a dog? Was the family really only slightly dented? Perhaps Annie had swept too much under the rug. Perhaps it was she who should have been in therapy.

The only thing she knew for sure was that Bertie was loved so much by all the Jordans, that he brought so much joy to their lives no matter what the reason for getting him in the first place, that when he went to doggie heaven at ten years of age, she went straight out the very next day and got Bertie (number two).

Her mother had been horrified at the lack of name change, saying it was bad luck, and disrespectful to number one, but Annie would not budge.

She just could not bear the thought of a world without a Bertie in it.

She still couldn't.

But if she went out and got another Bertie now, it was accepting that the missing one was gone forever and she just could not do that. Without proof, she couldn't do it.

Annie rolled over and looked at the photo on the nightstand of Ben and Daisy, taken the Christmas before as they clutched each other and kidded around, Daisy with her long blonde hair perfectly coiffed as usual, and Ben with Hugh's good looks and seriousness but that rampant streak of mischief no one could miss.

She imagined their lost child — she had always felt she was a girl — in that photo; at fifteen she would have been the annoying teenage sister. Would she have fair hair like Daisy or be dark like Ben? Be a flibbertigibbet obsessed with nails and necklaces or a buttoned-down scholar with a mind-boggling work ethic? Or a combination, or something entirely different?

Hugh groaned quietly in his sleep and she tried to pinpoint the last time they'd been anywhere together, done something special, just the two of them, but couldn't. They had visited the kids a few months back, quite a few when she thought about it, then she had gone away for the weekend with Rhona before her mother had gone so horribly downhill . . . and Hugh had continued to travel each month for work, but together? It didn't happen.

When he woke up, Annie was still watching him, pondering this. His sharp blue eyes sprang open, and although his body didn't move he was instantly alert, as though waiting for something terrible to happen. His mouth was immediately pulled back into its straight line, his eyebrows slightly raised to reduce the frown lines that gave away his worries as he slept.

He is worried, Annie thought, with a jolt. He was worried about her. He thought the something terrible was going to happen to her, or be her.

She knew that, just by looking at him, just by watching the way he gathered himself up in wakefulness to be prepared.

She was low, she knew that, beyond low. But she would never do anything terrible, anything stupid. She hadn't even begun to contemplate such a thing. She just couldn't, because of Daisy, because of Ben, because she was Mrs Goody Two-Shoes. And she could never put her children through the pain she felt now at the loss of her own mother.

Besides, couldn't Hugh remember the hell they went through when Daisy was pronounced by the school counselor to be suicidal when she had just turned seventeen? She'd been dumped by her boyfriend not long after another girl in her year died in a horrific car crash. At the time, Annie had put her daughter's moodiness and distance down to another 'phase'. She was definitely a phase sort of girl. So she was devastated to learn that she'd failed to recognize the far more chilling truth. After that, she was afraid to leave Daisy alone for even a moment. Her heart jumped out of her chest every time the phone rang. For a brief period she had to take anti-anxiety medication herself, she was so terrified for Daisy's safety.

Hugh knew the awful toll that had taken on them all.

Did he really think she would do anything, now, other than carry on? Carrying on was her only option. She was good when it came to carrying on. She always had been. Two small babies and a too-big mortgage: she carried on. Two school-age kids and a lost child: she carried on. A dearly departed mother and a much-beloved lost dog . . .

What Annie was currently doing was falling slightly short of carrying on. She saw that now, clear as crystal.

Bloody Bertie! It was his loss that was the nail in the coffin of her old life. She could still hear the echo of the hammer that drove it in ringing inside her, bouncing off the walls into all that empty nothingness.

Yes, she had the big house, the lovely — if slightly absent — family, the clothes, the shopping, the friends . . . but she wanted that stupid dog. And knowing that a scrawny terrier was at the bottom of her hollow pit of despair just threw a layer of shame over the nothingness. Other people in other places would think that Annie Jordan was the luckiest woman alive.

So perhaps she needed to find other people in other places.

Perhaps, she thought, staring deep into the dark blue oceans of Hugh's anxious eyes, other people in other places might help her find a point between this bland plateau she was balancing on right now and — if not happiness, then something like it. And perhaps it would be good for her and Hugh, too. Perhaps it would reignite their old spark to spend time together somewhere new and unfamiliar, where it might reek, but not of change or loss.

'About Mumbai,' she said. 'About Mumbai,' he

repeated. 'I'll come.'

He took this in, blinked, then a smile spread slowly across his face. His lovely mouth turned itself up to match his happy eyelashes.

But what she couldn't miss was that even when he smiled, he looked sad. It wasn't an expression, it was an atmosphere; it clung to him.

There was so much she wanted to say to him then, in the half- light of the morning, with all their history so fresh in her mind, with the sort of fleeting clarity that lying awake in the dark sometimes brought.

But was it clarity? Or was it insomniac madness? It was hard to tell.

And her grief was still too close to the surface while beneath it bubbled many complications. She couldn't decipher them herself, let alone explain them to anyone else, and anyway, over the years she had lost the art of speaking from the heart.

Actually, she'd never been much good at it — that's probably why she and Hugh had got on so well from the beginning — but maybe that was because there had been no need. And now when there was, when it would have felt like a release to articulate what she was having trouble even feeling, her heart felt like a stranger, any meaningful words too hard to come by.

Instead, she reached under the covers until she found her husband's hand and held it for a moment, sliding her fingers between his and squeezing.

'I'll go put the coffee on,' she said.

Chapter Four

Annie stepped out of the cool air-conditioned interior of the baggage claim area in Chhatrapati Shivaji Airport and into the furnace-like heat of the Mumbai arrivals hall.

Hugh was two steps ahead of her, which she tried not to find annoying. Once upon a time they walked everywhere side by side, holding hands, or holding children's hands. She couldn't remember when Hugh had moved ahead, but thought in India, of all places, they should be keeping in step.

India! What an assault on the ears and eyes!

Brown-skinned people dressed in a shock of different colors were five deep against the arrival-hall barriers, holding signs, flowers, balloons, each other. Someone, somewhere, was wailing, children were shrieking, a loud booming laugh floated over the crowd like a blimp.

'Sera, sera, sera, sera!' an old woman was shrieking, tears streaming down her face; another elderly woman clutched her from behind, also crying.

So much color and not a single white face anywhere, not in the crowd, behind it, in front of it. Even on the plane they'd been hard to spot. If Hugh had waited for her she would have asked him if that was always the case; if foreigners were always so few and far between, but instead, he was even further ahead and now greeting a short, rotund man with large, dark eyes, a slightly dusty toupee and a bright, white smile.

'Ali, my man, lovely to see you again,' Hugh said, turning to introduce Annie when she caught up. 'Annie, this is Ali, my faithful driver, isn't that right, Ali?'

Annie smiled although she didn't want to shake Ali's hand — she'd become more and more worried about germs the closer the trip got — but she could hardly ignore the one he proffered.

She grasped it and shook, imagining the amoebas jumping from him to her the way they did in disinfectant commercials, hoping that he — or anyone else who might have been looking — could not tell from her face how horrified she was.

When they found their white 4WD, jammed in the sweltering car park amid what seemed like thousands of other identical ones, Annie eschewed the front passenger seat that Hugh offered her and slid into the back, surreptitiously scrabbling in her handbag for a bottle of antiseptic, splurting it on her palms, rubbing them together. Hillary Clinton used it in far more developed countries than this, so it couldn't be that rude.

Still, when Ali looked at her in the rear-vision mirror, she lowered her hands and kept rubbing, distracting him with a smile. 'You OK?' Hugh asked, as they pulled away from the airport terminal.

She nodded, then looked out of the window, squinting and reaching for her sunglasses.

The flight had been made bearable by an empty seat next to her and a sleeping pill. She didn't know what day it was, or what time, but the world outside the SUV was dazzlingly bright.

And the scene that was now unfolding on the roads in front of, behind, and beside her was making her dizzy.

She'd felt sick ever since reading in the airline magazine that Mumbai was one of the world's biggest cities with a population of nearly twenty-four million people.

Twenty-four million? Just knowing that was bad enough, but what was worse was the fact that every single one of them seemed to be attempting to merge with the car she was in right at that very moment as they joined the freeway heading towards the central city.

Annie was a confident enough driver at home, but had been in a car accident with her father when she was very young so had always been a nervous passenger. In Mumbai, she realized, she was never going to be anything but a passenger. She was going to spend two weeks feeling on the brink of disaster. It was going to be a nightmare.

Shambolic didn't even begin to describe the battle that raged around her.

Uniform high-rise buildings lined the surprisingly modern wide road they were on, just as in any hectic metropolis, but every lane, not that they were recognized as such, was choked with cars, vans, trucks, buses, motorized rickshaws and everything in between.

The squealing of brakes and honking of horns was deafening. Every vehicle was trying to move at the same time, in the same direction, at the same pace. It was bedlam.

Two buses — one bright yellow and one wildly decorated orange — converged in front of their car, cutting them off. Annie jumped as Ali honked with such ferocity that she was surprised the steering wheel didn't disintegrate beneath his fist.

She gripped the seatbelt crossing her chest with both

hands.

Somehow, a motorcycle bearing two portly men in purple turbans squeezed between their car and the buses. Behind them, someone else — everyone else — was honking. On their other side, another motorcycle,

carrying a young couple — the woman riding pillion wearing a primrose sari — inched through an impossibly small gap.

Annie inhaled, as if she could make the whole car suck its stomach in, pull itself tighter, take up less room, just as the buses started to move. Ali took this fleeting opportunity to shoot forwards, right through the centre, honking for his life, parting the traffic like the Red Sea without — miraculously — touching another vehicle.

Annie closed her eyes. How would she ever cope with such chaos?

She could feel beads of sweat pooling on her skin beneath her shirt even though the air-conditioning was icy cold.

Her heart was beating too fast.

She should have stayed at home. She didn't want to be here. She had teetered on the brink of pulling out so many times since telling Hugh she would come to India with him. But every time she opened her mouth to tell him she needed to stay home, she had imagined him asking, 'What for?'

'Don't look out the front,' Hugh said. 'Look out your window. Look out the side.'

She opened her eyes and directed her gaze across the top of the torrid ocean of vehicles. The high-rise buildings further away from the airport looked like grimy apartments, not shiny new offices. Washing hung from nearly every dusty terrace like bright necklaces on weathered old necks.

In front of these buildings, which were only spitting distance from the many- laned freeway, crouched rows of temporary-looking shanty shops; they were nothing more than poles and old tarps, really, held together by grubby signs and rusty sheets of corrugated iron, but each selling something specific: garlands of flowers next to clay pipes, car tyres next to baby shoes, broken chairs, sewing machines, fruit, coconuts, carpets.

It was as if a giant hand had opened in the sky and just dropped everything it was holding down onto this one dusty strip.

In front of the shanty shops, a constantly moving sea of pedestrians flowed back and forth in a kaleidoscope of colors. They were close enough to touch and be touched by the traffic, yet no one seemed ruffled in the slightest.

Some tiny children were playing with an empty tin and a stick practically beneath the wheels of a gaudily painted bus that had stopped on the side of the road despite the bumpy snake of honking vehicles behind it.

One was a little girl with a short haircut, about three, Annie thought. When Daisy was three she had refused to wear anything but white, and would not so much as step outside even wearing gumboots if she thought she was going to get dirty. She still did not like the dirt.

Annie turned to look at Hugh.

'Not what you were expecting?' he asked.

'I don't know what I was expecting,' she said. 'Beggars, I suppose. But they wouldn't last a minute in this traffic. I hadn't thought about the traffic. It's unbelievable.'

'You'll see them,' said Hugh. 'The beggars. But there are not great armies of them. Not that I've seen anyway.'

'And are they missing limbs, and eyes, and all of that?'

'Occasionally, down in South Mumbai, the tourist part of town. But otherwise I think you'll find that Mumbaikars regard *Slumdog Millionaire* as somewhat misrepresenting the case. It's not like home, but it's not Hell on earth either.'

'But the poverty, Hugh.'

'Yes, there's a lot of it. And maybe I've just gotten used to it. But Mumbai's probably not that typical anyway, because there are also more billionaires here than in any other city in the world.'

'That doesn't make sense!'

'Not to us.'

'Not to anyone.'

'India's possibly not the best place to come to if you're looking for sense.'

Out the window, on the other side of the road, there was a hole in the never-ending stretch of high-rises, the ground level suddenly eaten up by a sprawl of small shabby mud-colored low- slung roofs undulating over the land like an enormous dirty carpet with an uneven pile.

'Speaking of poverty,' said Hugh. 'That's a real slum.'

'Oh, I saw one of these right by the runway as we landed,' Annie said. She still had the indents in her palms from clenching her fists so tightly. 'But they all have satellite dishes.'

'Welcome to Bombay, ma'am,' interjected Ali. 'Even the poor peoples have TV!'

'Bombay or Mumbai?'

'Both, madam. Bombay for the old ones such as me, and Mumbai for the young ones, such as everyone else.'

Annie sank back into the cool air-conditioning of the car, soured only slightly by the smell of Ali's armpits.

It occurred to her that she had not even seen *Slumdog Millionaire*. Hugh must have watched it on his own. On a plane, most likely. She certainly couldn't remember the last time they'd been to a movie together, or even watched one at home.

They jerked to a stop, the traffic snarled in front of them, the honking reaching a frightening crescendo. She looked up to see a half-finished empty high-rise building. She could see right through its unfinished door-and- window-shaped holes to the sky on the other side. A group of boys was playing cricket on one of the upper floors.

She turned to point this out to Hugh, but he was busy texting. Annie still resisted texting. It wasn't that she was against it in principle, it was more that her forty-nine-year-old fingers and matching eyes did not have the required co-ordination to spell things the way she meant to or send them to whom she intended.

The frenetic freeway continued, every mile almost identical to the one before, but eventually they turned off it — although Annie personally would not have picked the rocky slope covered in litter as an off-ramp — and descended into a different sort of landscape.

Here the buildings were not as tall and the wide dusty streets were also filled with battling traffic, but they were at least haphazardly tree-lined. The storefronts were enclosed, not shanty-like, although the sea of vibrantly clothed Indians was still in perpetual motion in front of them.

'Nearly there, ma'am,' Ali said, eyeing Annie in the rear-vision mirror again as they turned a corner, narrowly missing a straggling family of about twenty people of varying sizes who were crossing against the lights in front of them.

'On this left, very famous Bollywood movie star's house. Very famous. Lots of Bollywood stars stay here, madam. On this right, Arabian Sea.'

Annie hoped the Bollywood stars were better-looking than the sea; it was muddy and drab, its closest waves washing half- heartedly over jagged rocks near the road. A collection of rabid- looking dogs lounged in the shade of a dried-up tree circled by leaning motorbikes.

She really should have stayed at home even if all she did there was lie on the couch and stare out the window. This was all too . . . wrong, frightening, unfamiliar. She was just not the sort of person who went to India. She knew exactly what those women were like: they came home wearing colored muslin tunics and meditating and eating vegetarian curries until their pores started to ooze so much garlic and turmeric you could smell them a mile off.

There had been one such Indiophile in the short-lived book club she'd belonged to when the children were younger: Sandra, or Sandrine. She'd hosted the group one night to talk about The God of Small Things, which Annie hadn't even read, and had made a curry so hot that everyone apart from Sandra or Sandrine herself was catapulted into speechless hot flushes. She'd served beer instead of wine, and at the time Annie had thought her decor was gaudy, to say the least, all oranges and yellows and pinks.

Of course the colors made sense now, and Annie had only been in India an hour. With a pang she remembered that in those book- club days Sandra or Sandrine's only son had just moved to the other side of the country and she'd been almost hysterically bereft without him.

The other younger mothers, including Annie, had been unsympathetic in a 'come back when you've got a real problem' sort of a way. They'd joked about how they couldn't wait to get their children off their hands. A cheese board and something by Jackie Collins next time, thank you very much! Oh, the smugness of young mothers. She cringed even thinking about it.

She didn't know what had happened to Sandra or Sandrine. Or the book club, for that matter. It had fizzled out. Or she had.

A family on a motorbike pulled up beside them — a thin collection of dark- skinned people wearing a blooming garden of color.

A little girl, two at the most, was sandwiched between her father and an older brother, who was tickling her. She was wearing a synthetic Santa Claus hat despite it being May and thirty-five degrees.

The little girl wriggled around to escape her brother's teasing, laughing so hard her little white teeth glinted like a pearl bracelet in her mouth. Behind them, her mother smiled and turned, catching Annie's eye.

Annie smiled back, and the motorcycle lurched into the

traffic and disappeared.

Little girls were little girls no matter where they were, and mothers were mothers. Annie would no sooner have ridden with their children on a motorbike than left them overnight in a casino parking lot, but the way a mother feels seeing her babies erupt in unbridled joy? The same, everywhere.

And the way a mother feels when her babies grow up and she doesn't see them at all? Also the same. Just ask Sandra. Or Sandrine. At the end of the seaside boulevard the road terminated at the entrance to their hotel, the Taj Lands End, a tall, plain building whose external gates were studded with security officers.

They stopped Ali with white-gloved hands, checked the boot, the hood and underneath the chassis of the SUV with a mirror on a pole.

'Because of the terrorisms,' Ali said, cheerfully. Annie looked at Hugh.

'There were a couple of attacks a few years ago, but nothing you need to worry about now,' he said. 'Honestly.'

At the entrance to the hotel lobby, however, Annie had to surrender her handbag to an X-ray machine and walk through a security scanner, causing the waves of panic that had been shimmying up and down her body like flappers' tassels to return.

Just a few moments standing out in the searing heat and she was drained and anxious, but as she stepped out of the revolving door and into the pristine cool of the Taj lobby, the honking of horns was siphoned from her hearing, the hustle of the traffic replaced by the cool ballet of well-dressed staff and guests gliding across the vast marble floors.

She began to relax.

'Welcome to the Taj Lands End,' a handsome young man in hotel livery said to her, his eyes sparkling. 'And welcome back to you, Mr Hugh Jordan. Very, very nice to see your beautiful wife has been able to come with you this time. Very nice.'

He wobbled his head from side to side as he spoke, which Annie had assumed was a made-up thing, but she'd noticed Ali, the driver, doing it too.

Hugh moved towards the check-in desk, but the young man, Mahendra, according to his name badge, shook his head, the ordinary way. 'Oh, no need for such a valued customer as you, sir. Please, follow me, and I will take you and Mrs Hugh Jordan straight away to your room.'

'Room' was something of an understatement. It was a suite, with a vast king-sized bed, a writing desk, a walk-in closet, and a bigger bathroom than any at home. It had a view of an elegant curved bridge sweeping out into the Arabian Sea — which sparkled and glistened like a proper ocean from this vantage point — connecting the promontory on which the hotel sat to an island of skyscrapers on the other side.

'Lands End is in Bandra,' said Hugh, indicating the cityscape, 'and that over there is South Mumbai. That's the real deal.'

'If there is anything I can do for you, Mrs Hugh Jordan, while Mr Hugh Jordan is here for his work,' said Mahendra, 'please just ring the front desk and I will do my best to make sure your visit to Mumbai is the most top quality it can be.'

She thanked him, still transfixed by the head wobbling, and, eyes still sparkling, he left.

'Has he confused us with visiting royalty?' Annie asked.

'No, that's just the way the hotel staff are here. Very nice, don't you think?'

'Very nice.'

They ate that night in the most tourist-friendly of the hotel restaurants, Hugh having his 'usual' of some sort of fragrant chicken curry while Annie played it safe with a club sandwich — no lettuce or tomato. She'd read that eating vegetables that weren't washed properly was just as likely to end in the dreaded Delhi Belly as drinking the tap water, and she was not going to do either.

'They seem to know you so well,' she said, ordering a hot tea even though Hugh said the bottled water was safe. (Rhona had watched something on TV that claimed it was just swamp water in disguise, collected from the dripping drains of filthy slums by emaciated children and old women.)

'I guess it's their job to know me well,' Hugh said, with a half-smile that made her think he was pleased to be seen, to be remembered.

He nodded at someone else behind her, and the half-smile turned into a full one.

I understand that, she thought, sipping her tea: the need to have someone really see you.

She was just surprised to recognize the same thing in her husband.

Chapter Five

Annie slept like the dead, her body desperate to be supine and still. She barely woke even when Hugh rose to go to work, mumbling her goodbyes and falling straight back into a deep, dreamless sleep.

When she finally did get up, she pulled back the curtains and gazed out at the curved bridge and the spikes of South Mumbai across the water.

She could now see more flattened dull areas of low-rise housing on the rocks on the far side of the bridge, but in front of them brightly colored fishing boats were bobbing in the waves like ocean ornaments, and out to the west of the bridge, past the hazy skyline, cargo ships moved like tiny bugs along the horizon.

As far as views went, it was pretty impressive. She hadn't even known Mumbai was on the coast until Hugh mentioned it a few days before they left. She hadn't really thought of India as a seaside destination. But then again, she hadn't really thought of India at all.

She pressed her forehead against the cold glass of the massive window and looked down. There was a swimming pool nestled in the lush gardens eighteen floors below. It was round, with a mosaic star in the middle; a woman in a fluorescent green swimsuit was swimming lazy laps right through the middle of the star as she watched.

Striped umbrellas circled the pool like curls, with yellow and white towels laid neatly on blue loungers stacked on a terrace that faced out towards the sea. Coconut palms rimmed the area, and Annie thought that from ground level it probably looked like any five-star hotel pool anywhere in the world.

As she thought that, something caught her eye: a movement or a series of movements over the hotel fence on the patchy no-man's-land that stretched out to the rocks and sea.

She squinted. She was of an age where squinting just came with the territory. The ant-like procession turned out to be children, walking single-file over what looked like rubble towards a large mud-colored bank.

When they started disappearing inside holes in the bank, Annie squinted even harder and realized with a shock that it was in fact another slum, each hut a perfect shade of mud, some dug out of the side of a gentle rise in the land, and some shanties like the ones she'd seen coming in from the airport.

The pool might be generic, but she wondered how many other five-star hotels had a sprawling slum spreading like moss right over the fence.

She skipped breakfast, shy about going to the restaurant on her own, and instead went to the gym, where the treadmills faced out towards the ocean and she could imagine she was back home at the health club Daisy had made her join, and which she had been to only twice. Even then she'd only gone because Daisy went with her. How she'd admired her daughter's easy confidence with the buff young men lifting ridiculously heavy weights, with the chunky receptionist, the tanorexic on the treadmill next to her. Time with her daughter had become so precious in recent years that she would happily spend an hour pretending to climb stairs just for the pleasure of doing it next to her.

There were no other white people working out in the Taj gym, just a very overweight young Indian man being put through his paces by a bored-looking trainer. The young man was running from one side of the gym to the other with the sort of lethargy usually only demonstrated by people lying on sofas.

He wore an expensive watch, and a thick gold chain around his neck, and Annie got the impression that it wasn't his idea to be spending the morning sweating and pretending to lift barbells. The trainer had pretty much the same look.

The only other person in the gym was a sinewy woman of about Annie's age, also Indian, who was doing step-ups at a frightening speed in front of a mirror in one corner. It was as though there could only be so much motivation in the room at one time and she'd used it all, leaving the fat young man with nothing.

Annie wound up the speed on her treadmill. Through no fault of her own she had always been slender, able to eat whatever she wanted — which was never that much — without growing out of her clothes. Thus she was not prone to vast amounts of pretending to climb stairs. In recent years, though, she had been surprised by a certain sponginess around her belly, her thighs, her hips, her upper arms. She didn't weigh much more — well, not too much — but it was as though what she did weigh had given up paying attention. Her flesh was not bothering to hold itself together anymore, just as Eleanor's skin had not bothered.

There was probably a technical term for this, but it felt as though at a cellular level something had just rolled over instead of trying again.

Annie looked at the sinewy stepper, not an ounce of flab on her, her tight little biceps furiously lifting weights that would put a grown man to shame.

She pressed the 'up' arrow on the treadmill until it was going just a little bit faster than she was comfortable with. While she was here she could get fit: that was one thing she could do. She'd be crazy to waste the opportunity of having a huge well-equipped gym just a quick elevator ride from her room.

Buoyed by this, she managed another full three minutes on the treadmill before something clicked in her hip and it started to hurt. She limped on for another minute or two, but by then she was hot and bothered and dreaming of the enormous bathtub up in her suite.

She lounged in the tub's soothing water for a full hour; and once she'd dressed and done her hair it was lunchtime. Still not game to venture to the restaurant on her own — quietly blaming jetlag — she ordered lunch in her room, again opting for the safety of a club sandwich. She felt fine so far, healthy as an ox other than the hip, and she didn't want it any other way.

The meal was splendidly delivered by a beautiful-looking young man in a black tie and white gloves. When he smiled, Annie felt the whole room light up, as if her pleasure that what she ordered was what he had brought was not just a delight, but a miracle.

'I'm so sorry, I have no cash for a tip,' she said, at which the brilliance flickered a trifle. She supposed that begging happened inside the hotels as well as outside, and she would have given him something if she had it, but instead she was awkward, muttering her thanks and looking away as she waited for him to leave.

Actually, she had always been uncomfortable with tipping, even when she worked as a waitress during her student years and had been grateful for tips herself. It seemed so contrived to her to be extra nice to someone just to squeeze some more cash out of them. In an ideal world, being the normal amount of nice should have done it.

But the waitresses who did best at Crab & Co, where for three summers in a row she delivered jugs of beer and baskets of fried defrosted seafood, went way beyond the realms of normal. One of them stuffed her bra, another one took up the hem on her already obscenely short skirt, and a third changed her name label from Daphne to Daffy just so she had something fluffy to talk about. They flirted and simpered and bent over and fleetingly touched, but they could barely deliver a pepper grinder to the table without dropping it or putting it in the beer instead of the salad. Annie was probably the best waitress of all of them but she earned the worst tips.

'Well, darling, you can't eat principles,' her mother said when she complained about this, 'but you can certainly dine out on the memory of them, so good for you.'

When Hugh got back to the Taj that night it was already late. He'd had a day of meetings, he said, and wanted to take her out somewhere. There was a Mexican place nearby that he had heard was pretty good.

'Mexican food? In India?' Annie was doubtful, so instead they ate in the Chinese restaurant above the bar on the hotel's mezzanine floor.

She had vegetarian fried rice, which was very tasty, and which the waiter assured her was perfectly safe to eat. When the bill came, she asked Hugh how much he was going to tip and he explained that the service was included.

'With everything?'

'Yes, I suppose. What do you mean?'

'With room service?'

'Oh, yes, all the food, it's down here at the bottom. See?'

'So you never leave cash as well?'

'Sometimes I do, but the waiters seemed a bit embarrassed by it.

The thing about a country famous for its bribery is that the people who don't take bribes are very keen you know that about them.'

'India is famous for its bribery?'

'Ask a taxi driver,' Hugh laughed, and he looked properly happy, not like he was forcing it. 'So you had a good day? Not too bored?'

'No, not at all. It's . . . nice here.'

So nice that the next day she did it all again, although this time she ventured down to the pool.

After no more than ten minutes on a yellow striped towel she was so hot that she slid into the cool sapphire waters for a round of lazy laps. The water was delicious, but she didn't know how anyone lay out in the sun. As soon as she was dry she headed back to the icy air-conditioning in her room.

The same waiter — Valren, she noticed his name this time — brought her the same lunch and lavished on her the same lovely smile, which this time she at least returned.

After lunch, she lay on the bed, staring out the window at the Arabian Sea and the spikes of the curved bridge connecting Lands End to the rest of Mumbai.

She wished Rhona was there to talk to, lie by the pool with, or Daisy, even though Daisy had yet to grow back into wanting to be on holiday with her. If she ever did.

They did not have the sort of relationship Annie had always had with Eleanor. They were close, she thought, and cross words were rare, but they were not really friends.

Daisy was more — not aloof, exactly — but not inclined to include Annie in her life either. It hurt, sometimes, to think she didn't rate very highly on the totem pole of Daisy's priorities, not that she would ever let Daisy know that.

'Don't push it, my darling,' Eleanor had once counseled her. 'The things you want her to let you in on might be things you're happier not knowing.'

Not for the first time Annie's hand reached for the phone and she calculated the time difference before she remembered Eleanor, the person she wanted most to speak to, was gone.

Would she ever get used to that hole in her life? It didn't matter where she was in the world, the emptiness still swelled inside her, inky and dull.

She would email the kids instead, she decided, so ventured downstairs to find the business center. They'd be wondering, she was sure, just how old Mrs Goody Two-

Shoes was doing in India. When Hugh got home and asked if she felt like leaving the hotel, she was quick to say not tonight, maybe tomorrow, that she was happy with the Chinese restaurant again, but it was closed, so they ended up, reluctantly on her part, going to the smart Indian restaurant next to it: the hotel's flagship, Masala Bay.

She had white rice and a naan bread, while Hugh ate an enormous meaty curry and picked at a smorgasbord of chutneys she couldn't begin to describe.

It was a pleasant evening. They both started with a Kingfisher beer, and then Annie had a glass of Californian chardonnay, which cost more than a thousand rupees.

'How much is a rupee worth?'

'Well, wine's expensive here: you could probably get a taxi to and from the airport for the cost of what you are currently drinking. Not a private car like Ali's, but one of those battered old Fiats without air-conditioning.'

Annie was horrified, and savored every sip.

If Hugh seemed distracted, she put it down to tiredness. She'd given up years before asking him about his work, because the answers that agricultural engineers came up with were not easily digested. But he worked hard, put in long hours, took it seriously, as he did everything, and gave it one hundred per cent.

'Everything going well?' she asked, just to be polite.

'It's not the easiest place to do business,' Hugh said. 'A lot of promises have been made to the powers-that-be at home that can't exactly be delivered on when you're actually here. I won't bore you with the details. You like the hotel?'

'I do,' she said, passing on dessert. 'How could you not?'

They were in bed early, Hugh asleep almost straight away, Annie a few hours later, her mind restless, trying to come to grips with the time zone.

The next day she went to the gym, then the pool, then to check her emails. Neither Ben nor Daisy had answered her, and so she sent another chatty message to each of them, not mentioning that she had yet to leave the hotel or talk to anyone other than the man who tidied the room every day and the man who brought her lunch.

When she rang up to order another club sandwich, no salad, she realized she wasn't actually hungry for anything other than conversation.

Again, Valren brought it to her, setting up her table with a white cloth so that she could eat and look out at the sea at the same time.

'You are having a nice time here at the Taj, Mrs Hugh?'

'You can call me Annie, you know.'

'Yes, Mrs Hugh. Anything you would like.'

She started to say that she would like to be called Annie, but something about the way he was looking at her kept her from doing so. He seemed worried.

'Can I please ask, is everything to your satisfaction?'

'Yes, of course,' she answered, curious.

'Are you certain?'

'Yes, I'm certain. Is something wrong?'

'With me? Oh, no, ma'am. Not with me. I thought it was with you.'

'You thought what was with me?'

'The something wrong, Mrs Hugh.' He re-arranged her salt and pepper shakers and twisted off the lid of her bottled water (she trusted it now, and she had clarifying pills, plus he was wearing gloves).

'You think there's something wrong with me?'

'Oh, I do not mean for it to sound this way, ma'am. Please, forgive me. I should not say something. Please.'

Now he looked as though he was about to cry, and all of a sudden Annie wanted nothing more than to see that handsome face split once more by his beautiful smile. 'There's nothing to forgive, Valren.'

'Oh, thank you, ma'am.' There it was. 'In which case, I hope you do not mind me saying, but you do not seem as though nothing is wrong.'

'Oh, I'm sorry,' she said, embarrassed, because of course she did mind him saying.

'But it is I who should be sorry,' he said. 'It is my job to see that you are happy while you are here and you are not happy so I have not done my job.'

Annie would have laughed — an Indian waiter thought he was in charge of her happiness? Except that it wasn't funny.

She was not happy. She was sad. However hard she tried not to be, or didn't want to talk about it, with Rhona, with Hugh, with anyone — she was still desperately sad.

'Oh Valren, it's nothing to do with . . . lunch,' she said.

'Is it the room?' he persevered, still alarmed. 'Or the bed? Some guests find the mattress too hard. Or maybe the A/C is too hot? Or too cold? Any of these problems, Mrs Hugh Jordan, I can get them fixed for you.'

This time she did laugh, but it wasn't the sort of laughter that came with being tickled, or watching someone being tickled, or with even thinking that something was amusing. It was like a little explosion.

'The reason I am not happy,' she said, before she could stop the words escaping, 'is because my children have left home, my mother died, my dog disappeared, I don't seem to have anything to say to my husband and I just can't see the point in . . . much.'

Valren nodded his head almost as if that was what he had expected her to say, even though she did not herself expect to say it.

'But Mrs Hugh,' he said. 'I can fix all of that.'

Annie laughed again, although this time a little amusement had crept in. 'Do you really think so? How?'

'That is easy,' Valren said, his dazzling smile curving across his face, almost as wide and sweeping as the bridge over the Arabian Sea behind him. 'You just need Heavenly Hirani's School of Laughing Yoga.'

Chapter Six

Heavenly Hirani, as it turned out, was Valren's "auntie", although when pressed he revealed that every older woman he knew was considered an auntie. However, Heavenly was closer than some, he explained, because she was an old friend of his real aunt, who lived in Goa.

'My auntie in Goa is a nun and for me she wants that I am a priest,' Valren told her. He was still standing behind Annie's portable dining table, white- gloved hands crossed in front. 'But I don't have the vocation,' he continued.

He seemed quite chirpy about this. 'God has never tapped me on my shoulder, so I come to Mumbai instead and auntie sends me to Heavenly Hirani.'

'For spiritual guidance?' Annie asked, thinking he would actually make a wonderful priest. Some people had that sort of wisdom and kindness that made them excellent confessors, and he seemed to be one such person.

'No, for somewhere to stay,' Valren said. 'Auntie in Goa is still in charge of my spiritual guidance.'

'So, are we talking about being a Christian priest?'

'Yes, ma'am, in my village where I come from, everyone is Catholics. The Portuguese bring this many hundreds of years ago to Goa. You should come to Goa one day, especially the south. The peoples are very kind-hearted.'

But before she went to Goa, he said, she needed to go to Heavenly Hirani's School of Laughing Yoga.

Annie explained that she had a shoulder injury, which meant she couldn't do yoga — she'd finally given up after many painful years of trying. It was a lovely suggestion and she thanked him for being so helpful and for thinking of her, but yoga was not going to solve her problems.

'But Heavenly Hirani's yoga is mostly for the laughing,' Valren said. 'I do not think you will need your shoulders for that.'

'I just don't have anything to laugh about at the moment,' Annie said, sorry to disappoint him when he was so earnestly trying to help her.

'But this is the whole point of laughing yoga,' he replied, his smile firmly back in place, a friendly determination nonetheless exerting itself. 'You do not need a reason. Going there is the reason. That is what it is for. And after, you will feel much happier. If you cannot think of any reason to laugh, why would you not want to try it?'

He seemed truly perplexed by this, and as Annie tossed and turned in bed that night, waiting for the dawn, she found herself wondering why, indeed, she would not try it. She had come to India in a bid to stop being miserable, after all. How could she honestly turn down a chance at laughing?

At six she got up and quietly dressed, not quite believing that she was about to go through with it.

Hugh woke just as she was gathering her bits and pieces to leave. 'What's happening?' he asked. 'Are you all right?'

'Yes, fine, perfectly.' Annie smiled. 'Go back to sleep. I'm just going to try a yoga class.'

He looked surprised. 'Well, good for you. Do you need anything — money or, I don't know, does your phone work OK here?'

She hadn't tried it, but shrugged her shoulders, told him

she had everything she needed and went downstairs to find a taxi.

Valren had said the School of Laughing Yoga met every morning on the sand at Chowpatty Beach opposite Wilson College. Chowpatty Beach was in South Mumbai, he said, and very busy at night, but during the day it was very picturesque and empty and she would not be able to miss it or them. He would call Heavenly Hirani, he said, and tell her to expect a visitor — tourists were always welcome. Everyone was always welcome.

Still, Annie had not left the hotel since her arrival. She was nervous even about asking the valet to get her a taxi — and he was only two steps outside the revolving doors. He nodded his head at her request, but his focus remained elsewhere and she stood, anxious, and waited.

Exotically dressed businessmen were climbing into luxury limos wherever she looked on the hotel forecourt, even at that early hour. One of them was escorting a beautiful woman in a silver sari; her heels were high, her hair long and glossy. She looked to Annie to be around seventy, although she moved with the grace of someone half a century younger.

Annie was hot already, her leggings and sweatshirt too heavy for the heat, which even in the early morning bordered on oppressive. Another limo arrived in front of her, and another. She wiped at the back of her clammy neck and considered going back inside the hotel, but then she heard a honk and up between the cluster of fancy cars hurtled a boxy little taxi cab, black with a yellow roof and a body that looked as though it had been taken to over a very long period by a hundred angry ogres wielding giant studded clubs.

She hadn't known it was possible for a thing made of metal to be so crumpled yet retain its original overall shape. She looked at the parking valet, who was engrossed in a conversation with a group of businessmen. He turned briefly and pointed to the taxi.

Annie walked towards it, reached for the door, gingerly pulled it open, and slid inside.

The car smelled of stale smoke and something sour that she couldn't quite place — and didn't want to. The upholstery was covered in bright-pink plastic with yellow and turquoise daisies, further decorated with what looked like cigarette burns and irregular slashes caused, perhaps, by a sharpened knife.

The driver did not look like a bright-pink-with-yellow-and- turquoise-daisies sort of man. He was very small, dressed all in white, wearing a crocheted cap and perhaps just shy of two hundred.

He lurched off before she could even use her sweating palms to fasten the seatbelt.

'I can't find the bit to clip this into,' she said, but he did not seem to understand, instead suddenly braking just yards away from the hotel doors so he could indulge in a spirited coughing jag.

'Chowpatty Beach, please,' she said, her clamminess spreading, panic rising. 'By Wilson College?'

Again, the cab lurched, but at the bottom of the driveway the driver started hacking again. He was so small that his seat was pushed right forwards, his body pressed against the steering wheel, on which his head appeared to be leaning as his body was wracked by coughs.

'The seatbelt?' Annie asked, still scrabbling for it among the sticky daisies.

The driver didn't respond, but stopped coughing long enough to let a loud belch erupt. The security guards at the front gate were lowering the automatic barriers to let the car out onto the street.

Annie, her cheeks afire, could take no more.

She pulled a handful of rupees out of her purse, flung them at the driver, scratched at the handle until the door opened, then jumped out of the cab and scuttled back up the driveway.

Keeping her head down to avoid eye contact with the valet, she was nearly at the revolving door when she felt a hand on her elbow. She shrieked, thinking the taxi driver had chased her, jumping away from the grasping hand, clutching her bag to her chest.

But it wasn't the taxi driver; it was one of the security guards.

'So sorry, ma'am,' he said, looking mortified at having frightened her. 'So sorry. But I must have your bag for the machine.'

'Is everything all right, madam?' One of the liveried managers from inside the hotel was suddenly at her side. 'What has happened?'

'There is a problem with your taxi?' The valet was most certainly making eye contact with her now.

She knew how she must look: like a silly, old, hysterical foreigner, which is exactly what she was. 'No, I'm fine, really,' she said, biting her lip, hating the feeble sound of her voice. 'I just changed my mind. Really, it's fine.' She handed her bag over to the guard, stepped into the revolving door, and rotated at glacial speed away from all those concerned eyes, all that unwanted attention.

At least inside she was instantly cooled again, but as she collected her bag from security she realized she would have to go back to the room and Hugh would want to know what had happened.

She looked around the vast hotel lobby, her eyes resting briefly on the ceiling-height floral arrangement that had changed since the day before — the enormous sphere of roses was now pink, not purple. How had they done that without her noticing?

Up on the mezzanine level, she spotted the restrooms beside the spa. She would just go and use those, perhaps check out the menu at the spa, maybe go sit by the pool for a while, then go upstairs again.

Everything was all right. She was all right. It wasn't a disaster. She just needed to relax and pull herself together.

Hugh had indeed left for work by the time she got back to Room 1802.

She lay on the bed, trying hard not to think about her abortive attempt to leave the hotel, exhausted by the constant awful itch inside her to not be . . . like this.

Next thing she knew, housekeeping was knocking on the door and it was after ten.

She did not order lunch in her room that day, pretending to herself that she wasn't hungry rather than admitting that she was avoiding Valren. Instead she went to the gym, and afterwards made an afternoon appointment to have her hair done in the salon she'd only noticed while wasting time earlier in the day.

In the meantime, she went to the pool and, because she was starving by then, ordered a sandwich and settled under an umbrella waiting for it to arrive. When it did, she turned her back for a moment to get a sarong out of her bag and a crow flew down out of a nearby coconut tree and snatched half of the sandwich away.

The pool boy was insistent that she order another one, but Annie packed up her things and stomped back to her room.

She felt like crying, in fact she felt like a lifetime of tears was sitting right there behind her eyes, waiting for the dam to burst so they could flood her face, but she held them back. If she started she might never stop, and she didn't want to sit in the salon looking at her own red eyes and puffy face. That would just make her feel like the sort of woman who would cry because she got scared in a taxi and let a crow eat her lunch.

Had she not lost her mother and her dog, these minor setbacks would not rattle her so much: she knew that. But her grief was a Venus flytrap — snapping at passing slights to feed its constant gnawing hunger.

Surely Ben or Daisy would have answered her by now, she figured, so she stopped on the way to the salon to check her emails, but neither child had got back to her. She kept her Venus flytrap closed.

The salon turned out to be a good call. The staff were sweet and friendly, talking her into a manicure while she had her hair blow- dried.

She felt infinitely buoyed as she walked back down the hallway to 1802, but instantly deflated when she saw Valren up ahead, backing out of the room next to hers with an empty trolley.

'Madam!' It was impossible to believe that a face already so alight could light up any further, but his did. 'You look very beautiful today. I think you must have gone to laughing yoga.'

She considered lying, but Heavenly Hirani would know better, and anyway, lying would only make her feel more feeble and inadequate than she already did.

'I tried,' she said. 'Valren, I tried. But the taxi driver gave me the heebies and I lost my nerve.'

The illuminated face dimmed. 'The heebies? Oh, ma'am, what is this?'

'Don't panic, it's just an expression — the heebie-jeebies is what you get if your nerves play up and make you change your mind about something.'

The smile re-appeared. 'The heebie-jeebies? This does not sound so bad.' He moved the trolley to the side of the hallway. 'But what happened with the taxi?'

'It was nothing, really. It's just I always get a bit nervous in a car unless I'm driving and the driver was very old and he coughed a lot and I couldn't get the seatbelt to work and I couldn't tell if he knew where I wanted to go.'

'Oh, this would be giving you the heebie-jeebies,' Valren agreed, clearly taking to the idea. 'I understand. But tomorrow I will meet you at the front of the hotel and I will make sure you get a taxi that is not full of heebie-jeebies.'

'Oh, that's lovely, Valren, thank you, but there is no need. Really.'

'So how do you know you will not get the heebie-jeebies tomorrow?'

Annie had never thought of herself as timid before, but now she wondered if that was what she had become. Once upon a time she had hammered out convoluted contracts, wrangled difficult employees — she'd even fired people, not that she'd liked that part of her job. She'd taken persnickety math teachers to task, confronted overbearing sports coaches and fended off venomous stage mothers — all without thinking twice.

But now here she was — perfectly coiffed and manicured, lightly tanned and nicely turned out — in Mumbai, one of the largest cities in the world and no doubt a hotbed of fabulous life-changing experiences, but all she wanted to do was stay in her room, a room that could have been anywhere, that could have been in her house at home.

Nut up, Ben would have said if he was there, although probably not to her face.

'Don't be so pathetic,' Daisy — always a harsher critic — would have had no trouble spitting out.

Her children would be disgusted with her, and, although she was disappointed that they hadn't answered her emails, she did not like the thought of letting them down. She wanted them to be proud of her. She wanted them to be so proud of her that they would be desperate to slip back into her life and stay there forever.

'All right then,' she said. 'You'll be here anyway at 6.15 in the morning?'

'Yes, madam. I start at seven so I will come in early.'
'Oh, no, please, you don't have to do that for me.'
'Of course not. But I would very much like to.'

Chapter Seven

The next morning, there was Valren in the silvery morning light waiting for her. He'd already called a taxi, he said, one with air-conditioning and seatbelts, and within minutes a smart modern blue-and-grey taxi — a 'cool cab' Valren called it — was pulling up in front of her.

It did not look as though it had been taken to by angry ogres. It looked as though it had only just been cleaned and polished.

Valren leaned in towards the window and asked the driver to take Annie to Chowpatty Beach, opposite Wilson College.

'I should wait and bring the madam back?' the driver asked, in crystal-clear English.

Valren turned to Annie. 'I think this is a good idea for you?'

Annie looked at the driver. From what she could see he was about thirty, pleasant looking, wearing a crisp pale-blue shirt.

'Yes, thank you, I think this is good for me, too.'

She slid into the back seat, and clipped herself easily into the seatbelt. The seat coverings in this taxi were clean and a plain dark grey.

She turned and waved to Valren, who was smiling and waving back as though he'd just launched an ocean liner.

The taxi driver made his way smoothly down the driveway, past the security point, and out of the hotel compound, picking up speed as he drove along the boulevard beside the sea.

Annie gripped the cab's door handle even though the streets around the hotel were all but deserted this early in the morning, a far cry from when she'd arrived five days earlier and had barely seen the asphalt for the cars and bikes and people.

Now, a trickle of morning walkers and joggers pounded the uneven road but not even the marauding dogs were awake yet. No horns beeped, no trucks headed straight for them, and the only automated rickshaws she could see were lined up at the side of the road, not hurtling down the middle of it.

Despite this lack of other traffic, panic clawed at her. The driver wasn't speeding, and he wasn't half dead and hacking up a lung either, but he wasn't exactly crawling along and Annie needed to crawl. As he sped up, so did her heart rate. What was to stop him from taking her into the depths of Mumbai and dismembering her, or gang-raping her or selling her to slave traders?

She was sure she read that that happened in India. Or Africa. If she turned, she could still see the Taj tower behind her; it wasn't too late to ask him to take her back. She could say she felt ill.

But then he looked at her in the rear-vision mirror and smiled, and it was such a shy, lovely smile that she found it hard to believe he would do her harm.

'Do you want ceiling, ma'am?'

It didn't have garish daisies like the one the day before, but she was happy enough with it.

'Ceiling?'

'Seeee-ling,' he repeated more slowly.

'Ceiling? I'm sorry, I don't understand.'

'Sea Link, ma'am. Sea Link. Is bridge to South Mumbai. Over the seas.'

Of course! The graceful slice of modern engineering she could see from the hotel. 'It cost fifty-five rupees,' the driver said, 'or I can take you the long way. May be some cheaper, but Sea Link is quicker.'

'Yes, please, Sea Link. Thank you.'

They were at a wide open intersection now and there was more traffic, not all of it on the correct side of the road, but the honking was sedate, the general atmosphere far from fraught.

An empty bus had stopped in the middle of the road for no apparent reason, the rest of the traffic just pouring around it as though it were a boulder in a stream.

They were in the dusty suburban shopping area she recognized from the day she arrived, with the far side of the slum she could see from the hotel sprouting behind a higgledy-piggledy fence on her right. It had taken them this long just to get around to the back side of where she was staying.

She strained her eyes and thought she could see the heights of the Sea Link behind a tangle of elevated freeway up ahead, then her eyes slid down the fence and onto the grimy road edge, where an entire family was sleeping on what would be a footpath in any other city, laid out in a row, all five of them.

Annie bit her lip. What she had thought were flags hanging from the fence palings were clothes: a little boy's singlet, a little girl's shabby dress, a T-shirt.

The taxi driver looked idly in their direction, unmoved, before edging out into the traffic, despite the light remaining red, and putting his foot down, veering into a pot-holed coil of awful tarmac that soon emerged onto a wide empty road.

'Sea Link,' he said pointing ahead to the tollbooths; she fished the money out of her purse to pay the toll.

She had lost track completely of what the money was worth, but knew fifty- five rupees to be far less than the cost of a glass of wine. She'd given the taxi driver too much the day before, she knew that now, but at least in this taxi she was actually going somewhere.

And, if she could relax her brake foot enough, keep it from shooting through the floor, it was rather beautiful driving over the bridge so early. The sun was a tiny golden ball rising behind them, the light a lustrous silvery-grey. To her right was the same stretch of sea she could see from the hotel, far less murky from this angle; to her left, the seaside slum she had noticed perched on rocks on the peninsula, with its colored fishing boats bobbing in front of them. Somehow, the rickety slum buildings managed to look pretty in the morning glow — their different peeling pastels oddly co- ordinated. Martha Stewart would probably find them 'inspiring', Annie thought. She'd probably bring out a range of slum crockery based on the quaint paint jobs, with matching napkins referencing the bobbing boats.

Annie checked herself. She liked Martha Stewart. She would probably buy that slum crockery. And anyway, if rising sunlight turning a shantytown into a work of art wasn't inspiring, what was?

The orange ball of the sun was growing bigger, getting

higher, glowing through the morning haze — smog, Annie supposed, but atmospheric all the same. Its tangerine flare played peekaboo with the unfinished high-rises as they drove off the Sea Link and headed down the peninsula proper, throwing strange shadows onto the lower residential buildings in front, burning in staccato slices like forest fires behind the concrete skeletons.

The taxi soon veered away from the sea front and plunged into a built-up business area, the only traffic here a slew of other taxis in front of them and a single cow being cajoled the wrong way up the road by a wizened old man in an off-the-shoulder toga.

'Jaslok Hospital,' the taxi driver said, pointing to a modern building as they passed. 'Because if you go there, it is better to jas lok, not go in!'

Annie laughed and was rewarded with another of his shy, lovely smiles. 'Is very good hospital,' he added, 'but cost you arm and a leg.'

This man is definitely not going to dismember me, she thought, and anyway, she was too old for the slave traders. They wouldn't want her.

Her fingers, cramped from gripping the door handle and her seatbelt, started to relax as they drove through a smarter residential area past the hospital, although there was still the odd cow being fed a bunch of grass, even in this part of town.

'Is good luck,' the driver said. 'You pay to feed cow and is good luck for you, good luck for cow, and good luck for this mans who owns the cow.'

Eventually, they emerged onto some sort of flyover,

headed downhill, turned a wide corner towards the west and were disgorged onto a tree-lined parade parallel to a golden sandy beach.

'Chowpatty,' the driver said. 'I take you to Wilson College.' He stopped a couple of blocks further down outside a Victorian Gothic building not unlike Hogwarts. 'You go to funny yoga?'

'Laughing yoga, yes.'

She started to open the door.

'Oh, no, ma'am,' the driver said. 'I take you closer.'

He executed a careful U-turn and parked beneath a tree by an opening in the low concrete wall that separated the footpath (there actually was one) from the beach.

'Are you sure this is the right place?' she asked.

'Ma'am, I have never been to funny yoga, but I think that, yes, this is the right place.'

Annie looked at the vast, all-but-empty beach and heard Daisy's voice echoing in her head: 'Don't be pathetic, Mom.'

Teenage girls seemed to master the art of withering to perfection. Daisy at twenty-two had yet to outgrow it.

'You'll stay right here?' she asked the driver.

'Yes, ma'am. Right here.' He held up a newspaper. 'I catch up on all the briberies and corruptions.'

Annie got out of the car but turned back to him. 'I never even asked your name,' she said.

'Pinto, ma'am.'

'Thank you for getting me here, Pinto. My name is Annie.'

'Yes, ma'am.'

'I'm really not sure about this laughing yoga business,

so if I can't find it, I'll be right back.'

'I look out for you, ma'am.'

Chowpatty beach, with the sun licking at its golden edges and the city behind her, was truly something else to behold, Annie thought, as she walked gingerly onto the sand.

A group of young men were playing cricket closer to the water, which shimmered in the early morning light. A bedraggled family sat in front of a dumpster near the cricketers eating something they seemed to be cooking on the sand, as single runners criss-crossed the sand around them. In the opposite direction, a scraggly bunch of men were swinging their arms back and forth and bending to touch their toes. There did not appear to be anyone Heavenly among them, but perhaps Heavenly wasn't there yet. Annie was early.

She started to walk in their direction, sweating already, and not just because of the heat in the rising sun. The closer she got to the scraggly men, the more she could see of the beach that stretched towards the skyscrapers to the south.

The city seemed to go on forever. She had driven half an hour through its canyons coming from the north, and now there appeared to be just as much of it if not more to the south and east. Twenty-four million people — and she was nothing more in this vast landscape than a tiny grain of sand.

She glanced back towards the road.

Apart from the old guys, the runners, the cricketers and the bedraggled family, there was no one there. Anything could happen to her and only Valren would know where she was. And Pinto. Two men about whom she knew nothing except they were gifted with lovely smiles.

A shiver ran up her sweaty spine. Here she was on a vast Mumbai city beach all on her own in the early hours of the morning because a waiter at her hotel had told her to. So what if he had the sort of earnestness that made her want to adopt him and had talked of almost being a priest?

She hadn't told Hugh where she was going or anyone else at the hotel. Well, there was the parking valet yesterday, but would he remember? Was he even working today if she never came back and the police had to find her?

Maybe there was no laughing yoga. Maybe Valren was part of a gang and he was hiding in the shadows getting ready to pounce on her, rob her and leave her for dead. Lives were worth nothing in India, after all. Everyone knew that. How could she have been so stupid?

Just then, she heard clapping. She spun around to see a kaleidoscope of color streaming out from beneath the leafy trees back beside the road; a collection of women in bright saris and tunics, and men in colorful, casual summer clothes.

A woman in front, dressed in a lime-green tunic and matching trousers with a turquoise scarf slung over both shoulders, was leading the troupe across the sand, clapping vigorously and chanting 'Ha ha ha! He he he!'

They looked like a gang, but not of the pouncing variety. The woman looked like a Heavenly, and they looked like students of a laughing yoga school.

Annie peered back into the trees from whence they had emerged. She must have walked right past them. And now, standing there, looking at her and pointing at the chanting clappers, was Pinto. He wasn't going to rob her and kill her. She had to stop thinking the worst of everyone. Pinto was going to look out for her, just like he said. She was right to trust him. Her instincts were good — it was just a long time since she had put them to the test to quite this degree. If ever.

Chapter Eight

Annie abandoned the old men swinging their arms, walked away from the skyscrapers yawning into the neverland beyond, and headed towards the colorful clappers.

As she neared them, a plump woman in a bright-pink sari spotted her and stopped clapping to beckon her forwards.

'Ha ha ha, he he he,' she said, pulling Annie into the loose circle they had formed around the lime-green-and-turquoise-clad woman.

'Ha ha ha, he he he. Ha ha ha, he he he.' Her friend in pink nudged her to join in, and, even though she felt silly, she did, albeit quietly.

The supposed Heavenly could have been sixty or eighty or even ninety, Annie thought. She had that same ageless smoothness that she'd seen in the woman in silver the day before. Her body was small and lean, her hair long and dark grey with streaks of lighter grey, caught up in a loose bun at the nape of her neck. Her soft unlined face shone with pleasure as she stretched her mouth into the laughing chant and clapped.

She walked slowly around the inside of the circle peering into each face, stopping for a fraction longer to look at Annie. It was like having a bright torch shine on her — she wanted to turn away, but at the same time she craved the light.

Heavenly's eyes seemed to dance with laughter all on their own. Annie had never seen such eyes. They were like tiny little circuses. Finally, Heavenly stopped her chanting, moved back into the centre of the circle, lifted both arms high in the air and dropped them suddenly to her sides with a loud exhale. She did the same thing again, and again.

Everyone in the group followed suit, then broke into a round of applause as Heavenly bowed, then called to Annie.

'I think you must be Mrs Hugh Jordan,' she said. 'Welcome to our School of Laughing Yoga.'

'Welcome, welcome, welcome,' the group echoed. 'And welcome some more,' someone added.

Heavenly walked back towards Annie and took her hand, holding it in both of hers as though they were best friends and had been forever. 'I am Heavenly Hirani,' she said.

Annie thought of her mother, the softness of that hand, a hand that had held hers so many times over so many years, a hand that had stroked her fevered brow, or her cheek, or gently flicked her hair away from her face. A hand she would never feel again.

Perhaps there was something about the skin on the palms of kind old women everywhere that felt the same. The muscles in her body tensed as she battled to contain herself. Here she was at forty- nine wanting her mother! But if Heavenly noticed her struggle to stay composed, she didn't let it show.

'Let me explain what we will be doing this morning,' she said. 'I want you to stand in the circle between Kamalijit and Shruti, over there.' She let go of Annie to point at two plump middle-aged, almost identical, women standing nearby.

Kamalijit wore a gold sari, Shruti a purple floral one. They both waved, their grins stretching from ear to ear beneath identical spectacles, red dots in the centre of their foreheads.

'To begin with we will do some regular exercises,' Heavenly continued. 'All you need to do is follow what I do. This is just simple yoga, to move the body, to get the juices flowing, hey? Not for us the difficult poses, not for us the no- pain-no-gain, OK? Because to be truly happy you do not need to be a pretzel, you just need to walk without creaking. Am I right, everyone?'

'You are right, you are right, you are right,' they chanted, a titter running around the circle.

Heavenly turned back to Annie.

'After this simple yoga, we will do our laughing exercises. Do not worry, I will not leave you to do those on your own, either; I will take you through, step by step, little by little, as well.'

'Wonderful,' said Annie, 'although I'm not sure that—'

Heavenly grabbed her hand again and squeezed it with a ferocity that belied her age and size.

'You do not need to worry about being sure right now,' she said. 'You need to laugh, that is all. Just laugh. We will help you. Now, Mrs Hugh Jordan, go and stand between these lovely ladies.'

'Actually, it's Annie,' she said. 'My name.'

'And a beautiful name, too,' Heavenly agreed. 'Now move. First we start with cheerfulness exercise. How are you, how are you, how are you?' she chanted to her merry gang of followers.

'Very well, very well, very well!' the group chanted back. 'How are you, how are you, how are you?'

'Wonderful, wonderful, wonderful!'

'How are you, how are you, how are you?' 'Beautiful, beautiful, beautiful!'

The yoga that followed the cheerfulness exercise was simple, as Heavenly had predicted. They all stretched over to the side in one direction, then over to the other, arms above their heads, so the circle appeared to wave like moss in an ocean current, with only the odd interruption such as 'Left, left, I said left!' from Heavenly, which would be followed by an explosion of giggling as the errant bender changed course.

It was certainly far from the torturous yoga sessions at home. At those she'd always felt like it was a competition to feel the most pain and hold the most difficult poses for the longest time.

And it was a competition for which she was hardly able. Her shoulder, damaged from years as an eager but accident-prone tennis player and often painful, meant she felt awkward in many of the stretches, but too embarrassed not to attempt them. It was a struggle to feel enthusiastic about that sort of yoga, and she was always relieved when it finished, desperate to arrive at the boring relaxation bits so she could stop twisting her battered body and just lie still on the ground.

But in the rising sun on Chowpatty Beach, the movements flowed like the shallow waves on the edge of the sand, with them all going at their own levels. An elderly woman directly opposite Annie in the circle was bending hardly at all, while a younger woman (although not much younger) halfway between them could place her hands flat on the beach between her ramrod-straight legs.

Both looked utterly radiant. Now the sun had hit the sand, everyone was golden, their shadows long and elegant.

It was so hot that Annie was sweating, but it felt good.

Every time she made eye contact with anyone in the circle, she was rewarded with a welcoming grin. She'd been surprised to see men there, but they were just as friendly (and as mysteriously ageless) as the women.

'OK, now we are ready to laugh,' Heavenly eventually announced, to a further round of clapping.

'First we do the welcome laugh. Join hands at the front, like you are saying a prayer. Now nod your head and laugh.'

The whole group did just that and, although she felt ridiculous, Annie followed suit. It wasn't real laughter. It was forced, but as she kept doing it, it became less and less so.

'Eye contact, people,' Heavenly said. 'Do not forget eye contact. This is a big part of laughing yoga — looking at each other and laughing with each other. It is a group exercise, otherwise you may as well stay at home and laugh in the mirror.

'Now we do the laugh to complaining people. Point one finger and shake it, like you cannot believe someone would be complaining to you when we all know there is absolutely nothing to complain about.'

Annie wiggled her finger and laughed, catching the eyes of Kamalijit and Shruti, and the stiff elderly woman across the circle, followed by the bendy younger woman.

'Now, the Mumbai laugh,' cackled Heavenly. 'Close your mouth, stretch it wide, and laugh out your nose! This is how we do it in Mumbai!'

The circle rumbled with laughter, each person jiggling on the spot as they reeled around engaging with those beside and across from them.

'Now, Chinese/Japanese laughter. Close your eyes! Yes, screw them up! He he he! He he he!'

By Chinese/Japanese laughter, Annie was laughing for real. She looked at Kamalijit on her left and the two of them cracked up, then she looked across the circle at one of the men, who only had two teeth, both of them gold, and who looked to be having the laugh of his life.

'Laughter of apology,' instructed Heavenly. 'This is for when you realise that person you spoke to earlier really did have a reason to complain.'

Heavenly crossed her right arm over to pull on her left earlobe, then her left arm over to pull on her right.

Annie was laughing so much by now she had wet patches under her eyes, whether from the sun or tears of mirth she couldn't be sure. For the next few minutes, the whole circle shook with laughter. Heavenly moved clockwise around the inside again, laughing into the face of everyone there as they tugged on their earlobes, stopping again in front of Annie.

There she stayed, looking straight into Annie's light brown eyes with her dancing dark ones, as though she could see straight into her darkest thoughts.

Heavenly let go of her earlobes, and took both Annie's

hands away from hers.

'Laughter,' she said. 'That is all you need, Mrs Hugh Jordan. A little more laughter.'

Had anyone called her 'Mrs Hugh Jordan' at home it would most certainly not have been a laughing matter, but here it didn't seem to offend her at all. Besides, Heavenly just wasn't the offending type.

Kamalijit and Shruti were clamouring behind Heavenly to high- five her, as was Priyanka, the woman in pink who'd first beckoned her to join, while the rest of the women in the group high-fived each other.

'You vill come back,' the little old stiff woman said with a crooked smile. 'If I can,' Annie said.

'Is not a question,' said the little old woman.

The laughing school turned as one then to face the sun, and Heavenly led them in a brisk round of oms followed by a song in Hindi.

Annie stood among them, the same sun on her face, the extra warmth of an arm slung casually around her shoulder. It was the best she had felt in a long, long time.

After the prayer, the laughing school drifted back into the shade of the trees opposite Wilson College, Heavenly's students buzzing around her like bees around their queen.

'You will find us here every morning,' Heavenly said over their heads as Annie turned towards Pinto's taxi. 'We will see you again.'

'This is all right for you, this laughing yoga?' Pinto asked when she climbed into the back seat.

'Pinto, it was more than all right. It was completely wonderful. Did you watch?'

'Some small bit, ma'am,' he answered, pulling out into the traffic, which was building up now it was getting closer to rush hour.

'And what did you think?'

'I do not know, ma'am,' he answered, diplomatically.

'Not your cup of tea?' Annie asked. 'Do you have that expression?'

'Yes, we do, ma'am, only we do not say so much like that.'

'What do you say?'

'Ma'am, we say, "It is my cup of tea, just not right now."'

The taxi ride back to the hotel went some way to undoing the good of the laughing yoga even though Pinto was a considerate driver. (It wasn't him Annie was worried about; it was the other two million people on the road.) Only at one point did he lose his cool, and even then all he did was take both hands off the wheel to join them in prayer, then bow his head until it touched the steering wheel.

'Oh, please, no — no madam driver,' he prayed. 'Sorry, ma'am, but madam drivers in Mumbai is very bad. Look at her! She is not knowing where she is going and she is not going there very slow.'

The female driver in front was not doing her gender any favours with her erratic behaviour, Annie had to admit, but then she could not bear to look for very long. She spent as much of the trip home as she could with her eyes tightly closed.

When Pinto dropped her back at the hotel she realized she had never asked him what the fare would be.

'So, what do I owe you?' she asked.

'Ma'am, I am very shy about money,' Pinto replied, refusing to meet her gaze in the mirror.

That was not what she was expecting. 'Oh, but you have to tell me what you want or I might not give you enough,' she said. Or too much, she thought.

'I cannot do this, ma'am.'

'Well, how will I know?'

'If you like my job, then you decide and also then you maybe come in my taxi again.'

Now their eyes met. If it was some sort of trick, she couldn't say she minded. She thought she'd given the half-dead taxi driver five hundred rupees the day before to go nowhere, which had been silly of her, and she'd felt bad about it, but she'd thought that was about what the return trip would have cost had she gone through with it. So, working on that premise but worrying about the cost of a single glass of wine in the hotel bar . . .

'Here's a thousand,' she said. 'And if you're here at the same time tomorrow morning, we can do it all again.'

'Thank you, ma'am,' Pinto said, taking the notes she offered, nodding and looking at the handbrake.

'Is that enough, Pinto? Are you happy?'

'Yes, ma'am. I am happy.'

She very much suspected that a person who could not admit to something he didn't like not being his cup of tea, would similarly find it hard to confess to unhappiness.

But she would know tomorrow if she had done the right thing.

Chapter Nine

The residue of Heavenly Hirani's laughing yoga clung to Annie all day. She could barely keep the smile off her face. Even checking her emails in the hotel business center to find just a short *Awesome. Talk soon* from Ben, and nothing from Daisy, failed to dampen her mood.

Rhona had emailed a hurried hello and complaint about her youngest one, Caleb, pulling out the last of his baby teeth courtesy of a doorknob and a piece of string, as seen on YouTube.

In real life, Rhona reported, there was much more blood involved.

Annie had always had a soft spot for Caleb, even though in many ways he was the devil's own child, constantly in trouble with Rhona, other parents, his teachers, the neighbors . . . The list went on.

He was an eight-year-old who was blessed with choirboy good looks — golden curls, a smattering of freckles, enormous blue eyes — but who could not keep his hands to himself or the rest of his body out of trouble. He seemed to be able to break fragile ornaments just by looking at them, had already had his stomach pumped three times after eating or drinking different poisons, had broken his arm falling out of a tree outside the local police station, fractured his leg hiding under Rhona's sister's car just before she started it up, had two concussions on the football field even though he didn't actually play the sport, and had earned five stitches in his head after running into the refrigerator door at Annie's own house when he was tormenting Bertie one day.

Still, Bertie had loved him, as did Annie. He was a child full of mischief but without a nasty bone in his battered body. He'd told Annie once that she could be his mother if Rhona went to Heaven.

She knew that the special bond she had with the little horror helped keep his mother from strangling him when he tested her patience and that of Joe, Emma and Molly, who at fourteen, sixteen and eighteen were a close-knit group of which Caleb would never be part.

Annie was in awe of Rhona. Her friend had barely cracked once since her husband, Aidan, moved out, turning all her energy into making sure that the children, especially the older ones, emerged as unscathed as possible. (Caleb, Rhona said, was always going to be scathed, so she just needed to keep him out of hospital and herself out of the lunatic asylum until he was legal.)

Annie sent her friend an upbeat reply, saying she'd finally ventured out into the wilds of Mumbai and had returned in one piece. Then, instead of retreating to her room or the pool, she ventured into the hotel's main restaurant, a vast corner space with a busy buffet in the middle.

'What room, please?' a pretty young hostess asked her at the door. 'Oh, you must be Mrs Hugh Jordan,' she said when Annie told her. 'Your husband was telling us about you. Welcome to the Taj Lands End. Did you arrive today?'

Annie fudged the answer to that and asked if she could be seated in a corner, by the window, so she didn't feel so conspicuous on her own.

'Shall I bring you a newspaper?' the hostess suggested. 'If you do not want to read the news you can just pretend.'

Annie sat with her back to the rest of the room, her view out over the neighboring rooftops and onto the boulevard beside the Bandra sea front, or sea face as Pinto called it.

She couldn't remember eating alone in a restaurant ever before, although she thought she must have, surely, before Hugh.

Before Hugh.

She could barely remember that time. They'd met at university, after all. In the cafeteria, sitting across from each other, looking at trays of identical food, all of it only just this side of edible. They'd joked about how the chocolate milk was the one thing that kept them going and it had neither chocolate in it nor, most likely, milk.

She hadn't noticed him on campus before then — he was an engineering major and she was English Lit — but once she did notice him she was sort of surprised he hadn't crossed her radar before. He didn't wear trendy clothes, or have a fashionable haircut, or stick out particularly, except that he was very handsome, in an even-featured something-more-than-pleasant way.

It was his good fortune that Annie had just broken up with Carl Fenning, another good-looking guy who did wear trendy clothes and have a fashionable haircut and who did stick out — a little too much for Annie's liking. Her recent ex had been gregarious, charming — a real livewire — but had all the makings of being a hard dog to keep on the porch. And, although Annie had been very fond of Carl, she had felt exhausted after one night with him — a lifetime was not on the cards.

'He's your fun one, darling,' her mother had said. 'You'll know when you meet the real one.'

Eleanor had married her fun one, and he had exhausted her, although she stuck with him until his demise from lung cancer not long before Annie met Hugh.

Annie loved her father, but he was a man who was easily distracted, so, when she thought of her childhood, it was always her mother who swam into view. The two of them had been happily joined at the hip and could operate efficiently quite separately from Annie's father. Not that they bore him any ill will, it was just that sometimes, even Eleanor admitted, he seemed somewhat surplus to requirements.

Eleanor had met her 'real one' after she married Tony, she once confessed, and what's more she'd known it straight away. But she had taken her wedding vows seriously; and the real one waited for her, just not for long enough.

Right from the tiny toe plunge as she took her first sip of chocolate milk looking at Hugh across the cafeteria table, Annie had suspected Hugh was the real one. He was a man when her world at that point still seemed full of boys.

He told her after their first date that she was something special and that he saw them being together forever. At the time, she thought he was a silver- tongued Romeo and was charmed, but in fact he wasn't a flirt by nature at all. He was a man of few words (fewer and fewer as the years went by, as she was to discover) but he called things as he saw them, and right from the get- go he saw them, he saw her.

This dog was not leaving the porch unless she left with

him. She had no doubt about that whatsoever. Loyalty was one of Hugh's great strengths; she had lost track, she thought, sitting in the Taj Lands End breakfast room, of the others. He was a good provider. And a good father. But after twenty-five years of marriage was that enough?

The fact that she knew he would stay faithful to her should have made her feel better than it did.

Annie picked up the newspaper, the Hindustan Times, and skimmed the front page. The hostess was right to suspect there was not much in it of interest to her, and she got Pinto's joke now about the bribery and corruption: the paper was full of it. Sports players were charged with fixing matches, politicians with fixing their friends up with jobs, even Bollywood stars were being tarred with the bribery brush.

Every other story seemed to be a family feud that had ended with one less member of the family.

It wasn't exactly entertainment, although she did have to laugh at a story about a very successful bakery. This included mouth-watering descriptions of the delicacy for which it was famous, a sort of baklava, and even a recipe, plus detailed instructions on how to find the place. A rider in italics at the end of the story, however, said that at the time of going to press the hard-to-find bakery had closed down over a tenancy disagreement and was unlikely to ever open again.

She was also riveted by the taunting tone of the comments in the showbiz pages. Will she get it right this time? one caption asked of a beautiful model- turned-actress wearing a floral pantsuit. Or will she continue to look like something the cat dragged in?

Annie hardly wanted to keep reading, but she felt less obvious looking at something than just sitting there on her own waiting for a menu. When the children were little she'd rarely ventured out alone; she didn't think many mothers did. She always had the babies, and any time she got to herself she quickly found a purpose for at home: tidying up the linen press, organising the cluttered kitchen cupboards, re-upholstering a footstool, decorating the children's schoolbooks.

As they grew older she might have left the house more often, but it was usually to take them somewhere or pick them up from somewhere else, or run errands on their behalf. Ben had been sports-mad from a very young age, and Daisy had been in every after-school club, choir and theatre group imaginable. There was a seemingly endless list of things she needed Annie to get for her, and Annie never said no. She loved being a full-time mother, had never regretted a single moment, a single mile.

And if she'd ever had the time or inclination to go to a restaurant it would have been with her mother, or Rhona or another mom from the PTA, or — just someone. She didn't think she was that unusual in this regard — she doubted many women felt comfortable eating alone, even businesswomen. Just to prove her wrong, a woman in a dark suit bustled in and sat at the table next to her, briskly ordering from a passing waiter and pulling an iPad out of her handbag. She looked completely comfortable, but then in her corporate uniform she was clearly identified as someone for whom eating alone at a restaurant was a requirement of the job. No one would pity this woman, the same as they would not pity a man, or judge her. Not that Annie was worried about being pitied or judged, particularly. But she was obviously worried about something, because she felt supremely uncomfortable, even with the newspaper.

The whole notion of being herself, of sitting at a table on her own, was just too unfamiliar — another drop, in fact, in a sea of unfamiliarity.

'Mrs Hugh Jordan!' She looked up to see Valren. 'I am very happy to see you here. Did you go to Heavenly Hirani's School of Laughing Yoga?'

'Thank you, Valren, I did.'

'How are you, how are you, how are you?'

'Wonderful, wonderful, wonderful!'

They both laughed.

'You were absolutely right,' she conceded. 'It was just what I needed. In fact, it really was wonderful, wonderful, wonderful.'

'I can tell this from the looking of you, ma'am.'

He was so genuinely pleased with himself that she felt a sudden urge to write to his aunt in Goa that she should be very proud of him, this inspirational young man, despite him turning his back on the priesthood.

Instead she glanced at the menu. 'I think I'll branch out and have an egg- white omelet today.'

'Oh, but surely you would like to try some Indian food after your laughing yoga?' Valren said. 'A dhosa perhaps: I can prepare and bring it for you straight away.'

'Thanks, Valren, but I'm not even sure what a dhosa is.'

'Excellent! This is usually a breakfast food, but for tourists they can eat it anytime. I will bring it to you, and then you can not only find out what it is, but you can like it very much.'

And with that he walked quickly away, a man with a mission. Annie didn't want a dhosa, whatever it was, but his enthusiasm was, if not infectious, exactly, then at least impossible to deflate. Besides, she needed to toughen up. It was hardly a challenge to be sitting in a five-star hotel eating something she hadn't chosen when she had already caught a cab into the middle of Mumbai and been to laughing yoga with a group of local strangers on a city beach. A week earlier she had not even known that Mumbai was on a coast, let alone that it had beaches where something called laughing yoga might be practiced.

She smiled to herself, thinking of the earlobe-tugging apology laugh. 'I'm sorry, he he he. I'm sorry, he he he.'

Just remembering made her feel like she was standing in the sunshine all over again.

Chapter Ten

The dhosa turned out to be a stiff sort of a pancake, half of which stood up on the plate like a starched napkin, with a spicy potato mixture in the middle and a collection of chutneys to one side, along with a bowl of a bright-yellow, hot soup. A club-sandwich-hold-the-salad it was not, but Valren was so delighted to be introducing her to the delights of the Indian palate that she didn't feel she could send it away. Knowing that he might be collecting her plate, she didn't feel as though she could leave it intact either.

Once he had stopped beaming at her and gone to take someone else's order, she cut off the tiniest bit of pancake and gingerly lifted it to her mouth.

It wasn't fiery hot, which was her fear, but it did have a buttery spiciness that was actually very pleasant. She cut off a bigger bit of the pancake, and dipped it into the least scary-looking chutney, a chunky white one, which turned out to have a punchy coconut flavor.

The spiciness of the potato stopped just short of being sweet, and the crunch of the pancake complemented the soft mash of the filling.

She tried dipping another bite into the second chutney, which was mango, and the third one, which was a tangy sort of lime pesto. The bright-yellow soup tasted good, too, but she wasn't sure what to do with it, so dipped another few mouthfuls of the pancake in it, then ate the rest with a spoon. When Valren came back to clear the table she had all but licked the platter clean. The look on his face was worth the carbs.

When Valren brought her a cup of masala tea she suspected it came with an added white-sugar hit, to boot. The milky tea with cardamom, anise and cinnamon was not something she had even heard of, let alone contemplated before, but its spicy sweetness promised to become quite addictive.

As she drank it, she picked up the newspaper again and idly turned the pages, glossing over stories of striking retailers and feuding brothers, but stopping at a headline at the bottom of page five. YOUNG LIFE RUINED BY BANDRA ACID ATTACK the strap read. Below this was a story about a young nursing graduate from Delhi who had arrived at Bandra train station the day before to start her first-ever job at the navy base hospital in South Mumbai. As Preeti Rathi stepped off the train with the uncle who was escorting her, an unknown person threw acid in her face, Annie read, which she also swallowed, causing serious internal injuries as well as burns to her face, neck and arms. Preeti was now in an induced coma in the local hospital, breathing only with assistance.

Acid attacks were so common in India, the story went on, that a recent law now recognized them as a separate crime punishable by a minimum sentence of fourteen years in prison. This law had changed as a result of general outrage over such violence against women, the paper said, acid victims being solely female, usually young, and, in Preeti's case, very beautiful. Railway police were hopeful of nabbing the culprit, which Annie thought did not sound as though they were taking it terribly seriously. Preeti's parents and sister were on their way from Delhi to the

Mumbai hospital where she was in intensive care, her uncle too distraught to speak to the media.

Annie folded the newspaper, a chill running up her spine.

Laughing yoga aside, this was a very foreign country, and she must not forget that. Her heart ached for the young girl with the ruined life. At twenty- two, she was the same age as her own beautiful Daisy. The thought of her daughter's face burned off by acid that cost less than a dollar a gallon made Annie feel sick.

She pushed the image out of her mind.

Later in the afternoon she lolled about the pool, finishing her book, and finally commissioned a foot massage from Babu, the blind masseur, whom she had seen day after day crouched behind the pool boy's counter, waiting patiently under an umbrella. She didn't really like foot massages as a rule — or any sort of massage for that matter — but she'd seen Babu from her hotel window one day, tapping his way with his white cane out towards the pool, taking an errant left turn.

Standing at the window she'd sucked in her breath, desperate that he not fall into the flowerbed or down the stairs beside the garden, but out of nowhere a security guard had appeared, taken him by the elbow, leading him to his perch. She'd liked that the hotel would employ a blind person, and that other people who worked there would look out for him. Then when she found out his name was the impossibly endearing Babu, she buckled and paid the small fee for a fifteen-minute foot rub.

She reclined in the shade on a sun lounger, relaxing as

she watched the tendons in the smooth near-black skin on Babu's arms as they flexed when he rubbed frangipani cream into her legs.

He kept his eyes closed, his head turned up and to the side, as though her feet were some sort of instrument he was playing, and his cue from the orchestra was coming somewhere in the distance up above them. She was due a pedicure, so it was just as well he couldn't see her toes, she thought, as she all but drifted off to sleep.

In the distance, she could hear the honking of Lands End's crazy traffic outside the hotel.

Closer, those pesky crows were making themselves known. The bass in the music playing at the outside bar was turned up a little high, but that didn't annoy her as much as it normally would. She heard the espresso machine whoosh, and wondered if whoever had ordered a coffee knew about masala tea.

When Hugh called later that evening to say he'd been caught up in meetings and would probably not get home before nine, she realized that she had been waiting to tell him about her day; it had been such a good one. Deflated, and certainly in no mood to eat on her own for the second time, she opened the potato chips that were in the minibar and which proved so delicious that she ate a second packet as well.

Hugh got home closer to ten, hot and tired. His day had been hard, he said, and the traffic getting back to the hotel horrendous. A donkey had died on the other side of the railway lines and stopped traffic in both directions while the owner beat up the rickshaw driver who'd run into it even though he had only run into it after it had died.

He couldn't wait to get into the shower, he said, to wash the dust and dirt of the day off his skin.

It was almost eleven by the time he slipped into bed next to her, his hair still damp, smelling of the hotel shower-wash, which reminded Annie of the baby soap she'd used on the children when they were little.

'Do you want me to order you something from room service?' she asked him, but tiredness trumped hunger. He kissed her and fell almost instantly asleep.

He'd always had that ability. Get Hugh horizontal and he'd be out like a light, no matter if the TV was blaring, lights were blazing and two children were screaming their lungs out. It had irritated her, actually, always, but only because she envied him. Annie was more of a tosser and turner by nature, sometimes awake almost all night, only drifting off to sleep when the alarm was about to go off.

She sat up in the vast bed with its crisply laundered sheets and turned the TV on. Bollywood movies were playing on nearly every channel, so she tried to watch one, but only half understood it. It seemed to be some sort of take on The Taming of the Shrew, but there were two shrews. It was worth watching for the dancing and the colors alone.

Annie thought of Heavenly Hirani and the laughter on the beach.

She had never been anywhere as frightening and foreign as India, but it wasn't all gang rapes and acid attacks and sleeping husbands and thieving crows. There had been real happiness on that beach. Some of it, albeit briefly, hers.

She set her alarm for six. She would go to laughing yoga

again. Just thinking about it put her in a better mood.

Chapter Eleven

'Welcome, welcome, Mrs Hugh Jordan!' Heavenly Hirani called from the shade of the banyan tree, where she and the school were waiting when Annie arrived the following morning.

'Sit, sit,' insisted Shruti, who gathered today's pale-blue spotted sari up and moved over, almost squashing the little man next to her to make room for Annie.

'You came back,' Shruti said. 'You like us too much?'

'Just the right amount,' Annie laughed. 'Maybe a little more.'

A very elderly woman in a gold sari — she couldn't remember if she'd been there the day before or not — was looking at her as though she had never seen a white person before. Annie smiled, and the old woman's wrinkled face collapsed into a smile of her own, but she turned away, shielding her eyes.

'The last tourist lady who came to our school,' said Shruti, 'she was reading that book — you know, the one all the tourist ladies read. *Pasta Ponder Hanky Panky*.' She laughed. 'No, that is not it. What was it called, Priyanka? Italy, India and what was the other place?'

'You mean *Eat Pray Love*,' Priyanka answered, rolling her eyes. 'She's right. Every tourist lady who has come to laughing yoga is reading this book.'

'Are you?' Shruti asked Annie.

As it happened, Annie had read the pasta bit years before, but had lost interest with the pondering bit, and not bothered even proceeding to the hanky panky. She'd been a voracious reader once upon a time, but that had fallen along the wayside with the tennis, the movie-going, the book club. She didn't even keep in touch with her old work friends anymore. Her world had become so small. No wonder the holes in it felt so impossibly huge.

'No,' she said. 'Have you?'

'I have three children and seven grandchildren,' said Shruti. 'I do not have time to read a book let alone meditate and get a boyfriend.' The other women giggled. 'Besides, my husband would not like it very much if I did! But I do like Julia Roberts,' she said. 'Very pretty, you know, with nice big teeth.'

'What about meditation?' Annie asked. 'Does anyone here meditate?'

The women looked sheepishly from one to the other.

'Whoever started the rumour that all Indian people are good at meditating got it wrong,' said Malika, the youngest of the group, the flexible one Annie had noticed the day before. 'Most of us are too busy thinking about what we are going to cook for our next meal to seek enlightenment.'

'What about you, Heavenly?' Annie asked, turning her attention to the teacher, who was sitting next to the very old woman, holding her gnarled hand. 'Do you meditate?'

'I tried it once or twice,' Heavenly said, 'but for me it is too boring.' Annie laughed.

'Meditation is a practice to still the mind and promote relaxation,' Heavenly said, 'but in my experience most people's minds are already stuck in the mud and their bodies are stuck right there with them. Better to move both, eh? Now, since we are talking about moving, are we ready to get started?'

She stood up and started clapping her hands. 'Ha ha ha, he he he! Ha ha ha, ho ho ho!'

Heavenly's morning yoga was more energetic than it had been the previous day. They did their stretches, then the leaning this way and that, then they held hands and stepped back as far as they could while still hanging onto the people on either side.

Annie had Kamalijit, a vision in turquoise today, on one side, and a boy of about twelve on the other. He kept sneaking looks at her — she was clearly something of a novelty. He was wearing a red-and-blue-striped football shirt — but as with many of the people she had met so far his most striking feature was his smile.

Stepping back as far as she could and feeling her arms all but being pulled out of her sockets, she turned to see him with his head thrown back, eyes closed, laughing already.

'Are you ready, are you ready, are you ready?' asked Heavenly from across the circle.

'Yes, we are! Yes, we are! Yes, we are!' they answered, and the school of laughing yoga ran forwards, still holding hands, now borne aloft, into the middle of the circle where all their bags were stacked. They hooted and hollered, then ran backwards out again, stretching the circle as far as it could go, then raced back in.

'Beautiful and amazing!' Heavenly crowed. 'Beautiful and amazing!' the group echoed.

Beautiful and amazing isn't the half of it, Annie thought, turning to share a smile with her young friend in the striped top.

They repeated some of the laughing exercises from the day before, this time with the addition of the peeling-coconuts laugh. Annie had never peeled a coconut before, and couldn't really imagine how it would be done, but the boy, Sandeep, did her the great favor of peeling her imaginary coconut for her, to save her any embarrassment.

He was particularly good at the mobile-phone laugh, Annie told him, although Priyanka gave him a run for his money. Shruti, it was agreed, got top marks for her apology laugh because she had extra-large earlobes.

At one stage Heavenly beckoned the elderly woman in the beautiful gold sari, who was still sitting underneath the banyan tree, to come and join them. She took a long, long time to cross the sand, then stood in the circle for a short while, letting go of her walking frame only once to attempt the peeling- coconut laugh, and in so doing laughing for real so hard that Annie feared for her health.

After peeling less than one coconut, she turned and started the long, slow journey back to the shade, her bony shoulders shaking with laughter with every tiny step.

Heavenly certainly had a knack for drawing people in. A slightly ragged father and son who just happened to be passing by on the beach joined them for a while; a sad-looking middle-aged man in suit pants and a shirt and tie drifted in to the circle, then quickly out again. A fat Labrador even flopped down beside the bags in the middle at one stage, panting and drooling as it looked from one laughing human to the next.

People came and went on their own timetables. Heavenly certainly wasn't a stickler on that front. As she had said, laughing yoga was for everybody.

Except Pinto. He had been waiting in front of the hotel for her at 6.15, her thousand rupees obviously right on the money after all.

Today, he'd parked his car out of sight, perhaps worried that if he got any closer he could end up doing some unscheduled laughing himself.

'You like this again, ma'am?' he asked when she climbed back into the car to go back to the hotel.

'Yes, Pinto, I like it a lot. You should try it.'

'Oh, no, ma'am, not for me.'

'You don't like yoga?'

'I do not know, ma'am.'

'You've never done it?'

'We do not do so much this yoga where I come from, ma'am.'

'And where is that?'

'Jammu and Kashmir, ma'am.'

'This is the name of the state where I am from, ma'am. Most peoples hear only of Kashmir, but this is a valley and Jammu is another part of it also with a city, and the peoples in Mumbai do not care about this anyway.'

'People from Mumbai don't like people from Jammu and Kashmir?'

'Not so much, ma'am. And people from Jammu and Kashmir is the same.'

'So what brought you here then, Pinto?'

'I come here when I was twelve, ma'am.'

'Twelve!'

'Yes, ma'am. I come to Mumbai because I know that

Bollywood is here and I want to be a famous actor.'

'You came with your parents?'

'No, ma'am. With myself. My mum she cries so much when I leave my village that I think she damages her brains.'

'Oh, Pinto, I'm not surprised! Twelve is so young. You were just a little boy. However did you get here?'

'On the bus and on the train, ma'am. It takes a long time from Jammu, from my village. Maybe three days.'

'And what did you do when you arrived?'

'I looked for Bollywood, ma'am, but I could not find it. I thought it would be here to meet me and I had no money, not a single rupee. I did not think that Bollywood would be so hard to find and that so many other boys were also looking for it.'

'At least you weren't alone,' Annie said, although without much conviction.

'I was alone,' said Pinto. 'I do not have any friends and any money, so after not very long I get a job on a banana truck.'

'A banana truck?'

'Yes, ma'am, a truck full of bananas. But that boss was mean, ma'am, and he beat me because I was too small to lift the big heavy cover over the bananas. I try, but I have not got the muscles.'

Annie thought of Ben at twelve — a child no more capable of jumping on a train to Mumbai and getting a job on a banana truck than growing wings and flying to the sun. A baby never beaten by anyone, let alone his boss, not that he'd ever had one.

'Now I have barbells in the back of the taxi,' Pinto said.

'And if I have no customer, I go to the park and I do my exercises.' He took one hand off the steering wheel and flexed his bicep.

'Truck!' Annie cried, pointing to a large unwieldy lorry tearing towards them on the wrong side of the road.

Pinto just laughed and slowed to let it go past.

'What did you do next, after the bad banana boss?' Annie asked, her heart thumping.

'I take some of the bananas, ma'am; please do not be angry. I take some bananas from the bad boss and I try to sell them on the street, but because I had not put the cover on them, they were too ripe and no one would buy them, not even for one rupee, so I eat them myself even though I do not like bananas. But we have a saying in India: hunger does not have eyes.'

When Ben and Daisy were twelve, Annie was making them three meals a day, taking them to and from school, doing most of their homework and tucking them up in bed at night. She could not imagine a world in which they would have to eat rotten bananas or starve. 'Where did you sleep?'

'On the street, ma'am. Then after some days of no food, not even bananas, I get a job in a restaurant, washing up the dishes and I am doing this for eight years. I am doing this till my nails go away.'

He held both hands off the steering wheel and wiggled his fingers. 'But they have come back.'

'Please! Pinto! Both hands on the wheel! I need you to drive carefully.'

'Always I am careful, ma'am. Always.'

'Yes, but I prefer it when you are using those lovely fingernails to steer the car. Thank you. So, you washed dishes for eight years, then what happened?'

'Then I have saved up the money to get the licence for a taxi, ma'am, but I give it to a bad man and he runs away with it, so I go to work at a restaurant with more better money and in two more years I have the money again.'

'Oh, Pinto, you're breaking my heart.'

'Please, ma'am, do not make that happen. I have nine lives. Still three more to go.'

Pinto had graduated from sleeping on the street to in the back of his taxi, he told her. It was only for the past five that he'd been living in a guesthouse.

'Seriously?'

'Yes, ma'am, seriously. But for us, this is OK. For the tourist madams they see the mans asleep in his rickshaw and his bus and his car and they think he is taking a forty winks but this is his house! I was liking my taxi to be my house, but then there is a serial murderer in Mumbai killing the taxi drivers. They call him Beer Man because he leaves a can of beer behind after he kills the peoples. Bollywood is making a film, I think. You will see.'

'You must have been scared, Pinto.'

'Yes, ma'am, and once I am woken up by a crazy person on drugs with a knife in my face. He is not Beer Man but I need three stitches. And after that I go to a guesthouse, even though it means less money to send home and bed bugs, but I am happy there.'

'You're happy living thousands of miles from your parents, driving a taxi and sleeping in a guesthouse that has bed bugs?'

'Yes, ma'am. My small brother is an engineer because of me, and my next small brother is in the army because of me, and I can bring for my mother some beautiful dresses when I go home. This also makes me happy.'

Pinto turned around to smile at her, proving just how happy he was, not that she doubted him for a moment. He pointed cheerfully to a mark below his left eye. 'This is where I have the stitches.'

'Please, Pinto! Eyes on the road,' she said, tensing in her seat.

'Honestly. I'm not as lucky as you — I only have one life and I'm not quite ready for it to end.'

Pinto slowed to drive around a group of pre-teen boys playing what looked like marbles, with small rocks, in the middle of a busy intersection. Rickshaws careened around them, taxis honked, buses skidded, motorcyclists yelled, but the boys only had eyes for their game.

'Please excuse me, ma'am, for saying so,' Pinto said, 'but no one only has one life.'

Chapter Twelve

Outside the hotel, Annie handed over a thousand rupees, which Pinto took, shyly, thanking her, and asking if he should pick her up again the following day.

She said he should.

'If you have a local SIM card, ma'am, you can call me to take you somewhere anytime. We could go sightseeing. To Gateway of India, maybe, or Kanheri Caves.'

He carefully wrote his name and number on a piece of paper and handed it to her.

Annie thanked him, and said that was a good idea, although she didn't like to say she didn't know what a local SIM card was. Maybe she could email Rhona or, a slightly more practical idea in the circumstances, ask the concierge.

She skipped breakfast but went on her own to the restaurant for lunch, and after scanning the menu decided to try dahl, which was the cheapest offering and which she had at least heard of.

Valren was not working, but another handsome young man — was there an agency that provided them? — Adesh, who had a silky beard and was wearing a dark turban, took her order.

'Would you like some naan with that?' he asked. 'Or perhaps paratha?'

'What is that?'

'Paratha is bread, ma'am, like naan, but made with ghee and tastes very much better, although my wife is telling me it is not on her diet.'

'Please excuse my ignorance, but what's ghee?'

'This is Indian butter, ma'am. For many of us it is like medicine more than food.'

'So your wife doesn't have this medicine on her diet?'

'Ma'am, my wife says paratha is not on her diet, but this does not mean she does not eat paratha. My wife very much likes paratha because of the ghee.'

'I guess I'll try the paratha then,' Annie said. She liked the sound of Adesh's wife.

The dahl was like the yellow soup she'd had the day before with the dhosa, but thick with lentils and so full of flavour that before she knew what had happened she had emptied the entire bowl. As for the paratha, it was a cross between a croissant and a pita bread, and she could see why Adesh's wife was such a fan.

As she waited for her masala tea, she picked up the Hindustan Times and looked for news of Preeti.

The poor girl remained in a critical condition in the same Bandra hospital where she had been admitted, according to a small story well into the newspaper. The railway police were now looking at CCTV footage from the terminus at the time of the attack, and following a lead from police in Delhi, but the culprit was yet to be nabbed.

Preeti's parents had arrived at her bedside from Delhi, but she was still under sedation, the story read. Her lungs were damaged by the acid and doctors were not sure how long it would be until she could breathe on her own. Today there was a photo of Preeti before the attack — she was indeed a beautiful girl, with big eyes and full lips, wearing a green sari in front of a red background. She could have been one of the Bollywood stars featured in the paper's many celebrity pages.

Annie imagined her, full of excitement, travelling from Delhi to start her new life. She was not from a wealthy family — they could not pay the hospital bills, the story said, although the rail company had agreed to foot them. What promise Preeti must have felt, graduating from nursing school and being chosen to work at the naval hospital. What a different sort of life she must have imagined she was going to lead. This opportunity was going to completely change her world. And now it was changed again, without a moment's notice, for the worse.

Annie hoped they kept her under sedation for a while longer.

She couldn't read about Preeti without thinking of Daisy. She loved Daisy with all her heart, but never had it been more obvious what an easy life she had provided for her daughter. Not that this was a bad thing — it was what every parent dreamed of being able to do — but she wondered what would ever give Daisy that same sense of promise that Preeti must have had, setting off for Mumbai.

Daisy expected everything — from vacations to iPhones to university fees to eyelash tints — to fall in her lap, and why wouldn't she? It always had. Since the terrifying suicidal phase, all Annie had wanted to do was make her daughter happy. If she indulged her, tiptoed around her more than she should have — more than Eleanor ever would have — it was only because she remembered so clearly the fear of losing her.

Annie didn't know if Daisy ever stopped to wonder why she got everything she wanted, or if that might one day change.

At a pinch, she thought Ben could probably sleep in the back of a taxi for a night or two. But Daisy would likely not step foot inside one, let alone sit on the seat, or touch the door handles. Her headstrong daughter was quick to label others pathetic, but could effortlessly apply different standards to herself.

Still, thinking about her beautiful girl made Annie homesick, so she went back to the business centre after lunch to check her emails. Neither of the children had responded to her messages of the days before, but she sent them another anyway, this time telling them she had joined a yoga class and was starting to eat the local food.

Rhona, bless her, had emailed to say Caleb had learned how to spray his sisters with orange juice through the gap in his teeth and was so good at it that she was tempted to sell him to a passing circus, if only she could find one.

Aidan was acting weird, she wrote, which was not like him. The guy was a schmuck, but he'd at least had the decency to be wracked with guilt about leaving his family for the proverbial hot totty from the dental surgery.

He'd texted her to say that he couldn't take the kids for the weekend, she said, even though that had always been the deal. No explanation, just a terse sentence saying she'd have to deal with it.

There goes my lovely relaxing day of reading self-help books in the bath with only a bottle of pinot for company! Rhona wrote.

Annie typed into a return email that she wished she was back there to help out, but when she saw the words written down, she realized that she didn't. She was actually enjoying herself in Mumbai.

She deleted her original message and instead offered her condolences, then told Rhona about the laughing yoga group, the disdain at *Pasta Ponder Hanky Panky*, and the Indian women's skepticism about meditation. This would cheer her friend up, she knew.

Rhona had tried transcendental meditation on several occasions but failed spectacularly. Mothers of four just didn't have enough space left in their heads for quiet, was what she had figured. Also, she was gassy.

Mahendra at the front desk told Annie she would have to go into Bandra to buy a SIM card for her phone, which would then mean she could make local calls and send SMS messages. A lot of tourists did this, he said. She could get a taxi or she could walk out the front gates of the hotel and get one of the motorised rickshaws. It should cost no more than thirty rupees.

He said this as though it would be the easiest thing in the world to do, but the thought of climbing into one of those death traps held no appeal for Annie whatsoever. Still, when she got back to the room she was restless. She didn't want to stay there nor did she feel like going back out to the pool, so after glancing briefly at the book she'd been planning to return to, she scooped up her bag, checked her lipstick in the mirror and went back to ask Mahendra for a map. She wanted to walk to the mobile phone shop, she told him. He seemed doubtful about this, but Annie assured him she had a relatively good sense of direction and figured that the store was no more than twenty minutes away.

Once outside the safety of the hotel gates, however, she

started to lose her nerve. The rickshaws buzzed around her like flies, the drivers desperate to catch her attention, until they worked out she was striding on without them. It was just a matter of finding how to walk along the side of the road without there being a dog in the way, or a bus or a truck or five people walking abreast towards her.

She crossed the wide, busy street to walk along the boulevard next to the sea face, which was partly protected from the road by an ankle-high concrete lip. Families and couples gathered in occasional groups out on the jagged rocks, screaming as the coffee- colored water crashed around their feet and sprayed them. One old man was crouched in a loincloth doing his washing, although how he expected the dirty, salty water to clean anything Annie wasn't sure.

There was a pleasant breeze blowing down by the water, but within five minutes she was dripping in sweat. Her linen trousers and fitted shirt, perfect in the hotel air-conditioning, were no match for the near-forty-degree temperature and high humidity outside.

She could almost feel her hair crinkling as the moisture was sucked out of it. She should have brought bottled water from the hotel, as she was parched already. She passed a street wagon where two sulky-looking young men were selling samosas and something else that looked similar but was a different shape. They had water, too, but it was sitting directly in the sunlight and covered in a thick layer of dust.

By the time she turned away from the sea and started to walk in towards the shopping area, her hair felt frizzed and her shirt was stuck to her body, her shoulder bag leaving an even darker sodden stripe across her chest. She could feel the makeup sliding off her face, and her strappy white sandals were orange now with dust, creating little pouffy clouds of grime with every step she took.

In the absence of a footpath, she found herself jumping left and right to avoid the traffic, the pedestrians, the animals, the piles of debris, broken bricks or discarded pieces of plumbing that dotted the side of the road.

Behind her, in front of her, towards her, away from her, people streamed in every direction, walking, walking, walking, like a freshly painted mural smearing on a pavement in the rain.

Everywhere she looked screamed of thirst: paint peeled from walls, bark hung off trees, leaves sagged on branches, dogs panted in whatever meager shade they could find.

Was this why everyone dressed in such brilliant colors, she wondered? So they didn't feel as boiled dry and brown as the earth all around them? Her own neutral tones were decidedly bland, as well as dripping wet and unbearably hot.

She was entering the shopping district now, just a few boiling blocks away from the main street, but the dusty apartment buildings and private residences were giving way to the occasional storefront.

Across the road, an untended fruit stall provided an extra explosion of color on the side of the grimy street. Annie stopped in the shade of an abandoned building just to feast her eyes on it.

Luminous persimmons were displayed in boxes lined with bright-pink tissue paper next to oranges stacked in cartons of brilliant blue. Pears were neatly layered beneath piles of plump green grapes, dangling over the sides above the bananas. Fat green watermelons glistened in rows at the bottom of the display, with some other dark-red fruit — tamarillo? — climbing up the shelves behind them, lemons and limes filling in all the dull gaps.

Behind the stall, the corrugated-iron fencing had been painted in thick blue and white stripes. The whole scene looked like a work of art. And where the fencing ran out someone had made an attempt to brighten up an otherwise uninspired storefront with a collection of plastic containers — red, orange, green and white — tied together with string like balloons and clacking uninterestingly in the breeze.

The shop, Annie saw, was a clothing store called Nice Thread. Two Indian women swathed in different shades of mauve were standing in front of the window pointing up at something in one corner.

She could see that the door into the little shop was shut, which led her to believe it might be air-conditioned. The very thought started to lower her temperature, so when she felt brave enough to attempt a road crossing, she scuttled to the other side, pushed open the door and stepped into the small but blissfully cool space.

A thin boy in his early teens was sitting listlessly on a stool but jumped to attention. The store was tiny, with two racks on either side completely stuffed with colored cotton and muslin tops roughly organized in color.

'Can I try that on?' Annie said pointing to a pale-green tunic top. 'And that and that?'

Half an hour later she owned one in every color. Her

own oatmeal threads were shoved in a plastic bag and she was wearing a pair of white cotton pants and a pale pink top. The young boy had not spoken a single word to her during the whole process but had known exactly what she was looking for and kept delivering it to the tiny changing room, his thin brown arm poking through the curtains with anything he thought she might like.

Probably every *Pasta Ponder Hanky Panky* tourist who passed by did the exact same thing, she thought, but who could blame them? Over-dressed white women could only get so close to expiration before they were moved to outfit themselves the way the locals did.

Still, by the time she emerged from the phone shop, another ten minutes' walk away, with her new SIM card, she was once more overcome by the heat.

When a rickshaw stopped in front of her, she fought the urge to turn the hopeful-looking driver away, and instead climbed into the back seat, the heat on the black plastic burning through her new cotton trousers.

'Do you know where the Taj Lands End is?' she started to say, but the driver lurched out into the traffic before she could finish. He hurtled through the other rickshaws and cars and taxis as though he was the manic orb bouncing off the obstacles in a pinball machine, honking the whole way whether anyone was in front of them or not.

'Please, slow down,' Annie gasped, but the driver, sitting with one leg under his bum, seemed not to hear. 'Please,' she begged, 'I'm not in a hurry.'

But he was.

It had taken her half an hour to walk to the mobile-phone shop but it took fewer than five terrifying minutes to get back. She was so frightened as they barreled along the sea face, driving the wrong way into oncoming traffic, that she actually considered throwing herself out the side.

When the driver lurched to a halt outside the hotel gates, she could not get out quickly enough, not even stopping to debate the fare, which at one hundred rupees was three times as much as it should have been.

She just could not wait to get away from the heat, the noise, the dirt, the dust, and the fear of meeting a grisly end on a dusty Mumbai street, where starving dogs would lick at her corpse and Hugh, driving past, would fail to recognize her, dressed as she was in such an unfamiliar way.

Inside the hotel she clocked up another first, going straight to the lobby bar, sinking into a dark velvet sofa and ordering a double gin and tonic.

While she waited for it to arrive, her temperature lowering with each breath, she messaged Hugh that she now had a local number, then messaged Pinto the same thing, adding that she would see him tomorrow morning at the usual time.

From Hugh, she got no response. This rankled. She was tiring of the lack of response from the people who were supposedly closest to her. But from Pinto came the following: *Thunk U*. She took another long sip of her drink, grateful that, despite his lack of education, he still knew about manners.

She was cooler now, more comfortable, although her skin felt scorched and her hair was filthy from her outdoor excursion. The mere thought of washing and drying it exhausted her.

Annie leaned back on the velvet sofa in the bar, sipped her drink again and spotted the salon on the mezzanine floor. Damn Hugh. If he wasn't even going to bother answering her texts she would get her hair done again and charge it to the room. This time, when the hairdresser asked Annie if she would like a cut and color she said yes.

'It is very nice for me to work with hair so fair,' the hairdresser, Miti, said. 'Shall we do some highlights? I think you could be more blonde. I would be more blonde if I were you.'

It was funny to think of anyone imagining they were her. Would they still if they knew that before she came to Mumbai she spent most of the day staring out the window? That some evenings she started thinking of going to bed at six o'clock in the hope that she would sleep and dream about her mother? That she cried over the loss of a dog whose big claim to fame was that he could eat the crotch out of a pair of clean underpants in less than a minute?

'More blonde would be very nice with this pink color of your top, yes, ma'am?' The hairdresser was smiling hopefully at Annie's reflection in the mirror.

Annie did not think she had bought anything pale pink ever before, for herself anyway. Eleanor had made Daisy a pink gingham dress when she was little, doing the smocking herself. Daisy had loved it and been all but surgically removed from it when it grew so tight that the little pearl buttons down her back popped off, one by one, over the course of a single day.

Annie's wardrobe at home was filled with brown, navy

and neutrals. This simple cool top would be it for her on the pink front. There was really no sense in coloring her hair to match one tunic that had cost only ten dollars and would probably fall apart the first time she washed it. On the other hand, she looked so dull in the mirror compared to the hairdresser, whose own jet-black hair shone under the salon lights, and whose skin was as dark and smooth as chocolate ganache.

'You know what? I think you might be right,' she said. 'Blonde it is: knock yourself out.'

It wasn't quite a movie-style transformation, but Annie had to agree that being blonde certainly lifted her looks out of beige and into something brighter. The hairdresser did a lovely job, the highlights a honeyed gold, and the way she had trimmed Annie's fringe and styled her hair smooth but with a bit of bounce suited her face, took a year or two away from her features.

'This brings out your eyes,' the hairdresser said, draping Annie's hair this way and that with her comb. 'You have very beautiful eyes.' She could hardly wait for Hugh to get back from work to show herself off, but when she checked her phone she saw she had missed three calls from him.

Her heart skipped a beat. Could there be something wrong?

One of the children hurt, perhaps or—But no, she had sent them both her itinerary which included contact details for the hotel, and they'd have called her directly if it was a real emergency. They might be slippery when it came to communicating with home, but she was still the portal through what little there was arrived.

Back in the room the hotel phone was blinking that she had a message.

It was from Hugh: a piece of machinery had gone missing on its way from Pune. No one seemed to know its whereabouts and, as Hugh was the company's man on the ground in India, he was being sent to find it.

He hoped to be back the following day.

'I'm so sorry, Annie,' he said, before turning to someone else and muttering something she couldn't hear. From the honking in the background, she assumed he was in a car. 'I had hoped we'd have more time.'

For what? she thought, tossing her new smooth blonde hair over her shoulder, trying to smother the irritation she felt. More time for what?

She wondered why he had bothered bringing her to Mumbai in the first place. If it wasn't for laughing yoga, Pinto, and the hairdresser, she'd be having the worst trip of her life.

She called room service and ordered two desserts, one a fresh mango sorbet and the other a chocolate torte. Annie knew from experience that it was impossible to stay irritated when chocolate torte was involved.

She was licking the last of the silky stuff off the spoon when her aggravation subsided enough for her to remember the morning she had noticed that her husband was sad, even in his sleep. She'd sailed adrift from her own good fortune. She needed to remember why she was lucky.

Annie thought of Preeti, unconscious in her hospital bed, she thought of the hairdresser who loved her eyes and envied her hair, of Pinto who'd been alone on the streets of this crazy city for more than twenty years, of the ladies on the sand in their saris at Chowpatty Beach doing Heavenly Hirani's laughing yoga.

Daisy wasn't the only one who'd had an easy life: Annie had one too, most of the time. Hugh's absence was unfortunate, but she needed to keep it in perspective.

That didn't exactly stop the irritation, but she thought that perhaps another peeled coconut or two might help her move closer once again to the good fortune she kept forgetting.

Chapter Thirteen

'You look very nice today, ma'am,' Pinto said when he picked her up in the morning.

She was not wearing the same sweats that she'd sweltered in on other days, but had gone for a pastel-green tunic, the new cotton pants, an orange silk scarf Rhona had given her and the flip-flops she'd brought to wear around the hotel room.

'When in Rome . . .' she told Pinto, by way of explaining her attire, but she could tell by his nervous laugh that he didn't get the reference.

'Your hair is good.'

'Thank you, Pinto, and thank you for your text,' she said. Another nervous laugh.

'Did I make some mistake?'

'No! Not at all.'

'I am not going to school when I come to Mumbai. I tell you this yesterday, ma'am?'

'No, but I imagined that you didn't. You taught yourself English?'

'To speak, yes, but to write takes much longer. It take me ten minutes to write for you,' he said.

'Well, I certainly got the message, as we like to say.'

'I have something to show you on the way this morning,' he said as they drove onto the Sea Link. 'I see it when I come to get you and I think this makes you laugh.'

They were driving down the marine parade in South Mumbai when Pinto slowed the cab and pointed to his great find. It was a bus parked at the gates of a large building called St Mary's Primary. The bus was yellow with the word SHCOOL painted across the back and side in big black letters. It did make her laugh.

'It might have taken you a while to learn, but there's nothing wrong with your spelling,' she told Pinto.

'I did not go to school, but I did not go to sh-cool either,' he agreed, pleased that she'd got his joke.

'You sure you don't want to come and try the yoga today?'

'No, ma'am. I sleep in my car, thank you.'

'You didn't get a good night's sleep?'

'Ma'am, I stay now in guesthouse in Colaba, but I share a room with two other taxi drivers. One of them takes a lot of medicines and he is up several times in the night. Other one is very old and he drinks a lot of Kingfisher beer, then when he is drunk he eats his food at sometimes four in the morning. It is hard for me to stay to sleep sometimes.'

Annie was hardly surprised, in those circumstances. 'You're not married, Pinto?'

'Yes, ma'am, and I have three children. A big son and a small son and a very tiny baby.' He fidgeted in his pocket to pull out his phone. 'My eyes are on the road, ma'am,' he said, before she could suggest otherwise, but when they stopped at the lights, he scrolled through the images on his camera and passed the phone back to her.

'This is my very tiny baby,' he said. 'I just come back from visiting her in Jammu. This is where my wife and childrens live.'

The photo was of a sleeping fat peach of a girl, with skin much paler than Pinto's, wrapped up in a pale lemon blanket. She was beautiful and Annie told him so.

'Yes, ma'am. Thank you, ma'am.'

'You must miss them so much. When you go to visit, do you fly?'

'No, ma'am, I have never been in a plane. Now it is still three days in the bus and train — Jammu does not get any closer!'

This morning when they stopped at the lights at the bottom of the hill before turning in towards Chowpatty Beach, a young girl carrying a baby on her hip scratched at the window and made feeding motions with her hand.

She couldn't have been much older than thirteen, and the baby was maybe six months.

Annie started to scramble in her bag for her purse.

'Do not give her money, ma'am,' Pinto said. 'She has gold in her teeth this one. She is a rich girl and her family has many investments.'

'But she's begging, Pinto. And the baby! The money would be for the baby. Surely you must feel sorry for her when you have a baby of your own?'

'The baby is fat, ma'am. The baby does not know about the money. Please do not give anything to this girl. Please do not look at this girl.'

Annie did not look at the girl; she looked at the baby, and as she did, it smiled, a big happy grin accompanied by the wriggle of the pudgy fingers on one chubby hand.

Annie laughed, and the baby grinned even more. Maybe Pinto was right, the baby did not know about money. The baby probably didn't even know it was begging. It was just a baby, wanting what all babies do — to be loved and taken care of.

'I want to take the baby with me,' she said.

'I know, ma'am — all the madams want to take the baby with them. This is why the baby is here.'

The madams, as it turned out, were just as predictable as everything else.

There was so much more she wanted to ask Pinto, but they were already at Wilson College. Annie had barely put her brake foot through the floor the whole drive — she'd hardly noticed the traffic at all.

'I must be getting used to it,' she said.

'You are very safe with me, ma'am,' he said. 'I am down the street catching some winks.'

She had no doubt about that — ever since he'd told her about taxis being houses she'd spotted locals who shared Hugh's uncanny ability to fall asleep wherever he lay, only they were in the back of rickshaws or slumped on chairs or park benches. She'd even seen a man sleeping precariously on the concrete railing of a freeway on-ramp.

'Good morning, everyone,' she said, to those gathered under the banyan tree. 'Lovely to see you all again.'

'Lovely to see you all again,' echoed Shruti, giving her a high- five.

Annie relaxed quickly into the yoga, enjoying the slow stretches, cajoling her muscles into going that extra inch before sliding back to being relaxed. The leaning into each other was wonderful. The more she let go, refused to tense, the more she felt supported by the person next to her, Sandeep on one side, as always, and a short but solid woman she had not met before, but whose name she was told was Kirti, on the other.

She kicked off her flip-flops and tossed them into the middle of the circle the way the other women had, noticing that the other footwear in the pile was mostly tattered sandals, enjoying the feeling of the fine dusty sand beneath her toes.

This morning, the laughter started early, when the two oldest members of the group, a couple called Pooja and Suraj, forgot what they were doing and let go of each other during a tandem balancing stretch.

Instead of holding wrists while they squatted to hold each other up, they both plopped back on the sand like shuttlecocks, exhaling with matching puffs of surprise. The laughing school laughed.

'Well then, we may as well take it from here,' Heavenly Hirani said. 'I was going to do some sun salutations but it looks like the laughter is ready and waiting for us today.'

This time she forgot to speak in English, so Annie did her best to follow without verbal instructions.

The first exercise was obviously a mirror laugh, with each person holding up one hand and looking into it, shaking a finger and laughing. The apology laugh came next, and a variation on the Chinese/Japanese laugh which included blowing out the cheeks and squinting.

In between, Annie kept laughing because across the circle Shruti did, too, flying into a fresh gale every time she looked at Pooja and Suraj, who were still slapping at each other and blaming the other one for the tip-up.

The last laugh involved the school forming a human train and Swedish massaging the shoulders of the person in front of them, then turning in the other direction and doing it again.

By quarter to eight the sun could have fallen out of the sky and light would still have radiated from the north end of Chowpatty Beach.

After the oms and the hymn, Kirti turned to Annie and said something she couldn't understand, repeating it over and over.

'What's she saying?' Annie turned to ask Sandeep, whom she could usually find right behind her.

'She is saying, "Do you speak Hindi?" ' Sandeep reported.

No, I just smile and nod, Annie acted out, making Kirti laugh. Back under the tree, Priyanka produced a large plastic bag full of spiced nuts and started dishing them out into the open hands of the laughing yoga school.

Annie thought about pretending to be looking for something in her own purse so she could avoid being given any, but felt ashamed. She loved the company these women provided she told herself as she opened her palms to receive the snacks, and if she got Delhi Belly? Well, it was a price worth paying.

The nuts were fiery to begin with, and she almost choked on the first mouthful, but after that first burst they proved quite addictive. She ate them all.

The men sat separately, over on the wall that separated the beach from the pavement, ribbing one of them, Ashor, who had just revealed that he had, as of that day, 'completed' fifty years of marriage.

Fifty years, thought Annie. Now that was a milestone,

although 'completing' it didn't make it sound like much fun, more of a chore. And to look at him, she would have pegged him as one of the younger ones in the group, but if he'd been married half a century he was probably closer to seventy.

It occurred to her then that Heavenly Hirani's School of Laughing Yoga, while it was ostensibly for everyone, might actually only be popular with old people.

'Is this a senior citizens' group?' she asked Shruti. 'Are you a senior citizen?'

'No, but . . . '

'Everyone else is?'

'I am only sixty-two,' said Malika.

'I am sixty-three,' said Priyanka.

'Meera is ninety-three,' Shruti said, indicating the woman with the walking frame, who had stayed in the shade today. 'Although she has been ninety- three for a few years now.'

Annie wasn't sure how she felt about joining a senior citizens' group when she was only forty-nine, and her doubt must have registered on her face because Heavenly turned to her and said: 'You are only as old as you feel, Mrs Hugh. And when you come here, you feel much younger. No need for facelifts at Heavenly Hirani's School of Laughing Yoga.'

'But where are all the actual young people?' Annie couldn't believe she hadn't noticed this before.

'They do not want to do yoga,' sighed Malika. 'They want to work in IT and move to America.' Malika wasn't married, but had two nephews who had done just that, she said. 'And my sister is praying fourteen times a day that they will see the light and come home, but I do not think this will happen. They go to a gym and do spin classes where they are now.'

'Not easy coming back to the slum after living in a big fancy apartment in New York, hmm?' Shruti was shaking her head. 'Remember how my cousin Tabrez complained every day for six years when he came back?'

'Anyone would think the slum is a bad place to live,' said Priyanka, and they all laughed.

'But isn't the slum a bad place to live?' Annie was confused. 'Not Dharavi slum,' said Malika. 'It is five-star.'

'It depends what you mean by bad,' said Shruti.

'I thought all slums were bad.'

They laughed again.

'How many have you been to?' Malika wanted to know.

'I'm sorry.' Annie was embarrassed. 'I don't mean to offend, but where I come from a slum is not somewhere that has an option to be good.'

'You have slums where you come from?'

'No, I mean slums in India. I thought they were terrible places to live.'

'That Mother Teresa,' Shruti said. 'She has a lot to answer for, eh?' 'Calcutta — giving all of India a bad name!'

'Do not tease,' Heavenly said. 'Have you been to the slum here, Mrs Hugh Jordan?'

'No, of course not.' The very idea of it turned her stomach. 'That wiped the smile off her face, did you see?' chortled Priyanka, but not unkindly.

'So then, tell me,' Heavenly said. 'What do you think of with this word "slum"?'

'Oh, I'm so sorry, I'm putting my foot in it.'

'No! Your foot is where it should be. But tell me what you think when you hear this word.'

Annie's cheeks, already flushed by the sun and her mortification, colored further. 'Well, I think of poverty, I suppose. And dirt. And open drains. And beggars. And sickness. And crying babies. Just . . . misery.'

The women nodded enthusiastically in agreement. 'Yes, this is what most Westerners think,' agreed Heavenly.

'Although rich white babies cry, too,' said Malika. 'I sat next to one on the plane when I went to Chennai to visit my auntie. Ay ay ay, that tiny little thing could scream.'

'Yes, yes, of course, I don't mean just the crying part,' Annie said. 'With the babies. It's the hunger. And anyway, it's just what I think. I'm sure I've got it all completely wrong.'

'Would you like to get it all completely right?' Heavenly asked. 'Of course. The last thing I want to do is upset anyone.'

'Good. Is your taxi driver coming back for you today?'

'He's sleeping in the car just down the road.'

'Excellent,' said Heavenly. 'Would anybody else like to come with Mrs Hugh Jordan and me to Dharavi slum?'

'Oh, I couldn't!' Annie said. A slum! That was her worst nightmare — the very reason why she'd never wanted to come to India in the first place.

'Good idea. I can visit my niece,' said Shruti. 'I need to get my eyes checked.'

'She is a doctor at the hospital there,' Priyanka explained to Annie, not seeming to notice her panic.

'I tried to get them checked at the fancy-pantsy hospital in Colaba, but they put me on a waiting list a mile long. At Dharavi hospital I just go in and pester Shriva until she does it.'

'The slum has a hospital?'

'And schools, and a university, and it is where you will find the best poppadums and samosas.'

'And the prettiest girls!' piped up Ashor.

'And the tastiest goats,' added the grinning man sitting next to him.

'I can see that you are perhaps a little reluctant to see this for yourself,' Heavenly Hirani said, reaching for Annie's hand, taking it in hers again.

A lump rose in Annie's throat. Heavenly's touch seemed to transport her right back into the figurative arms of her mother. She had the same gentle but assured approach. Even coming from a yoga teacher she barely knew, it felt so much like love it was uncanny.

'What are you afraid of, Mrs Hugh Jordan?'

'I'm not afraid,' Annie said. 'I just wasn't expecting . . . '

'But some of the best things in the world are not expected! Were you expecting to discover laughing yoga when you came to Mumbai?'

'No, I wasn't even expecting to come to Mumbai and I didn't know there was such a thing as laughing yoga.'

'Were you expecting to watch the sunrise on a golden city beach every morning?'

'I didn't know there was a beach.'

'Do you think you will not be safe with us? Do you think we will not take good care of you?'

Annie looked around the group. Now she had figured it out, she couldn't believe she hadn't noticed they were seniors. For a start, they were so small. Sandeep was the tallest and he only came up to her shoulder, but Pooja and Suraj barely made it to her waist. If she was going to get set upon by angry beggars, this crowd was not going to be much help.

'You have a lot to do today?' Shruti asked, innocently. 'Back at the Taj Lands End?'

'There is a very nice pool at the Taj Lands End, I think,' said Malika. 'And three restaurants,' chipped in Priyanka.

'Expensive restaurants,' added Ashor.

'But I think the Indian one, Masala Bay, is very good, is it not?

My brother's next-door-neighbour's driver son worked there and said it was very good but that a glass of wine costs fifteen hundred rupees.'

'Your brother's next-door-neighbour has a driver?' asked one of the men.

'He is the driver. We are talking about my brother, not Mukesh Ambani!'

'So, what are you going to do today?' Sandeep asked Annie, not interested in the adult banter.

Annie's plan for the rest of the day had, in fact, got no further than taking care of her laundry, which involved putting it all in a canvas bag, ticking off on a list what she wanted done to which, and calling housekeeping to come and collect it.

She had nothing to cook, nothing to clean, no one to talk to, nowhere to go other than the pool, and she happened to know it was Babu's day off. She'd thought Valren might be about to chat with at lunch and . . . Well, she had to go to the business center in case Hell had frozen over and Daisy or Ben had answered her emails.

Then she had assumed she would while away the hours until her husband came home so she could watch him fall asleep at the drop of a hat.

It was a schedule that, on reflection, had very little going for it. But still — a slum?

'We are very proud of Dharavi,' Heavenly said. 'Or we would not wish to take you there. But it is a very wonderful small city within a very wonderful big city, and I promise you that after you see it you will not be afraid to visit again. You will also never complain about having a small house.'

'Or about working too hard,' said Priyanka.

Once more Heavenly squeezed her hand. Annie still did not want to go.

And yet, here were these smiling faces looking at her, their heads wobbling like dashboard dinguses. She supposed that all the pale- faced tourists who had come to laughing yoga after reading *Pasta Ponder Hanky Panky* had jumped at the chance for a guided tour of a bona fide slum.

But they had come to India hoping to 'find' themselves and she hadn't.

Not really.

Although strangely enough, Annie had to admit that she was already somehow a slightly different person. Heavenly was right, she hadn't expected to be doing laughing yoga with a gang of geriatrics as the sun came up on Chowpatty Beach.

Yet she had, and she had loved it. Today she had even let go and leaned as far as she could go into the shoulder next to her without worrying about falling over, without worrying about anything.

She thought of Ben, quiet like his Dad, but a rock climber and a surfer, a spirited debater, a sensible kid who nonetheless took risks, someone who would eat hot chillies and have steam coming out of his ears before he would complain, who stood up for his friends when they were being bullied, who didn't believe in being cool, to such an intense degree that he ended up with a cool all of his own.

Ben would have leaned into those laughing yoga shoulders the first time around. Ben would not hesitate for a moment at being asked to go to the Dharavi slum.

'OK, then,' she said. 'I'm in.'

Chapter Fourteen

After much to-ing and fro-ing it was a group of five that ended up going to the slum — Annie, Heavenly, Shruti, Pooja and Suraj. And as Annie had a taxi driver on standby, it was decided that Pinto should take them.

Pinto did not seem impressed. 'Ma'am, I am not that sort of taxi,' he said as Heavenly and Shruti climbed in the back anyway.

Suraj had something to say to him about that, as did his wife, and judging by the tone and the level, it was shaping up to be a right old ding-dong.

Annie stood nervously on the curb while they argued. 'I don't think he wants to take us,' she said, but Heavenly just motioned for her to get in the front.

'He is a taxi driver, this is a taxi, we are wanting to go somewhere, so he will be taking us,' Heavenly said. 'It makes perfect sense.'

Pinto couldn't argue with that, although he certainly looked as though he wanted to. 'Sorry, ma'am,' he said to Annie.

She wasn't sure what for. She was luxuriating in the space of the front seat while the other four were crammed like doughnuts in a box in the rear.

'This is very nice taxi,' he said, by way of explanation. 'Very nice taxi usually only take three peoples.'

'Don't be ridiculous, we could get twelve more in here, at least,' Shruti said.

'Maybe in one of your old dirty city taxis, but not my cool cab,' Pinto said. 'This is very nice taxi.'

'She is teasing you,' Heavenly soothed. 'Come on now. We promise not to let anyone else in.'

Pinto pulled out into the traffic, which was getting heavier now the city was waking up. The Ganesh elephant god glued on a spring to the dashboard was bobbing every which way, as was the crew in the back.

Every bump in the road — and there were many — led to an eruption of laughter.

'Sudden movements at my age — oh dear,' said Shruti. 'Suraj, you need to get your elbow out of my ribs.'

'He could not find your ribs if he tried,' Pooja said, looking at the rolls of flesh tumbling down Shruti's middle beneath her tunic. 'Mind you, he cannot find his own bum some days.'

This made them laugh even harder.

'Oh, sudden noises, too,' hooted Shruti. 'No more. No more.' Annie's right leg quickly grew numb from braking on the carpet in front of her. The traffic had grown to a frightening level, the honk of every horn like a hundred fingernails down a single blackboard. I'm going to die, she thought, as they hurtled around corners and sped past other speeding traffic, the motorbikes swarming around them like bees, a woman pillion passenger in a burka on one side, three laughing boys concertinaed together on the other. Scarves flapped from necks, and packages dangled from panniers and passengers. They whisked past colorful trucks and bus after bus, half of them stopped in the middle of the road so passengers could pour out like porridge.

If Pinto crashes the taxi, the passengers pulled from the wreckage will be described in the Hindustan Times as 'a group of elderly Indians and one middle-aged Western woman', Annie thought. Hugh could read a firsthand account of the smash in the paper and not even know it referred to her.

That was if he even noticed she wasn't at the hotel when he got home. He would probably just lie down and go to sleep and perhaps even get up and go to work the next day before it occurred to him that anything was amiss.

There would be no photo of Annie in the paper, like there was of poor Preeti. Annie's passport and driver license were sensibly in the safe back at the hotel. If everyone else in the car died without first whispering to the paramedics at the scene 'What has happened to Mrs Hugh Jordan?', then she would be alone in a Mumbai hospital bed until who knew when? Her family wouldn't be gathered around, devastated, trying to figure out how to pay the bills. They would be oblivious.

How long would it take Hugh to find her? Did he even read the Hindustan Times?

It was definitely he who would have to notice she was gone, who would have to look for her. If anything happened to him — if he was in another car crash in whichever bit of India his machinery had disappeared in, or got on the wrong train and couldn't get back from some remote province except by riding a donkey which might drop dead at any moment — she could lie dying in a slum hospital for weeks before the children noticed they hadn't heard from her. But then, she could lie at home, dying, for that matter, without them knowing, or thinking to check up on her.

She thought about the time the year before when she

had bumped into a friend who'd casually mentioned Daisy was in town for her own daughter's birthday celebrations. Annie had smiled and fudged it in the store, but cried in the car afterwards, although when she checked her phone there was a message from her daughter saying she'd made the last-minute decision to come to the party. But still, it hurt.

'Am I such an awful mother?' she'd wailed to Rhona. 'Have I being getting it all wrong?'

Rhona! Rhona would notice my death, she realized, as a BMW cut off their taxi with only an inch to spare. Oh, the relief. Even with four children and a weird-acting husband, Rhona would come searching for her.

'Are you feel all right?' Pinto asked, the taxi stopped for a red light, his face creased and anxious as he looked at her, the occupants of the back seat silent.

'Yes,' she said, without much conviction.

'You look like cow who ate cheese,' Pooja said, earning a slap and an earful of Hindi from Suraj.

'This is not right,' Pinto said, agitated. 'Cow who ate cheese? What is this?'

'I know what you look, you look pale,' said Shruti. 'This is funny for us because, you know, in India it is very good to look pale. It is very compliment. We like to look pale.'

'But the tourists like to be in the sun to make their skin darker,' Heavenly said. 'For them pale is not good. This is an upside-down world, eh?'

'You are all right for me to keep driving, ma'am?' Pinto's concern was heart-warming.

Annie forced a smile and nodded. It was an upside-down world.

They were driving down the Mumbai version of a high street now, with shanty-style shops on either side, the usual ebb and flow of colorful pedestrians blurring the street's busy edges.

In front of them she could see nothing but taxis, a sea of black and gold and blue-grey cool cabs. She felt as though they had been driving forever.

Then Pinto jammed on the brakes and, to her surprise, the occupants of the back seat opened the doors and started getting out.

'We are here,' said Pinto.

But the scene into which the colorful group was disgorging seemed no more slum-like than many of the other parts of the city through which Annie had driven on the way to and from Chowpatty Beach.

'I wait,' he said, repeating it louder to make sure Heavenly could hear. 'I wait for madam here.'

'I'll text you, Pinto,' Annie said. 'In case you want to get another fare, or do your exercises.'

'No, ma'am, I wait for you. I always wait for you.'

Annie followed her friends as they navigated the other pedestrians on the main drag, soon turning off down a smaller side street.

It was as though the same number of people, objects, sights and sounds had suddenly squeezed into a fraction of the space.

Chaos reigned on either side of the lane, where tiny makeshift stalls were selling anything and everything. A cow stood outside what appeared to be a butcher's shop, right in front of a wiry young man wielding a cleaver and hacking at a large rack of meaty ribs on a wooden block.

Next to that, a minute, very dark-skinned woman was selling used pots and pans; next to her a boy was hawking what looked like wedding invitations. Across the lane, a flower stall and a spice stall complemented each other's colors perfectly, while a pile of only-just-removed sheepskins broke up the party, bringing with them their very own village of flies.

The lane smelled ripe, thanks mainly to the fleeces, but it did not reek as Annie had expected. The further she got away from the skins, the more she could pick up other, spicier aromas — cardamom, cinnamon, nutmeg — intercepted every now and then by a whiff of jasmine or the odd cloud of laundry detergent.

In between a handcart loaded with a towering stack of what looked like tea towels and a pile, literally, of motor-scooter parts, three small children were sitting in the gutter playing with a stick. They stopped what they were doing to stare at Annie. 'Hello!' the little boy shouted with a grin.

They were beautiful children: two girls with pixie crops and the shirtless boy — three pairs of black eyes above tiny white teeth in perfect brown faces. They were not begging, far from it, they seemed engrossed in their game. In fact, they had all their body parts, seemed well-fed and, despite the dust between their toes and the bedraggled chicken that played peekaboo behind them, happy.

'Hello,' Annie said and waved, at which the two little girls hid their faces behind their hands, peals of laughter soaking into the shoddy walls around them.

'They'll be candidates for the laughing school in another

sixty or seventy years,' she said to Shruti.

'Not so scary for you now, Mrs Hugh Jordan? Think you will survive here for a couple of hours?'

A couple of hours! Heavenly saw the look on Annie's face, but just smiled.

'Mrs Hugh Jordan, you must learn to relax.' And with that she reached for Annie's hand once more and pulled her off the narrow lane into the darkness, leaving the other three to follow.

Dharavi Slum was a maze, with tiny topsy-turvy alleyways leading this way and that, disappearing around corners and criss- crossing each other seemingly ad infinitum. The buildings were only two storeys high and appeared to have either been dropped from space or been haphazardly added so that nothing was quite flush or the same height or even made of the same materials. If she hadn't known they were houses she might have thought they were just piles of discarded building trash.

In places, the alleys were so narrow that Annie could not see how the light would ever get in — but then with the light, she supposed, came heat. There was certainly no air-conditioning in this corner of Mumbai.

Open drains crossed the ground in some parts, but they ran with water, often soapy water, and when she released her nostrils, they didn't smell putrid although she never risked it for long.

It was impossible to keep from looking in the open doorways as they passed because they were sometimes less than a step or two away. Whole families sat on the floor of spaces exactly the size of the bathroom at the Taj.

Some rooms had a bench that ran down the length of one wall where a body or two or even three might be slumbering. At the back, single gas- burners on narrow counters made up the entire kitchen, with pots hanging from the ceiling. Between the doorways, rickety bamboo ladders led to the top floors, where similar-sized rooms she guessed housed similar numbers.

Children ran up and down the ladders like monkeys, or sat in doorways while their mothers, crouched, swept their tiny floors with brush brooms.

Their spaces were minuscule, but Heavenly was right, these women were proud of where they lived. As proud if not more so than many of the women Annie could think of who lived in giant McMansions at home and still moaned about cupboard space.

To think she had been investigating a new island bench for her own kitchen! The kitchen she barely used now the children and her mother were gone and she didn't even need to make up Bertie's special rice dinner or bother with the occasional chicken stew.

She couldn't believe it had been more than a day since she had thought of her poor dog, but before her eyes could well with tears, a baby goat about Bertie's size ran on wobbly legs right in front of her across the alley. A chicken popped out of a doorway in front of it and gave it such a fright that all four of its little hoofs left the ground. It then skittered and galloped back between her legs and into another doorway, where it squeezed under a wooden stool and poked its head out to look up at her.

For a mad second Annie actually thought it could have

been Bertie.

Something about the eyes, the comedy scamper, the checking to see if she was pleased or not.

'Do animals get reincarnated?' she asked Heavenly, who had stopped to talk to a young woman in the house next door to the chicken.

Heavenly was unfazed. 'You think you know this one?'

'I'm sure it must sound silly but my dog, Bertie, he's been missing for a while and Mr Hugh Jordan thinks he is gone, so I was thinking that maybe . . . ' Now she said it out loud it definitely did seem silly. And besides, what help would it be to her to know that Bertie was now a baby goat in a Mumbai slum? He'd only end up in a korma.

'The animals here lead a good life,' Heavenly said, as though reading her thoughts. 'And when they finish it, they lead another one.'

So a korma would not be the end of it. Annie wasn't sure how comforting that was.

'But anyway, in India, you do not need to die to be reincarnated,' Heavenly continued brightly. 'Some prefer to do it while they are still right here on this great good earth.'

Bertie would probably have preferred to be a live preppy Ivy League type with a trust fund, Annie thought. So if he was no more, as Hugh suspected, and if he had a choice, she hoped that's the one he'd made. Although now the baby goat was playing with a potato, rolling it across the floor with its nose, and she had to admit the little dear looked pretty darn happy exactly where it was.

Shruti bustled up behind them, carrying a plastic bag full of onions she'd bought along the way. Pooja and Suraj were slowing her down, she said, because they had bumped into an old friend and were arguing about where they were when they'd last met him.

She would wait for them, she said, they wanted to go to the hospital anyway, in case they saw anyone they knew there.

'You OK, Mrs Hugh?' she asked.

'She is fine,' answered Heavenly. 'Come on, now I show you our industry area.'

They waved goodbye to Shruti and crossed another lane, wider than those in the residential maze, but still impossibly thick with cows, bicycles, motorbikes, cars, trucks, rickshaws, taxis and the constant pumping wave of pedestrians that made Mumbai seem alive, like a heart, the people passing through it this way and that in fat ribbons like blood through veins.

On the other side of this lane, the open doorways led into far less domestic views — the first one was full of rubbish piled right up to the ceiling and had three people sitting on their haunches sifting through it. So did the next one, and the next one, and the next.

'What are they doing?'

'You will see,' said Heavenly. 'Out on the streets there are people collecting the garbage. You have seen these people? Maybe with big bags full of garbage? They bring it to Dharavi to sell it to one of these families. Then the families sort the plastics into different colors, then the different colors will be taken to different machines and will be melted down to little pellets, then the little pellets will be sent all around India and the world to factories where they will be made into other things of that same color.'

'So this pile of pink could end up being a Barbie doll?'

'Exactly,' said Heavenly, smiling. 'In India, your trash is our treasure, but it might also one day be once more your treasure.'

'So even plastic is being reincarnated.'

'While it is still with us here on this great good earth, yes,' said Heavenly. 'This is a perfect example of what I am telling you.'

They turned left down an even grimier alley, this one thick with grey dust and hotter than the ones through which they had already passed. At the first doorway, Heavenly leaned in to address a small man poking at the embers of a smoldering fire. Everything including him was the same shade of ash.

'Behind you, look.' Heavenly pointed to a stack of shiny silver bars, like gold ingots but bigger, that were stacked against the wall. 'Each one is fourteen kilograms of melted aluminum cans!'

'But surely it's too hot for him to work in here,' Annie said, smiling at the man, who smiled back, revealing a mouth entirely free of teeth.

Heavenly shook her head. 'He makes good money,' she said. 'So for him is good temperature.' She said something to the man that made him laugh. 'I tell him he will be retiring to Kerala before we know it.'

Beyond every doorway in the next alley sat rows of men working on old Singer sewing machines, the sort that Eleanor had used when Annie was a child, with a foot treadle operating the needle.

In the last doorway, the whole room seemed to be taken up with bright- green leafy cotton fabric that covered the floor and billowed between the machinists.

'Dresses for Africa,' said Heavenly after a quick chat with the closest machinist. 'Made right here in Dharavi.'

There were fifteen thousand one-room factories in the slum, Heavenly told her. It was the best place in the world to buy suitcases. Or Levi's. Or leather jackets.

'But isn't it slave labor?'

The men bent over their sewing machines making the African caftans looked fresh from the sort of scenes that flashed up in TV news stories about sweatshops.

Heavenly shook her head. 'Do you know, there is almost no unemployment in Dharavi. These people who live here come from out of Mumbai where there are no jobs at all and they work hard. It may not seem much money to you, or me even, but it is enough for them to save and go back to their villages one day and get on with their lives.'

'So no one lives here all the time?'

'Oh yes, doctors and lawyers and air hostesses live here all the time. But these people making the dresses and the leather bags, they come and go.'

Chapter Fifteen

The next alley they passed through led into an airy square. Every doorway that opened onto it was painted a different color, and in one corner there was a raised pergola featuring a Hindu shrine wreathed in flowers and crawling with ginger kittens.

Dotted around the square were large inverted wicker domes on which poppadums were drying in the sun.

'You probably eat these in your hotel,' Heavenly said. 'Best poppadum in India come from Dharavi.'

Annie tried to look enthusiastic yet could not help but feel concern over the proximity of the kittens to the uncovered poppadums.

Heavenly didn't miss this. 'Maybe they are royal princes in a past life, eh?'

The two women perched on the edge of the pergola in the shade, watching as a middle-aged man stepped out of his doorway wrapped in nothing but a towel, brushing his teeth.

'Do the houses have bathrooms?' Annie asked.

'There is running water, not all day, but in most houses,' Heavenly said. 'But the toilets are shared.'

'By how many?'

'Oh, about a thousand,' Heavenly said. 'Tourist ladies love that.'

Two neighbours were sitting on their doorstep to Annie's left, chatting. One was peeling garlic, and the other chopping potatoes on a board on the ground.

The man cleaning his teeth had wandered over to them

and was spitting out his toothpaste next to the potatoes.

An older woman emerged from the room behind the garlic peeler; a teenage boy slipped out after her and disappeared down the alley.

'How many people live in these little places?' Annie asked.

'We like to keep the family together,' Heavenly said. 'So maybe there is a mum and a dad, and their mums and dads, and some children.'

'Six adults? And then the kids?'

'Yes, and we sleep side by side like sardines in a tin,' said Heavenly. 'You have children?'

'Yes, two, but they don't live with me anymore. They're away at university.'

'And your mum and dad?'

'My father died years ago, and my mother, just a few months ago. We didn't sleep like sardines but she did live with us, in our house.'

'Your house is big, yes? She had her own room?'

'Yes, she had her own room.'

Annie had not changed a thing in it. She still slipped in there some days and lay on the bed, pressing her face into her mother's pillow, closing her eyes and sinking into the faint cloud of White Linen she had convinced herself was still there.

'Come on,' Heavenly Hirani said, jumping to her sandaled feet. 'The pottery district is next — it is my favorite.'

They entered the darkest part of the maze yet, slithering between buildings, Heavenly greeting every second occupant as she negotiated their way, warning Annie when to duck her head, when to make way for another small animal, when to peek inside a doorway at a particularly tidy or interesting home.

There were no maps of Dharavi, she said, no street names, no method to its madness.

At one stage they emerged into a large open area which to Annie's horror was piled with garbage almost as high as the two-story slum buildings beside it. Children ran up and down the rubbish hills, chasing and playing, dogs barking, chickens squawking.

'But, Heavenly, this cannot be safe,' she said.

'Maybe,' Heavenly agreed, merely raising an eyebrow. 'The charities people did clean it up once or twice, but the people here filled it in again.'

'Why?'

'Because if it is cleaned up someone will build more houses on it and then there is nowhere for the children to run and sometimes we like to see the sky.'

Annie looked up at the hazy blue above them as a train rattled past behind the rubbish hills.

Heavenly Hirani turned down another alley, this one so narrow that she felt her shoulders could almost touch either side; it was barely a person wide.

In through one doorway, she saw a family of sardines, flat out on the floor, all lying on their sides, just as Heavenly had described. There were four adults and three children in descending size, each with an arm slung over the one in front, the smallest clutching a towel.

It grabbed at her heart, that sight, and squeezed. She

fought the urge to stay and just watch them sleeping, but Heavenly was moving quickly up ahead, and Annie knew that if she was left behind she would never find her way out again.

The narrow alley spat them out into another square, but nearly every inch of this one was covered in teetering stacks of terracotta pots of every shape and size, from something Annie might put her earrings in to something she might plant a tree in.

The doorways here opened into rooms full of loose clay, some of it in various stages of being made into something else, some of it just piled, wet, in a corner. As they walked away from the square, more pots lined the sides of the alleys, which were interrupted every now and then by a smoking pit. Annie assumed they were where the clay was baked.

Wherever she looked — in doorways, down halls, in crowded rooms, on stoops — clutches of people were gathered, chatting, combing each other's hair, passing fruit or children around, or newspapers, ribbons, glasses.

The generations were all here together, mixed up in this part of the slum with the terracotta pots and clay, everyone all in together, talking, laughing, sharing.

You would not lie on your deathbed in Dharavi without anybody noticing, thought Annie. You would not be a sad story in a newspaper: a lonely corpse sniffed out by hungry dogs weeks after your death.

This was what families were supposed to be like.

'What about your family, Heavenly?' she asked the little woman. 'Oh, they are everywhere,' she said. 'Always. Here and there.' They passed a tannery, a chai tea stall, a samosa stand; and just as they threaded their way back closer to the railway lines Heavenly pointed out a movie cinema held together with nothing more than some old rope, a few sheets of corrugated iron and a peeling collection of ancient Bollywood posters.

'You see, we have everything here,' Heavenly said. 'We are very busy.' 'It's kind of amazing,' Annie said.

'An eye-opener would you say?'

'I don't think I would have believed it without seeing it.'

'This is what the people tell us,' Heavenly said. 'There is not a lot of personal space in Dharavi, but there are a lot of other things.'

'At the very least it's a lesson in getting along,' Annie agreed. 'But the people who live here — if they haven't got villages to go back to — they're happy staying here? They don't want to move anywhere else in Mumbai?'

'There is nowhere else in Mumbai. And Dharavi is in the middle of three big railway lines, only twenty-five minutes from an international airport, and provides the city with so much that if everybody here stopped doing what they are doing for even one day the whole city would collapse. There are three hundred bakeries here in this slum. Three hundred! And you know how we like our breads. Besides, what would all those ladies in Africa do for dresses, hmm? Strut around with nothing on?'

'I just assumed that it would be a place people were desperate to escape from.'

'Mrs Hugh Jordan, people are breaking their necks to get into Dharavi. It is a government-designated five-star slum,' said Heavenly. 'That is right, government-designated! It might look ramshackle to you, but it is location, location, location. You have that where you come from?'

'But surely not all slums are like this?'

'Of course not. Mumbai is a rich city compared to most and there are a lot of very poor people in India — you know this already — but there are a lot of very poor people in other countries, too. I think what Dharavi shows is that to be poor is not the worst thing. It is not the best — but it is not the worst.'

'We don't have anything like this where I come from,' Annie said.

'Then you are very lucky,' Heavenly replied.

At this they emerged back onto the same stretch of Indian high street where they'd left Pinto, and on hearing a cackle Annie turned to find Shruti standing behind her, proudly sporting a pair of bright-blue spectacles.

'So, what do you think? They will do me till I can get a pair of Dolce and Gabbanas, eh?'

Pooja and Suraj were staying, she reported, to go to a movie. She would have gone to it herself, she said, but the glasses were too strong and made her feel queasy.

'Your niece couldn't find you a different pair?'

'She is a doctor, not a miracle worker,' Shruti said. 'And the ones that were better to see through did not go with my sari.'

A loud honk rose out of the sea of other loud honks as Pinto's taxi pulled up and the three of them climbed into it.

Pinto looked rested and relieved to have found her, agreeing to drop Heavenly and Shruti back to Chowpatty

Beach.

'You like this slum?' he asked her, as they headed back to Lands End.

'I don't know if "like" is the right word, but I was amazed by it.'

'Amaze good or amaze bad?'

'Amaze good! I thought it would be sad, but it wasn't.'

'No one in the slums has time for sad, ma'am.'

'Exactly.'

'And the tourist madams like that it is not so disgusting as they think.'

He was right about that. She'd been scared of what she might see at Dharavi and, because of that, what she had seen had an extra rose-tinted glow to it.

'But now I show you something different.' They were near Jaslok Hospital, in the middle of four lanes of traffic, but Pinto started to slow the car down.

'Look up there to your right, ma'am,' he said. 'See this big building that rises in the sky much higher than all the other buildings around it?'

Annie looked, but the traffic hurtling around them made it hard to concentrate.

'Pinto, should we be holding up all these cars?'

'Yes, is fine. But do you see this building, ma'am?'

She looked again. 'Yes, I see it. I couldn't miss it.'

'Ma'am, before at Dharavi you have seen one square mile with one million peoples living on it, yes?'

'Yes, Pinto, but please, speed up.'

'Look out the back window at this building while I speed up, ma'am. OK? Now you are seeing one twenty-seven-storey building that has just five peoples living in it.'

'Five people?'

'Yes, ma'am. Very rich man, Mukesh Ambani. Him, his wife, his very beautiful daughter and his two very fat sons.'

'What, one family lives in a twenty-seven-story building?'

'There are five hundred servants also, ma'am. The saying is that some days when the sun is going one way the building's shadow falls across Dharavi slum, but I am not sure that this is true because the slum is not so close.'

'Whether it's true or not, there is something seriously not right about one family living there and a million living in the slum, even if it is a five-star slum.'

'Yes, ma'am,' Pinto answered. 'Government-designated! This very rich man, Mukesh Ambani, he is not so popular in Mumbai, although his cricket team is getting better.'

Pinto sped up and joined the flow of heaving traffic, although with every vehicle seeming to go in a slightly different direction, it was hardly a flow.

Annie bit her lip twice and broke a nail grabbing the back of the front seat somewhere between the twenty-seven-story house and getting back to the hotel, but she paid him triple the usual, as he had been so patient with the other passengers.

When she looked at her watch, she could hardly believe it was only just midday. She'd been away for so little time yet she felt as though she'd entered a whole new world — like Narnia.

As she walked down the hallway to Room 1802, she felt her phone buzz in her bag to tell her she had a message.

Hoping it was Hugh, she scrabbled to find it, but it wasn't from her husband; again it was from Pinto.

Thunk u so much. If u happey. I'm veary happey every think naice because of u. thunk again far halp me, god help u

So, she was giving him the right money, and she felt stupidly happy at finally knowing that for sure.

She texted back: *My pleasure, Pinto.* And then, after a moment's thought: *See you tomorrow morning, and after yoga let's go sightseeing.*

Chapter Sixteen

To Annie's delight there was an email from Daisy waiting for her when she logged on at the business center.

However, her excitement was short-lived.

Hey, Mom. All good here but I need a new dress to wear to this uber-cool party that Freya is having next Saturday. I've seen one for $349 — looks awesome on. Could you pay that amount into my account? Pretty please? I'll wear my old silver heels, the ones I wore to that dorky wedding last summer, unless you want to pay in extra for a new pair lol! Dx

Annie sat back in her chair and re-read the email. Not a word about India, about yoga, about her, Annie, at all. Just another attempted withdrawal from the Bank of Jordan. She'd bought Daisy a dress a few months before, she recalled, to wear to another one of Freya's parties, whoever Freya was.

She had paid it, last time, the however much it was for the dress. She had paid it without even thinking. She had been pleased to be asked. Now, she was not. Now she had a lump in her throat and was trying not to admit how hurt she was. She wanted her daughter to look beautiful and feel confident and happy when she went out, but she also wanted her to at least ask how Annie was doing on the other side of the world in India, a matter of weeks after her own mother's death. It wasn't as though she'd just popped out to get the groceries; it wasn't as though this was an ordinary time in her life.

Pinto, who had never even been to school let alone studied marketing at university while living in a flat and eating food paid for by his parents, had just managed to thank her properly for paying him the equivalent of $30 — and he had actually done something to earn it.

She had made him happy and he had told her.

She couldn't even remember if Daisy had thanked her for the last dress, let alone told her how happy it made her for Annie to buy it for her.

The lump in her throat turned to a rare burning fury, smoking away the goodness from the morning's laughing yoga. That spoiled little madam!

But no sooner had she thought that than she felt the dreary burden of guilt settling around her shoulders like a wet blanket. Daisy was her daughter. Her precious, living daughter. It was a mother's job to love and spoil her children. Wasn't it? She'd lost one and come close to losing Daisy, after all. And if she'd got into the habit of spoiling her, in a way she herself had never been spoiled, there was a very good reason for it. She could hardly blame Daisy for her selfishness, but nor was she in the mood to further indulge it.

Hi darling, not sure about the dress: seems a lot when I only just bought you one, she wrote. Busy getting out and about in Mumbai. I think you'd be impressed by what I've been up to over here. Did you get my other emails? Dad is very busy with work so I'm left to my own devices. It's a whole new world. Talk soon, love Mom.

She pressed send, then clicked on an email from Rhona. Rhona would cheer her up, she was sure.

She was also wrong.

Annie, the hot totty is pregnant!!!!! her friend wrote.

Four months gone!!!! That's why the bastard has been acting so weird. Afraid that I would see her tiny little baby bump, I suppose. Although it's so small that none of the big kids even noticed it. He told me yesterday. By text!!!!! And I've been a wreck ever since. I mean it's not like I want him back or anything, the low-down disgusting FAT loud filthy piece of scum, but I just wasn't prepared for this. The grief he gave me about getting pregnant with Caleb! Do you remember that? The backtracking and brownie-pointing I had to scrabble around with to make up for that. I could never even ask him to look after the kids on his own because he'd made it so clear that it was my choice to have a fourth. (Choice? Huh! The Pill AND a condom? That kid was coming whether I liked it or not.) So I had to do all the work. And I did! And it was bloody hard and I was tired all the time so no wonder I didn't want sex and he was 'forced' to get it from that slut at the dentist's. If he'd helped out around the house every now and then it might have all ended differently. Why do I feel like this? I can't stop crying, Annie. The kids are freaked out, too. They won't say much — well, Joe won't say anything, but the girls are all red-eyed and dramatic and I think they think it means he doesn't love them anymore. Does it mean that? I can cope with him not loving me, but not them. And now I'm not sure I can cope with him not loving me either. He must love HER much, much more if he let her have a baby. Just like that. A baby, Annie!!!! I don't want him back, honestly, but I want something. God, sorry to rant, but just be pleased you can't see me. I look disgusting. My hair is doing something weird and the crown fell off my tooth yesterday so I look like a witch, and not the sexy, fun sort, but the hubble, bubble, toil and trouble sort. Better go. Caleb's got a cold which means he's not running around as much as usual, but every time he coughs it sounds like a demolition ball hitting a brick wall. Email me. Please!!! I miss you!!!!

Annie felt wretched on her friend's behalf. Rhona was never a wreck. Never. She was as solid as a rock — and for her to be crying and using multiple exclamation points, against which she often railed? Bad news.

Annie wished she were there, to squeeze her friend's hand and reassure her that everything was going to be OK. Since she'd lost Eleanor, Annie knew only too well the feeling of having no one who understood, no one who wanted anything more than to make the bad things go away. Eleanor had always been that person for Annie, and sometimes for Rhona, too, and now they just had each other and here they were on opposite sides of the world.

She certainly did remember how tough Rhona had it when Caleb was born. Aidan was a funny chap at the best of times: great fun when there were other people around, but always jiggling and restless when there wasn't anything much going on. He loved having friends over at the drop of a hat, going to parties, organizing outings, conjuring up plans for weekends away. It was always lively, but he could be tiring, and Annie knew that, although his kids loved him and thought he was a riot, it was Rhona who picked up after him, who picked up after them all.

But that was what wives did, what mothers did. Annie had done it, too. Younger men might be more useful around the house these days but Hugh, like Aidan, was not domesticated at all. He would no sooner be able to do a load of laundry than crochet a pot-plant holder. He never cooked, he never cleaned, he didn't even mow the lawn — they paid someone else to do that. He didn't take the kids to their after-school commitments or ever join the PTA or help with their projects or take them to the doctor when they were sick. That was her: she had done all that. And she hadn't minded. Then. But looking back, after reading her daughter's email and her friend's, she minded now.

When had she and Hugh struck that deal, exactly? At least Aidan had told Rhona he wasn't going to help after Caleb was born (the man really was an arse), but with Hugh he had somehow assumed, and she had assumed right along with him.

Had there even been a discussion about her not going back to work?

She'd been so happy to leave her HR job to have Daisy, and then before she could even think about going back to work she'd been pregnant with Ben, and she truly could not remember ever talking about what would happen after that.

They had been difficult days, the most physically demanding Annie could remember. A thirteen-month-old and a newborn? There were weeks when she felt like a cow, being milked around the clock by angry sucking machines. When she thought of that time now she saw herself in a black room, like a modernist Madonna: lonely, bleak, hollow-eyed, pale.

It had been such a good morning in Mumbai, so full of color and surprise and unexpected delight. She had come back to the hotel buzzing, but how quickly a good mood could blow away — like the fine top layer of sand across a beach, disappearing at the first suggestion of a breeze into a vast dark ocean never to be seen again.

Annie felt her old emptiness start to work its way into her crevices, but then Heavenly Hirani floated into her mind, just like a cloud. 'You need to laugh, that is all. Just laugh.'

Annie had been about to answer Rhona by scorning Aidan and his poor taste in cheap sluts. Misery loved company, after all, and in the wake of Daisy's email, she had a few exclamation points of her own to get rid of.

But with Heavenly's words ringing in her ears she decided to take a different approach.

Oh, sweetie. No wonder you're upset. What is he — competing in the Double Standard Olympics? And to tell you by text? What a nutless wonder! But you know, I've been thinking. It could end up working out VERY WELL for you. This way you are going to get a brand-new baby to cuddle and kiss (don't think they won't want to palm it off on you every time they can) and you didn't even have to have sex with the filthy piece of scum to get it. Plus you can hand it back whenever it poops. Rhona, this is going to be a blast! Caleb won't be the youngest anymore, which he will LOVE. The girls will get firsthand experience of what it's like to be in charge of a vomiting mini-troll, so they will never ever want to have sex, ever, for fear of winding up with one of their own. And Joe will probably become a priest. The good kind. On top of that, the hot totty will end up pudgy and tired like we all did. And Aidan doesn't know what's about to hit him. Young moms aren't like we were. He'll be up feeding it expressed milk at 3am and wandering around wearing a Baby Bjorn every Saturday and Sunday so she can sleep in. Within a year he will look 105 and be thoroughly tapped out and exhausted, while you will be the windswept and interesting wrinkle-free ex who can lounge in the bath with a good book and a glass of pinot. Chin up, darling. You're about to get all the Schadenfreude you so richly deserve.

Annie pressed send, feeling mildly elated, but another layer of sand was blown off the surface of her mood when she got back to her room and picked up the Hindustan Times.

Doctors at the hospital had reduced the medication that had been keeping Preeti in a coma, and she had regained consciousness, Annie read, her heart hammering. Damage to the young woman's lips and throat meant she could not speak, but she had been able to communicate with her father using a notepad and pen.

This treatment must be very expensive, Dada, her first message had said. *I am so sorry, my ATM card is in my bag and there is money in my account.*

The wind blew, another layer gone. How different from the message Annie had been given by her own daughter. It was ridiculous to compare the two, but also impossible not to.

Who would do this to me? Preeti asked, on her notepad, the paper reported. *My life is over. My future is gone.*

The culprits, needless to say, had yet to be nabbed.

By the time Hugh got back to the hotel it was dark. He looked exhausted.

'You would not believe the time I've had,' he said bending to kiss Annie on the forehead as she sat on the bed with the newspaper. 'Talk about a wild goose chase.'

She was not going to tell him what she had been doing while he was chasing banana-pickers around the countryside; she was not going to tell him about Daisy or

Rhona or poor Preeti. She was going to wait and see how long it took for him to ask. 'You didn't find it?'

He took off his tie and loosened his shirt collar. 'Well, we know where it isn't. It isn't in Chennai, where it was made. It isn't in Bangalore, although it was between 11am and 1pm yesterday, and it isn't in Pune, where it's supposed to be now, but hasn't arrived. How a twenty-ton machine could go missing I seriously don't know. The Indian suppliers are good guys, but they seem just as mystified as I am, which is a worry because they're in charge of the thing.'

He kicked his shoes off and lay back on the bed. 'They are going bananas, excuse the pun, back at the office at home, but all I can do is rely on what I'm being told here, which is "Yes, Mr Hugh, it is on its way."' Hugh wobbled his head as he spoke. 'On its way where is the question.'

He closed his eyes, sinking into the pillows. 'Oh, that feels good.'

Earlier in the day Annie had talked herself into suggesting they brave the traffic and go out for dinner, but looking at her tired husband lying back in the bed half-asleep already, she realized that was not going to happen.

She felt anger stirring with sympathy in her belly, and then his phone rang.

His eyes sprang open and he jumped out of bed to answer it. The banana- picker was still AWOL.

Ten minutes later he was still talking, although Annie had stopped listening.

She changed into her gym clothes and slipped out the door. She didn't think Hugh even noticed.

Chapter Seventeen

Annie slept fitfully, her stomach churning, her mind whirring, and was awake well before the alarm went off.

She considered texting Pinto to say she wasn't going to laughing yoga.

She felt more like crying.

In the end, though, she dithered so long that it was too late to pull out: he would already have been on his way to meet her. She knew that, even with no traffic, it took him half an hour to get from the guesthouse to the Taj Lands End.

And her mood began to lift, as always, just at the sight of the city as they swept over the Sea Link, the sun rising behind her, the Arabian Sea rippling beside her.

She felt even better when she saw that half the laughing yoga school had coincidentally turned up dressed in a similar shade of burgundy.

Three were in saris — one with gold threads shot through it, one with blue flowers, one with green flowers — and four in tunics — one spotty, two floral, and one plain.

The ladies seemed to find this hilarious, particularly Heavenly, who re- arranged the circle so that every second person was wearing the same color.

'Like rubies in a friendship ring,' she said. 'Like lovely laughing rubies.'

By the time Annie was through the first round of 'very well, wonderful, beautiful' she was positively uplifted.

It was physically impossible to hold onto her own personal dark cloud when she was surrounded by lovely rubies on Chowpatty Beach, all chanting their hearts out and smiling at the sun.

I am very well, wonderful, beautiful, not miserable, she told herself as the exercises began.

This time, Heavenly got the entire school sprinting up and down the beach, from the shore to the banyan trees. It may not have started as a laughing exercise, but it certainly turned into one very quickly. It wasn't just that saris weren't made to sprint in; it was that the elderly bodies contained by saris weren't made to be doing the sprinting.

Shruti was bright red in the face from the exertion of laughing, rather than running, and a new woman Annie hadn't seen before was clutching onto Priyanka's arm, her legs crossed, as if in danger of an embarrassing accident — which only seemed to be making her laugh more.

The different speeds at which everyone was running meant that they were coming towards each other instead of all going in the same direction, which led to a lot of collisions in the middle.

Pooja and Suraj had stopped to have a row up near the trees, and Annie was laughing so hard, she was just about on the brink of an embarrassing episode of her own.

'OK, OK, I am thinking the running exercise is not working so well for us today,' Heavenly finally said, gathering them all back into a circle. Laughter continued to ripple around them in waves, rising and falling with heaving shoulders and upturned mouths. 'For now, I would like us to do a special friendship exercise.'

'To go with our friendship ring,' called out one of the rubies.

'Yes,' said Heavenly. 'This is very easy. Now, everybody, off with your shoes. Everybody. That means you, too, Mikhila.'

'Veejay doesn't want me to take off my shoes,' said Mikhila, the newcomer who had been avoiding the embarrassing accident. 'Because then you will see I have a very long second toe.'

'We don't need to see your toes to know that you wear the churidars in your house,' said Priyanka.

'What does that mean?' Annie asked Sandeep, who was, as usual, standing next to her.

'In India if you have a big second toe it means you are very bossy,' he said. 'All the mothers do not want their sons to marry the lady with a big second toe.'

He wiggled his own smooth brown toes, and Annie looked down at hers, neatly manicured, none of them too short or too long.

'You are a good and loyal friend,' said Shruti, peering over from her position further around the circle. 'Very practical.'

'Goodness, that sounds boring.'

'Hmmm. Can you wiggle your little toe separately from the fourth one?' Annie could on her left foot but not her right.

'Interesting,' said Mikhila, looking on. 'It means one half of you is adventurous and not to be trusted with my husband, and the other half of you is very predictable.'

'OK, I want you to push your feet as hard as you can up against the person standing next to you,' ordered Heavenly. 'Up against their feet, OK? So the outsides of your feet are right up against the outsides of their feet and you are pressing into them, into the sand. Then I want you to cross your arms in front of your body and grab a hand on either side.'

The circle did as it was told.

'Now, press against those feet, and pull those hands. Press and pull. Press and pull. Press and pull!'

For a kid, Sandeep was surprisingly strong, and Annie fought to keep her balance as he pressed and pulled.

On her other side, Pooja was far more frail, and the side of her foot was calloused and hard, but she was also remarkably solid in the sand. At first Annie feared she would pull the old woman's arm out of her socket, but Pooja was pulling her, too, the energy in her palms hot and definite.

With her own arms being pulled across her body, it was like being locked in a very intense hug.

She felt suddenly emotional. It was the connection, the physical connection of being part of something, someone, a group of someones.

A warmth rose up, radiating out from some small dark place inside her and reaching to her edges, as if for air, the sun, the tingle in the atmosphere of a random group of separates all somehow briefly but certainly tuned in to each other, to make one lovely, smooth, magnificent, single something.

This was what she was missing at home.

Here, on the other side of the world, with a bunch of almost complete strangers, Annie did not feel lonely.

After laughing yoga, when the group found out Pinto

was taking her sightseeing, everybody had a suggestion as to where she should go and in which order, but her taxi driver had it worked out anyway.

'I show you my top five,' he said, as Annie buckled herself in. 'First we go to Gateway of India because now is good time. No peoples.'

The Gateway of India was a beautiful basalt arch perched on the edge of the harbor down in Colaba, which Pinto said was the heart of South Mumbai. He was surprised that Annie had never heard of it, because it was the city's number-one tourist attraction.

'I'd barely heard of Mumbai before I got here,' she reminded him as they drove down a wide road with grand if past-their-use-by art deco apartment buildings on one side and a vast dusty cricket ground on the other.

The Gateway had been built during the British Raj, more than a hundred years before, especially for a visit by King George and Queen Mary, Pinto said. 'Although the king and queen arrive some years before it is here.'

'So it was built for them — but later?'

'Yes, ma'am. This is sometimes the way in Mumbai.'

Once upon a time the harbor had been a rough place for poor fishermen to come and go, he said, but now it was where all the famous people arrived in the city if they were coming by boat.

Annie could see, as they parked the taxi, that the harbor was peppered with bright ferries tied together in groups, bobbing up and down, their red lifesavers strung along the sides like open mouths.

The boats took tourists on short trips around the harbor,

Pinto said, or to Elephanta Island to see the famous Hindu caves.

'Should I go to the famous Hindu caves?'

'Ma'am, you should go where you want, but there are more better caves in Sanjay Gandhi National Park. Not Hindu, but Buddhist, from when the monks live there many long time ago. We can go there one other day.'

She and Pinto separated to go through different security gates — his and hers — to enter the concourse in front of the Gateway.

He was right: the ferry-boat rides didn't start till nine, so there was barely another soul there.

Annie stopped to take in the Gateway itself, which — with the vast empty concourse in front of it and the harbor behind it — seemed somehow otherworldly to her. At twenty-five yards high with four square turrets on top and an elegant arch in the middle, it was a staggering sight, although at a slightly odd angle to the rest of the city.

'The politicians run out of money to build the good road all the way up to it,' Pinto said. 'This is also sometimes the way in Mumbai.'

To their right, in a fenced-off square surrounded by lush flowering bushes, was a towering statue of a man on a horse. This was Chhatrapati Shivaji, Pinto told her; the great Maratha king from the seventeenth century.

'Very good fighter Hindu king, ma'am. We do not care about him so much in Jammu, but he is very popular here in Maharashtra state. The airport as you know is named Chhatrapati Shivaji now, and so is the train station. I will take you to the train station after.'

Annie walked up to the Gateway. Security guards prevented anyone from walking through the arch, so she walked around to the front of it, where the Arabian Sea stretched into the distance.

The ferries were impossibly jolly, fresh out of a children's book about little boats that could, while container ships and industrial vessels slid mysteriously across the water further out.

She could hear the sea slapping against the rock of the landing in front of her, and the distant call of one ferryman to another out in front somewhere, but otherwise it seemed impossibly peaceful. This gentle haze was as far from the India she had imagined, when she had ever thought to, as she could possibly get. The slum had possessed a mad sort of beauty or charm, which was a surprise, but still matched her expectation of chaos and commotion. Here, though, she could sense a kind of serenity that she had not believed a place like Mumbai, a country like India, could ever possess.

Pinto emerged from behind the Gateway, flicking his cigarette butt onto the ground. Annie wanted to tell him not to smoke or litter, but had to remind herself that he was a grown man and didn't need mothering. No one she knew needed that, it seemed.

A couple of Indian women, sisters perhaps, walked in front of her, smiling shyly. The older woman had a sari on, red and orange in a modern pattern, while the younger one had a bright-pink tunic-style dress with a blue scarf that the breeze had picked up and was lifting out behind her like a sail.

They both had black shiny thick hair caught up in loose

buns at the back, and they stopped at the edge of the jetty to look at the majestic building to the right of the Gateway on the sea face that curved to the north. It was a grand construction, almost gothic in style, with small turrets on each corner and a large one in the center.

'This one is Taj Mahal Palace,' Pinto said following her gaze. 'This is very famous hotel in Mumbai. Brangelina stay here. And Oprah.'

'It's beautiful,' Annie said, as a little girl ran up to the woman in the pink tunic and clutched her legs.

The girl was about four, with a cute bobbed haircut, wearing a white halter- neck dress with plump red strawberries on it and a frill around the bottom. She had a row of tiny pearls around her neck, an armful of bracelets, and yellow sandals with flowers over the toes and around the ankles.

When she looked up and smiled, full of mischief, Annie smiled back, thinking her heart might just break. She wanted to tell the woman in pink that this gorgeous little vision would one day grow up to ignore her mother's emails and turn septic if there wasn't the right sort of hummus in the refrigerator. She wanted to tell the woman in pink that she should try and cling onto who she was before she had the little strawberry princess, because when sequins replaced the strawberries, she would struggle to remember. What she, Annie, wouldn't give now to have a child seek her out, to cling to her like that. Children grew up so quickly, she wanted to tell the woman in pink. Before you have the chance to relax and truly enjoy them — poof! — all of a sudden, they are gone.

She watched a man walk along the sea face in front of the hotel balancing a tray of nuts and a pile of mangoes on his head. He dropped something out of his pocket and slowly lowered himself to the ground — back ramrod straight — to pick it up, effortlessly rising again and moving on.

The vast space in front of the Gateway was starting to fill with people, Indian families mostly, and couples comparing pictures on their phones, holding hands, sharing iPod earphones.

'Part of the Taj Mahal Palace looks newer than the rest of it,' Annie said to Pinto, pointing to a section to the left of the middle dome.

'Yes, ma'am, this happens after India's 9/11. The bad terrorists hit many places at the same time and kill many people.'

This must have been what Hugh had been referring to when they first arrived in Mumbai, but Annie was ashamed to not know more, so she didn't press Pinto for further details other than to ask who was behind the attacks.

'The bad peoples in Pakistan probably,' he said, with a shrug.

'What have they got against India?'

'Ma'am, this is very complicated for you, but for me when I go back to my village, my old friends sometimes they are mean to me because I can pay money to my family and now I have a nice shirt from driving my taxi in Mumbai. Sometimes I think Pakistan is like my old friends.'

Annie thought she could quite well ask Pinto to explain the iCloud and Keynesian economics. He seemed to have a knack for distilling the most convoluted matters into an easily cracked nutshell.

'OK, then, where to next?' she said instead.

'Since we talk about Chhatrapati Shivaji I take you to the train station,' he answered.

The traffic in the city center was getting worse, rising with the temperature from a comfortable level to something verging on unpleasant. Still, Annie found herself distracted by the buildings in this part of Mumbai. Some were broken-down, all but derelict, with damaged shutters, peeling paint and shattered windows, while others were staggeringly beautiful: graceful, ornate and clearly well looked-after.

These unlikely bedfellows nestled next to each other on wide roads choked with buses, taxis, cars, bicycles, handcarts and pedestrians. At one intersection, Annie jumped with fright as a goat leapt onto the hood of a limousine parked on the road beside them.

Be it buildings, cars or people, Mumbai was a mish-mash of opposites.

Nowhere was this more apparent than when out of the mayhem of downtown Mumbai rose the gloriously gothic Chhatrapati Shivaji Terminus with its spikes and domes, its central clock, its collection of columns and turrets.

'Wow' was all she could say as Pinto slowed in the moving traffic for her to get a better look. 'Can I have a look inside?'

'Yes, ma'am, but I must stay with taxi or police will want my money.'

He pulled over, ignoring the honking behind and beside him. 'Go to booking hall, ma'am, and have a look at train platforms, but please to not get close. There are many peoples there at this time of the day and some of them like to do full body massage on the womens.'

'I'll be five minutes,' she said, getting out of the car.

'I will be here,' Pinto said. 'And do not forget to look up.'

The station was across the street so, head down, Annie ventured into the sea of people coming and going from the busy terminal, moving like pebbles in a shallow tide, dragging her across the blue stone floor of the extraordinary building.

By comparison the booking hall was relatively empty, most of the commuters veering off to go straight to the platforms.

She looked up. The grace of the space was in the height — maybe twenty yards, she thought, standing with her back against one of the hall's red marble pillars and following its smooth surface up to the curved ceiling, its ornate trusses meeting in the center like stars; the arches around it covered with carved foliage and tiny gargoyles.

Through one of the lower porticoes opposite the ticket windows she could see the trains arriving at two of the platforms, the ceiling on that side of the building low, the signage modern and ugly, the commuters moving, moving, moving.

But there in the near-empty booking hall, the world froze for a moment, quite perfectly, and Annie, a small speck in a sumptuous vault staring over into a sea of workers, felt a sort of snapshot brand itself on her memory. As a tourist she would never really know what it felt like to come from here, to be part of this throbbing metropolis, but she would know more than anyone who had stayed at home. Or in her hotel.

I've changed, she thought, as a group of little boys ran past her, shrieking, an old man brandishing a walking stick bringing up the rear. In a short time in a strange place, she had changed.

Pinto was waiting anxiously outside the taxi when she emerged from the station, clearly relieved to see she had not been sucked up onto a local train and delivered somewhere out of his reach.

'Do the locals call it Chhatrapati Shivaji Terminus?' she asked as they merged back into the traffic.

'No, ma'am. They call it VT after Victoria Terminus, because otherwise by the time they say Chha-tra-pa-ti Shi-va-ji Ter-min- us the train has gone.'

She laughed. 'Now where?'

'Now, ma'am, I show you something quick on the way to something else very special. This something quick is not for me so good, but for the tourist madams, they like this a lot. Oh, no! Not again!'

He clapped his hands together in prayer pose, resting them on the top of the steering wheel. 'Oh, my god, please what have I done for you to put me behind another madam driver?'

Annie quite liked being behind another madam driver as it slowed Pinto down, if not for long.

'Oh, she has no idea. She goes this way and that.'

The madam driver didn't seem to be any more haphazard in her lane- changing skills than anyone else on the road, but Pinto was determined to get around her and did. If there was one reason to avoid madam drivers it was because their very existence seemed to bring out the worst in the otherwise mild-mannered Pinto.

Annie shuddered as they careened close to another bus, her hands balled in fists at her side, but her heart no longer lurched at these near-misses. If she was getting used to Mumbai traffic then she had changed even more than she thought.

They crossed a cluttered bridge, after which Pinto pulled a U-turn in front of a delivery truck, but so unfazed was the truck driver that he didn't even honk.

Annie looked out the rear window and saw a snake of other taxis doing the same thing behind them.

They slowed down to pass a railway station far less spectacular than VT, and on the far side of it Pinto pulled over to the side of the road and turned to look at her.

'Did auntie at the funny yoga say to you at Dharavi that once you see this slum you will never again say your house is too small or your work is too hard?'

Annie nodded.

'Now, when I show you this thing, you will also never say that you have too much laundries to do.'

He jumped out of the car and she followed him over to the concrete railing on the side of the bridge.

There, below her, stretching between the familiar ramshackle corrugated- iron rooftops to the skyscrapers beyond, was a scene of industry that her eyes could barely decipher.

Washing lines stretched from building to building, hung

with hundreds of white shirts in one direction, blue in the other, green in the distance. Great swathes of printed pink and purple cloth stretched over square concrete pools that were a patchwork of different shades of white-to-grey water.

In one pool a small boy was swimming, in another a large man was lathering himself in suds, above them, on a rooftop, a blue- turbaned wallah was spreading out sheaths of bright-red fabric in piles like ketchup.

The closer she looked, the more she saw.

Down to her left, another turbaned man was beating his washing against the side of a concrete tub. To the right, yet another launderer was stripping off and jumping into a milky-looking bath. Piles of wet whites sat on one rooftop, wet oranges on another, layers of blue pants flapped in the breeze between.

'The world's biggest outdoor laundry,' Pinto said, pleased to see her jaw drop. 'Most of the clothes come here from all Mumbai and from your hotel, too.'

It was mad. And beautiful. Like a beehive.

Her eye would catch the slightest movement, and on closer scrutiny she would see something being wrung out or twisted or beaten or soaked. The lines weren't even, there didn't seem to be a system, it was laundry mayhem.

And yet . . .

'They never make mistakes,' Pinto said. 'They never give the womens back the black pants if she gives them the white pants. Dhobi wallahs, we call them. This is good job.'

'Better than a taxi driver?'

'No, ma'am, and the dhobis stay in the family. So your

father is a dhobi and then you are one, too. Hard work, but good work.'

'And you can go for a swim at lunchtime.'

'Yes, ma'am, although I think this is not the best thing for laundry.'

Annie thought of her washing machine at home, and the dryer that she used more and more. Once upon a time she had dried everything outside, just like this but in two neat, tidy rows, not two thousand. She remembered pressing her face into Daisy's little onesies as they hung on the line, soaking up the delicious sunshine smell. She had stared at her daughter's little dresses hanging up for hours at a time when she was a baby; the wonder of having produced such a perfect specimen.

Ben still brought his laundry home when he visited: two bags full of funky socks and underpants, sports gear and sweats. She loved doing it for him, but she didn't marvel at it hanging on the clothesline.

Now, she didn't even have a clothesline. It had been taken down to make way for a new garden shed years before and never put up again.

'Look,' Pinto said, pointing behind her, away from the laundry. A man approached them along the bridge carrying a huge round ball of laundry on his head. It was almost the same height again as he was. He looked like the stalk of a dandelion.

'This could be the laundries from the Taj Lands End,' Pinto said. 'Ma'am, this is very hot outside now, so I would want you to come with me back in the cool cab.'

As he said the words, Annie realized she was melting.

'You OK, ma'am? You would like water?'

She would, and off into the madness of the city they lurched, but after less than five minutes Pinto stopped and got out, returning moments later with a cold bottle of water and a mango.

'Mango season,' he said. 'You take for later, ma'am. Very good quality. Now I have something else to show that I think you will like even better.'

As they drove through the city, avoiding the snarl-ups where they could, Pinto explained that the sight she was going to see she would see nowhere else in the world but in Mumbai.

'And not even at Harvard can the peoples work out how it happens!'

'Harvard University?'

'Yes, ma'am. I take you now to Churchgate station to see the dabbawallahs. The laundrymen are dhobi wallahs: they do the laundry. These men are dabbawallahs: they do the lunches. These are uneducated men from the villages, but they are more clever than the smart peoples at Harvard.'

Pinto parked his taxi under the shade of the trees lining the street opposite the Churchgate railway station and jumped out to open her door. 'You must cross the road here, but please to look at the traffic because it might not look at you.'

Annie obliged, the sun instantly soaking through her top and heating her skin, sweat running down her spine by the time she got to the other side of the road.

'Hurry, ma'am, come on, come inside.'

She didn't need to be asked twice: being outside was

like standing in an oven. But inside the station was not much cooler, nor quieter — the air was alive and it was a grungy squat affair compared to the beautiful booking hall she'd seen earlier.

Still, trains arrived every two minutes, disgorging thousands of passengers onto the platforms to flow back out onto the street through the entrance Annie had just used. There were so many of them they became a separate entity, a single thing, like a flow of lava.

Interrupting them every now and then were shoe shiners, sitting on the floor behind little wooden boxes at which they tapped sharply with their brushes, between customers, to attract attention. Annie was amazed at how successful this was and at how many men wanted shiny shoes.

'They make a lot of money,' Pinto said of the shiners. 'And don't pay any taxes.'

'But you'd rather be a taxi driver, right?' 'Yes, ma'am! I would rather be a taxi driver.' 'With A/C.'

'With A/C!'

'The shoe shiners are the ones who are too smart for Harvard?' 'No, ma'am. Not that I know of. Wait one moment and you will see.' A dog started howling somewhere inside the station, brakes squeaked outside amid the incessantly honking horns, the shoe shiners clicked their brushes, a man standing behind them gabbled into his cellphone.

The noise was overwhelming and the heat oppressive, but just as Annie was losing the will to live Pinto leaned closer and whispered, 'Look, ma'am, coming towards you down the platform. The dabbawallahs.'

From the midst of the vibrantly colored throng of streaming passengers appeared a steady streak of white-jacketed men carrying trays on their heads, about the length and width of surfboards, but with squared-off corners.

On top of these trays sat dozens of round tiffin tins, each one several layers — about a foot and a half high.

The tiffin-tray bearers swarmed either side of her, like canoes in the rapids, moving impossibly smoothly considering the weights they were bearing.

'Every day, this happens here,' Pinto said. 'Now come outside and watch.'

As the dabbawallahs exited the station and reached the footpath, there were other men in white coats to meet them and help get the trays on the ground, although Annie saw one practically throw his off his head so that one end hit the pedestrian railing while he caught the other end with his hands and lowered it to the pavement.

'He must have thirty tiffins on that tray!'

'Yes, ma'am, and each one is maybe half a kilo.'

'What's in them?'

'Curry, rice, chapatti, a vegetarian dish, like that.'

'And where do they go?'

'This is the secret of the dabbawallahs' system, ma'am. They go to the people who order the tiffin.'

Behind them, a heavily laden tray was turning the corner on the head of a stocky young man. He stepped across the sidewalk and out into the traffic, ignoring the oncoming buses and taxis and bikes, and crossed to the other side of the street, near Pinto's taxi.

'Why is he going over there?'

'Yes, ma'am, on this side of the street the tiffins go to this side of the city and on that side of the street, to the rest of the city. There are one hundred and fifty thousand tiffins delivered every day.'

'How?'

The men on the sidewalk were busy swapping the tiffins around, switching trays and grouping the tins together in different lots, directing the dabbawallahs here and there.

An old man with a weathered face and a silver walrus moustache was stacking his on a wooden handcart.

'Like that,' said Pinto pointing at him, as another dabbawallah passed with his tiffins hanging from his shoulders. 'And like that. Look he is carrying maybe forty of them, ma'am.'

Another tall, thin young man was tying tiffins to his brightly decorated bicycle. Pinto exchanged a few words in Hindi.

'He has fifty tiffins, ma'am.'

'But how does he know where they're going?'

More words were exchanged and Annie moved closer to the bike, where Pinto pointed out the markings on each tin, or each bag the tin was kept in. They looked like scribbles.

'That first number is for the street,' Pinto said, pointing, 'and that second mark there is the building. And this third one is maybe for the mans's name. Like a code.'

The tiffins would be delivered to the registered customers, and the dabbawallahs would pick up the empty tins from the day before, bring those back to the station and be on the train back to the village by four, he explained.

Most were completely uneducated, illiterate, yet studies had shown they made fewer than one mistake every six million deliveries.

'Where does the food come from?'

'Sometimes from the customer's own house, ma'am, but sometimes from the caterers. Beyond the city, ma'am. Because the dabbawallahs have to fit on the train and so they must get on it when there are lesser other peoples.'

As the local wallahs collected their tiffins and started filtering out into the city on foot, by bike, pushing a cart, the street reclaimed its regular chaos.

'Pinto, each thing you show me is more amazing than the last,' Annie said as she climbed, soaked in sweat but enthralled, into the taxi. 'I don't know how you do it.'

'I do not do anything, ma'am. This is India, that is all. This is Mumbai.'

Chapter Eighteen

The news of Preeti was worse, not better.

Her father and the railway company were arguing over who should be paying the hospital bills, while the federal police and the railway company were arguing over who should be dealing with the investigation.

The railway police had arrested a former boyfriend of Preeti's in Delhi, but her father was saying that it could not possibly have been him because not only was he a good boy, from a respectable family, but he had not been in Mumbai when the acid attack took place.

The federal police were asking for the CCTV tapes from Bandra station, but the railway officials were stalling them, saying there was no need now they had their culprit.

In the meantime, Preeti had been too distressed to continue writing and her doctors had once again increased her medication to sedate her.

There were burns to her entire face, it was revealed, and forty per cent of her upper body, including the whole of one arm. The navy hospital where she had been due to start work was being non-committal about what it could offer her should she recover.

My daughter's life is ruined and no one is doing anything about it except bickering, her father said. *My heart is broken.*

Annie was still upset about Preeti when Hugh got back to the hotel, although at least he was in time for them to make a reservation at Masala Bay for dinner.

She showed him the story after he'd taken a shower and dressed, and he read it but was distracted, or at least not visibly affected by it. 'Things like that happen here all the time,' he said. 'Are you ready? I'm starving.'

Annie was floored. 'That's it? Things like this happen? Are you serious?'

Her husband looked surprised. 'I'm sorry, Annie. I didn't mean to upset you.'

'Upset me? We're talking about a promising young woman our daughter's age whose future has been snatched away from her by some completely evil random attacker whom nobody's even trying that hard to find and you're not horrified?'

'I'm sorry, darling. Yes, it is terrible, you're right. I'm just preoccupied by work. Please, let's go to the restaurant. I haven't eaten all day and I'm sure I'm just hungry.'

Annie and Hugh were not arguers, they never had been. Annie was sometimes annoyed, but had learned many years before that there was no point venting her fury at Hugh because that just made him clam up even more. On the odd occasion she'd been furious enough to give him the silent treatment, he hadn't even noticed.

Now, she did not feel like giving him the silent treatment; she felt like slapping him, clawing at his face, pulling his hair, demanding some sort of reaction, any sort of a reaction. She could not remember ever having felt so angry. But if she threw a hissy fit and refused to go to dinner, she knew Hugh would be completely mystified. He would probably think she was sick and call the doctor.

There was no point in even attempting to tell him what was wrong. Besides, it wasn't really about Preeti. It was about Daisy. And how could she be angry at their own daughter, whom she loved so much?

So she swallowed her feelings — they seemed so misplaced, after all — and followed him down to the restaurant for dinner. She drank two glasses of the expensive wine and sat patiently while he took three work phone calls in a row, even smiling as he mouthed his apologies.

But her anger didn't go away. It hid.

Back in the hotel room later that night she texted Pinto that she wanted to go the next day, Sunday, to the monks' caves in the national park. It was Heavenly Hirani's day off, so there was no laughing yoga, but Hugh would once more be setting out to track down his missing banana-picker and Annie wanted to go somewhere, to do something, where she would feel better than she did right now in that hotel room, her husband snoring next to her.

I see you then, Pinto texted back. *Thunk u. I am heppy to do some.*

The Sanjay Gandhi National Park was yet another surprise, not the least because the entrance to it was straight off a major highway along which they had sped for the better part of an hour.

Pinto literally made a turn in the middle of the freeway, crossing a lane of oncoming traffic, and there between the high-rise apartment buildings and a string of make-do shops were the rather scraggy-looking gates to the park.

It seemed unlikely that through them would be anything park- like, let alone a spectacular collection of caves, but if there was one thing Annie had learned since she had arrived in Mumbai it was to be prepared for a surprise.

Pinto parked his taxi and they walked to the ticket office, where he seemed to haggle for her ticket. As they moved on he explained that he was not allowed to drive in there, but had negotiated for another taxi to take them to the caves, unless they wanted to walk seven kilometres in the claustrophobic heat to get to the heart of the park. 'That's the only option?'

'Yes, ma'am, so this taxi is not a good price and it is not a good taxi, but to walk is a long time and also there could be a tiger but only if you pay some more.'

'For a tiger?'

'For the chance of a tiger.'

'Is that very expensive?'

'Yes, ma'am.'

'And am I likely to see a tiger?'

'No, ma'am. The money is just for the chance.'

'Right, well, I think it is my cup of tea but perhaps not right now.'

'Yes, ma'am.' He grinned as he led her to a small clapped-out van with a serious lean to one side. She climbed in the back, where three people were already sitting, sweating and waiting, while Pinto got in the front and continued bargaining with the driver, although he had already paid the fare.

The van then proceeded to hurtle up the unpaved road through the national park as though they were racing every other taxi in Mumbai, although theirs was the only car on the road.

Annie clutched at the musty moth-eaten curtains

hanging in the window beside her, too terrified to look out the front, her head touching the ceiling every time the van bounced over another pot- hole or speed hump.

Bits of the city were still clearly evident as they sped through the outskirts of the park — pylons sprouted out of weed patches, satellite slum buildings grew like mushrooms between the massive trunks of big gnarled trees.

But as they got further away from the entrance, the city disappeared, leaving only the dusty dry forest bed and gently sloping tree-covered hills. They wound their way up, hurtling around the corners with squealing tires, the driver never changing gear, never slowing down, never noticing that his passengers were being flung around behind him like coconuts in a sack.

Finally, he screeched to a halt and the sweating occupants of the van clambered gratefully out.

Pinto pointed up behind Annie as she shook off the dust that had collected on her during the drive. 'Look, ma'am, right there!'

The closest tree had monkeys hanging from it like mangoes. One had a tiny baby clinging to her so tightly that it was all but indistinguishable from its mother, who looked like she had extra hands and feet and a tiny head sprouting from her torso.

'Oh, they're so sweet!'

'All the tourists madams like the monkeys,' Pinto agreed. 'Look at the very small babies. Twins, I think ma'am, up there — look!'

At the top of the tree one monkey sat on an outer branch with two identical babies on either side, each pulling at different bits of her but trying to keep their balance, a battle one of them lost.

Annie gasped as the baby monkey, hardly bigger than a piece of fruit, fell, but swung onto the branch below and then scampered back up for a cuddle with its mother: so like a human child.

Pinto's smile had dropped off his face, and Annie wondered if he was thinking of his own children back home in Jammu. What must it be like being separated from them for so much of the time?

They walked up to yet another ticket office, where he had to negotiate yet another fee — another time-consuming exercise, but Annie didn't mind. She was happy to sit and watch the monkeys playing in the trees.

'I think each tree has its own monkeys,' Pinto said when he finally got the tickets and returned. 'And its own boss. See this one: I think he is in charge.' He pointed to a branch above them where a big monkey was stretched out on a branch, sleeping. Leaning on him, also sleeping, was a smaller monkey, his lady friend, Annie assumed, and leaning on her was a little one.

They were perched on a single branch, clipped to each other like toys, and their three tails hung down parallel to each other but in different sizes. She took a photo with her phone, and the big monkey opened his eyes and looked at her, scratched his belly, then closed his eyes again.

She would have been happy to go home right then, it was such a wonderful thing to see, but Pinto was having none of that.

'There are many caves and a view at the top that is some

big thing special,' he said. He seemed more excited than usual.

'You don't come here very often, Pinto?'

'Yes, ma'am. But usually the peoples I bring here is very, very old or very, very fat and they cannot do the walking, but today we can do the walking.'

She was pleased he didn't consider her very, very old, because she knew from an earlier idle chat that his benchmark for this was fifty-eight and she wasn't far enough away from there to assume she didn't fall into the category.

They walked up a steep path cut into the rock and turned up a hand-carved set of steps. At the top, built into the basalt, were three dwellings, each with a pillared entrance, three interior rooms and the remains of what looked like shrines built into the walls.

'People lived here?'

'Yes, ma'am, I think it is the crazy Janians. For some thousand years.'

'What's a crazy Janian?'

'Like a Buddhist but with different karma, ma'am. I'm not sure more.'

What he was sure of was that whatever sort of Buddhists they were they had lived in the Kanheri rock caves for hundreds of years. It was like a university for monks, he said, with more than one hundred hollows scattered across the hills.

'Come up, ma'am, because the caves get more better up higher, and also empty because the old fat peoples never go.'

They climbed higher, passing more cave homes, with Pinto stopping to point out various touches, such as the channels carved into the rock that had delivered water to the monks as far back, he thought, as the third century.

A vast temple halfway up with huge stone pillars carved into its interior took Annie's breath away. It wasn't just the beautiful simplicity of the large phallic shrine at the far end of the carved- out cavern that transfixed her: the light coming in through the entrance cast a spectacular glow on the pillars' intricate gargoyles, the floor's carefully pocked texture, the shrine's smooth curves.

'This is beautiful,' she said. 'Absolutely beautiful.'

'Maybe the crazy Janians get married in here,' Pinto said. 'I think this. Come on, we go higher.'

They kept climbing, sometimes taking hand-carved steps, sometimes just clambering over rocks. As Pinto had predicted, the other tourists fell away. It was the heat more than the height that made it difficult. Annie was dripping. Pinto took her bag and slung it over his shoulder.

'You will be happy to come to the top,' he said.

And when they got there, she was.

'Look, ma'am,' Pinto said, turning around and pointing back in the direction from which they had come. 'Mumbai.'

They were on top of a large rock face, with smaller rocks scattered around it, one of which formed a perfect throne. Annie sat on it. Below the rock face, the national park spread like a lush green blanket, falling away into the distance, where Annie could just make out the faraway outline of the city. Otherwise she could have been on the moon, she felt so far away from the traffic of Colaba.

'I can't believe this is only an hour away from Mumbai,' she said.

'It's good,' agreed Pinto. 'I like coming here.'

He walked to the edge of the rock face and held up both arms.

'I'm king of the world!' he shouted. 'I'm king of the world.'

He turned to Annie. 'Ma'am, can you take photo of me? To send to my village.'

He handed over his phone and she took one and showed it to him.

'Maybe one more where I look better for my wife,' he said. 'Has your wife ever been to Mumbai?' Annie asked as they made their way back down from the highest point.

'No, ma'am. She has never been away from the village.'

'Does she want to come?'

'I don't know, ma'am. I am not asking her.'

Husbands everywhere seemed not in the habit of asking their wives much, it would seem, Annie thought, as they clambered back down the hill.

'Who was Sanjay Gandhi?' she asked as they started the drive towards the city.

'He was son of Indira Gandhi, our very famous prime minister,' Pinto answered.

'And she was the daughter of the other Gandhi? The really famous one?'

'No, ma'am. You know about this other Gandhi? This really famous one?' He eyed her in the rear-vision mirror.

'Would you hate me if I said no?'

'Ma'am, I would never hate you because you are always

making me happy by coming in my taxi. But if you would like to know more about this other Gandhi I can take you to my favorite place. I like this one better than the dabbawallahs and VT.'

'What is it?'

'The Gandhi house, ma'am. Is a small museum. Very good. I think you will like it.'

Annie was not usually much of a museum person. The world's larger collections tended to leave her overwhelmed. But she was indeed hazy about the significance of this other Gandhi, and Pinto had not steered her in the wrong direction yet. 'Lead on,' she said. 'Gandhi house it is.'

The museum was in a charming three-story house in a lovely, leafy street not that far inland from Chowpatty Beach.

'This is where Gandhi lives while he is in Mumbai in the olden times,' Pinto said, pulling up outside. 'Although he spends much of his time walking through India, talking with the peoples, teaching them not to fight and telling Britain to go home.'

He escorted her to the door of the house, then said he had already been there so many times there was nothing he did not know already about the father of the nation, so she should explore the place herself. He would be waiting under the tree across the road having a smoke.

'Start on the top floor,' he said, 'where Gandhi sleeps, then go to puppets.' 'Puppets?'

But desperate for his smoke, Pinto was already heading for the shady tree.

The ground floor of the museum was a research center

and library, but not the glossy and pristine sort. It was still just a house, to all intents and purposes, with the rooms turned into offices.

Annie loved the place just for the worn wooden stairs, for the peeling paint on the walls, adorned with photos of Gandhi as a boy, a teenager, a young man. The interior designers where she came from would be in hysterics at the very sight of the original mosaic tiles on the floor of the rooms she peered into. They would have been just as at home in a grand palazzo in Rome as beneath Gandhi's bare feet.

The house, she read, when she arrived on the top floor, was where Gandhi had stayed whenever he was in Bombay, as it was then, between 1917 and 1934. His room had been preserved as he had lived in it. The crisp white walls and dark wooden shutters gave it a tropical feel, but it was sparsely furnished, with just a mattress on the floor, a writing desk, a bookshelf, and a small traditional cotton loom.

There was hardly anyone else in the museum, and it was so quiet Annie could hear the rustle of the leaves on the trees on the terrace outside the door of Gandhi's room.

In the space across from this she started to piece together more of Gandhi's life, looking at photos, mementoes and copies of various documents. He was born into a relatively well-to-do family, she read, travelled to London to study law, then went to South Africa, where he was thrown off a train for being colored.

This inspired a lifelong battle for equality, not just for himself, but for everyone.

All she really knew of Gandhi was that Ben Kingsley had played him in a movie she had never bothered to see. Now she at least knew why he deserved a movie. Gandhi had been an advocate for all the downtrodden — the peasants, the persecuted, women, even vegetarians, although she wasn't quite sure how downtrodden vegetarians were.

He was ahead of his time in some ways, she thought, or maybe he was part of the reason why the times ended up where they were. Ghandi was a fan of civil disobedience but only if it was non- violent, and he was a poet: or at least he wrote soul-scorching prose in beautiful handwriting which as far as Annie was concerned was as good as poetry ever got. Framed on one wall in lovely open, cursive script was the simple motto: Be truthful, gentle and fearless. The simplicity of this gave her goose bumps. Did she try hard enough, she wondered, to be truthful, gentle and fearless? It seemed so straightforward written down like that: a blunt little instruction on how to live a worthwhile life.

It was easy enough to be gentle — for her anyway — but being truthful was hard. It required work. And it came with risk. She supposed that was where the fearlessness came in.

I lack that sort of bravery, she thought, moving into the next room, so it was one out of three for her as far as Gandhi's recipe for living was concerned.

He, however, was truly a man of his wise words, and nowhere was there a clearer example of this than in a neatly typed single- page letter on a different wall, dated 23 July 1939, and addressed to Herr Hitler.

Dear friend, Gandhi began, before very politely asking the Führer to please not start a war which may reduce humanity to the savage state. Tears welled in Annie's eyes. The chutzpah of a man halfway across the world, asking the leader of the Third Reich to take his foot off the gas.

Gentle and fearless, indeed.

A lot of the weightier political issues for which Gandhi fought long and hard proved somewhat beyond her, but the basics were spelled out in an adjoining room devoted to a series of miniature tableaux.

These, she figured, were the puppets to which Pinto had referred.

Doll-like creatures formed dramatic scenes behind glass-fronted boxes about the size of an old-fashioned color TV set such as the Philips K9 of Annie's youth.

The first scene depicted Gandhi leaving India after gaining the approval of his doll-sized mother and her sari-wearing friends only by vowing not to touch wine, women or meat, in that order, according to the plaque on the front of the glass box containing the tableau.

The Gandhi doll then went on to South Africa, where he was turfed from the train, started advocating for the downtrodden, and eventually travelled to London to meet the king in Buckingham Palace. This doll house made Annie laugh out loud — not because Gandhi was wearing his traditional garb, which by then was just a loin cloth, so he must have been freezing cold in London — but because the queen doll looked so much like the real thing.

The scene showing Gandhi's wife, Kasturba, dying in his arms in prison sobered her somewhat.

And the gruesome scene of Gandhi's assassination proved equally heart- wrenching, even as played out by puppets. In this tableau, the dolls were crowded around their hero, the closest ones holding him up, the bullet wound in his chest marked by splotches of red paint.

Even though the characters were only eight inches tall, each one had a different look on its face — shock, bewilderment, sadness. Some arms stretched towards the heavens, some towards the man himself, some comforted the dolls standing next to them.

So that's where being truthful, gentle and fearless got him, Annie thought. What a terrible tragedy, but then again, there she was, a white woman from the suburbs on the other side of the world, standing nearly seventy years later where he too had stood, with goose bumps.

The museum was free, but Annie made a donation and bought a handmade book of Gandhi's wisdom and 'glimpses of life'.

She needed all the wisdom and glimpses of life she could get her hands on.

Driving back to the hotel, she realized that she was able to drift off for minutes at a time without imagining being mangled in a car wreck. Then a honk, or a swerve, or the bashing of human hand or motorcyclist's leg against the taxi would bring her back to earth with a thump. Her best moments remained when they were stopped at the traffic lights.

'Oh, ma'am!' Pinto said, during one such lull, pointing to a massive billboard for an upmarket watch company. 'This man, with this watch! Who is this man? Lino? Lilo?'

'Leo,' Annie offered. 'Leonardo di Caprio.'

'Yes, ma'am, Leo di Caprio.' Pinto was dancing in his seat with excitement. 'This man with this watch is in my favorite movie of all times.'

'Let me guess — *Titanic*?'

'Yes, ma'am, *Titanic*. I watch this movie three times. Jack, come back. Jack, come back! And I cry and cry and cry, ma'am. Jack, come back!'

He did as good a Kate Winslet impersonation as any Indian taxi driver could pull off, Annie was sure, and with such enthusiasm she couldn't help but join in.

'Jack, come back! Jack, come back!' the two of them pleaded together.

'She had the whistle, remember, Pinto? She had the whistle, but she could barely blow it.'

'And it is too late for Jack anyway. He is all frozen on the thing. Oh, ma'am, I love this film so much. Jack, come back!'

'You're a romantic, Pinto.'

'I do not think so, ma'am.'

'But you love the story of Jack and Rose.'

'Yes, ma'am, but this is in the movies. For me it is not like Jack and Rose, because for me my parents have chosen my wife.'

'Oh, and this isn't good?'

'It is not good or bad, ma'am, it is just the way it happens. I go back to Jammu one time and my parents have choosed my wife and so we get married, and sometimes I can visit and then we have my big son, my small son, and now the tiny little baby.'

It obviously wasn't going too badly.

'So it was an arranged marriage?'

'This is not a choice in my village to have a love marriage.'

'But you would have wanted one?'

'There is no sense to want one when this is not a choice.'

This struck Annie as being equal parts stunningly pragmatic and hopelessly sad.

'But you love your wife, Pinto.'

'Yes, ma'am. She is nice. But she is a very simple woman. She does not read or write or speak English or go to the ATM. She has never been out of our very small village.'

'But you talk to her on the phone?'

'Sometimes, ma'am, but usually I talk to my father and he says all the things.'

Annie wondered if perhaps she had been wrong, if rather than missing his family Pinto preferred his job driving taxis in Mumbai to the simple life in a distant village with a wife he hadn't chosen and his three children.

'Do you think love marriages are better than arranged marriages?'

'Is different,' he said. 'Even for Jack and Rose, this would have been love marriage when her mother wants for her arranged marriage.'

'So do you think she was wrong to fall in love with Jack?'

'I think that this will make her mother very sad, ma'am, and for me I would not want to make my mother very sad, so I will say arranged marriages are better because you can make your parents happy and then also your parents can help you in your marriage to be happy in your whole family.'

'You really think that?'

'Ma'am, sometimes a while ago I think love marriage would be better, but then my mother and my dad help my wife with all the things when I am not there and this is good for everyone.'

Pinto was not a man to waste too much time questioning what he didn't have, concentrating instead on what he did have, no matter how inferior a situation it seemed to Annie.

She could learn something from him.

'Jack, come back,' he was saying up front, with a chuckle. 'Jack, come back.'

Chapter Nineteen

Preeti's alleged attacker had been released, Annie read when she got back to the Taj Lands End. The police had no evidence against him and were now back at square one, the culprit still un-nabbed.

Nearly a week after the acid attack, the space being devoted to the story was shrinking, the emphasis now on who would pay for what and when. The injured woman's condition was noted as critical but stable and her father disappointed that the only arrest made was of someone the family knew well and whom they never thought for a moment was involved. Preeti had not written any more messages and needed much rest to make a recovery, the doctors had said. At least they were talking about a recovery, Annie thought, as she made her daily trek to the business center.

There was another message from Daisy: *Did you think about the dress?*

Annie cried when she read it.

Was it just the contrast with Preeti that was making her see her beautiful daughter in this new ugly light? Or had Daisy been like this all along and Annie blind to her faults, blind to everyone's faults, including her own? What would Gandhi do if his daughter only talked to him when she wanted something?

She wiped away her tears.

Gandhi would be too busy defending the vegetarians to bother with such a trifling affair.

'Talk about a first-world problem,' Daisy herself would

no doubt say, with a languid eye-roll.

Hi darling, Annie wrote back.

I hope everything's all right back at home. How are the studies going? About the dress, to be honest I feel a bit disappointed that you would ask about that again, but not about what I've been up to, or how I'm feeling after such a big couple of months. I'm in Mumbai, after all — in India! It's like nothing I've ever imagined — hot, dirty, busy, yes — those things I was expecting, but there is so much to see here, so much to do, and exploring it has been a real joy. I wish you were here with me. You'd get through the wet wipes, but I think you would love it, too. Talk soon, love, Mom.

Truthful, tick. Gentle, tick. Fearless? Well, she'd never told her daughter she'd disappointed her before, so tick, tick, tick.

Next she opened a message from Rhona.

Her friend sounded much more like her usual self, saying that she was getting her shizz together and that Annie was right, if she didn't have to have sex with Aidan but could still get to smell the head of a newborn baby she could perhaps start to look at the bright side. Although having sex with someone would be good, she added, if she could find someone who didn't mind her private parts having been quite such a popular delivery route for large humans.

But how are YOU? Rhona asked, *You know, REALLY — as in a not-disappearing way.*

Annie thought about that on her way out to the pool. Since she'd been in India some things had become more muddled in her mind than ever. Her feelings for Hugh and for her children, which she'd never really doubted before, for example: she was doubting now, that was for sure.

And in doing that, she doubted herself. What sort of a woman didn't know whether she loved her husband, and wondered if her daughter was a spoiled brat and her son — — ? Well, she didn't wonder so much about Ben. He was like Hugh, just not a talker. But if she was going to be truthful, thank you Gandhi, he had been in the grunt-only phase for about seven years now and she was tired of it.

She was tired of cleaning up after everyone even though she wanted to because that would mean they had a better time. But what about the time she was having? Basically, it boiled down to having the people she loved most in the world disregarding her, for want of a better expression. And it was pathetic to feel that way, but that didn't make it hurt less.

However, in terms of disappearing, she thought, as she swam lazy laps across the middle of the circular swimming pool, in some ways she felt more definite than she had in years.

It seemed that a lot of what she was thinking about now wasn't exactly new: it had just settled at the bottom of her life like sediment while she got on with things. Now the sediment had been stirred by grief and change.

She was still in a muddle — unsure what the final mix was going to be — but surely it was progress to be even this much clearer about what lurked beneath her own skin?

Congratulating herself on this small revelation, she decided on a pedicure.

The salon receptionist led her over to a leather recliner,

which faced out, just like the treadmills on the floor above, towards the Arabian Sea.

Her manicurist was a man with the spa-appropriate name of Placid. He barely spoke, but had a very gentle touch. He was just starting to work on her toenails when another customer bustled in and flopped into the recliner next to her.

She was stunningly beautiful, about thirty, Annie thought, with glossy dark hair, a red-and-gold sari and spiky high heels, which her manicurist slipped off as she lay back.

'Hi, I'm Maya,' she said. 'You are a guest at the hotel?'

'Yes. Annie,' she answered, stopping just short of calling herself Mrs Hugh Jordan. 'You're a guest, too?'

'I wish,' Maya said. 'I work here. Or for the Taj group anyway. In PR. Down at the Taj Palace mostly. But every now and then I feel it essential to come and do some quality control at the Lands End salon with Rajesh here, don't I, Rajesh?'

Rajesh nodded, hiding a smile as he gently placed both Maya's feet in warm water.

'So, what brings you to Mumbai, Annie?'

'My husband is working here, or somewhere near here, and I just came along for the ride.'

'And do you like it?'

'Do you know what? I actually love it.'

Maya threw back her gorgeous head of hair and laughed. 'You know the best people are always the ones who are so surprised by this crazy city. You are surprised, no?'

'In just about every way imaginable.'

'You expected much more excrement and much less Hinglish, right?' 'Hinglish!' Annie laughed. 'I like that.'

'Hey, what color are you getting?' Maya asked, leaning over to grab the bottle she had selected. 'Ladies On The Town. That sounds about right. See this, Rajesh? I will go Ladies On The Town as well.'

As Rajesh and Placid worked on their toes the two women talked, or rather Maya talked and Annie listened, which was fine by both of them.

'Do you have kids?' Maya began by asking, then she put her hand up to stop herself. 'OK, so you might have noticed by now that Mumbaikars are very nosy. Here is how it works: they will start by asking you if you are married, then proceed to asking whether you have children. Then they will ask if you have boys or girls and if you say only two girls they will suddenly look very happy and say, "Oh, that's a shame!" Because basically what they want is to keep going until they find something wrong. Quite often I will walk away from a conversation thinking, I was a very content, happy woman until that person started asking me about my life. Now I feel like a disaster area!'

'I have a boy and a girl,' Annie said. 'Both in their twenties. Nothing wrong with either, although I would like to hear from them a bit more often.'

'Oh, that is a shame,' Maya said. 'See what I mean. Thanks for making it so easy!'

She had a lovely laugh and found plenty of excuses to use it. Annie found herself envying this woman. She was so content: she sparkled with it.

'I live next door to my parents and I talk to them a hundred times a day,' she said. 'They probably do not want to hear from me anywhere near as much as they do, but that is their bad luck.'

She was married, she told Annie, to a Bollywood actor but not an A-lister, because you had to come from one of a small handful of Bollywood bloodlines to be an A-lister and her husband came from hoteliers in Rajasthan.

'Was it an arranged marriage?' Annie asked, since nosiness was allowed.

'No, it was a love marriage,' Maya said. 'My sister and I — just the two of us, no boys, oh, what a shame! — we both have love marriages. My sister had this big fancy wedding for three thousand people, oh my goodness, you would not believe it. We only had a hundred and fifty, but we did take them all to Goa.'

'So, I hope you don't mind me asking, but are love marriages for the wealthy and arranged marriages for the less wealthy?'

'No, I do not think so,' said Maya. 'I grew up in Mumbai, which as you can tell is fairly cosmopolitan, and my father is a businessman plus we lived in the US for a while; I went to college there. So I suppose we have lived a less traditional life than many others in India. My parents were happy for me to have a love marriage, but they would have arranged one if I had wanted them to. And also, I wanted to marry someone they approved of, so it was sort of like I arranged it myself. This is becoming more common, I think, and it is not much different from how it is done anywhere else.'

'Is one better than the other?'

'I do not know. I think the statistics show that arranged couples do not get divorced that often, but then the divorce rate is low in India anyway. It is all a matter of perspective. Like age. You know, my dad was telling me this morning about his driver who had to go home to his village because some relative or other was sick, and when he got back my dad asked him what happened. "Oh, she died," the driver said, "but it is OK because she was very, very old." Then my dad asked how old, and the driver said, "Forty-two. Like I told you. Very, very old."'

'I thought my taxi driver was being a bit presumptuous thinking fifty-eight was very, very old, but forty-two is something else!'

Maya laughed, wriggled her toes and checked her watch. 'Hey, Ladies On The Town is looking good but I should go. Will it dry on the hop, Rajesh? I had a conference call I was supposed to make ten minutes ago.'

'There's just one more thing I want to ask you,' Annie said. 'Since I have your ear. The beggars on the street: there haven't been that many of them — that's been another surprise — but there was a little girl the other day with a baby on her hip, and my driver said not to give them money, that they have plenty already, that it's a waste.'

Maya laughed again. 'It is a tear-jerker I know and you will notice that the beggars only cling to the tourists because they do not get much sympathy from the locals. All I know is this, Annie: I got my MBA from Harvard, came back to India for a very good job in PR, was promoted twice over a three-year period and only then was I making as much as a

Mumbai beggar.'

She stood and re-arranged her sari. 'You cannot believe everything you hear about India,' she said. 'But you can believe some of it.' She handed over her business card. 'If there is anything I can do for you while you are here, or anything the hotel can do — organize cars, planes, boats, trains, you name it — just let me know. My people will be happy to help.'

Thrilled to have found someone so engaging to while away an hour or so with, Annie was in good spirits for the early part of the evening, but her mood soured when Hugh was home late again.

She ordered room service for the two of them, but let her dahl and roti sit untouched while he talked on the phone and ate his.

When he finally hung up, she could no longer contain her fury. 'Why did you bring me here if all you're going to do is talk on the phone to someone else?'

'But it's work,' he said, surprised.

'And that's an excuse?'

'For working? Of course.'

'Not an excuse for working, Hugh. An excuse for this: for ignoring me. For spending more time on your phone than talking to me when the work day is actually over. Or should be. For not even asking how I'm doing or what I'm doing or if there's anything that's worrying me or if every bloody thing is OK.'

Her voice was getting louder and louder. Hugh looked horrified. 'I just assumed . . . '

'What? You just assumed what?'

'I just assumed that everything was OK.'

'And why would you assume that?'

'Because you never said anything.'

'When did I never say anything, Hugh? When you asked me? Oh, that's funny, because I don't remember you asking me.'

'Annie, I don't mean to upset you. I'm sorry, but this bloody machine—'

'I don't want to hear about the bloody machine!'

'But it's basically twenty million dollars of the firm's money missing in action so—'

'I said I don't want to hear about it!'

They were sitting on either side of the room-service table that had been wheeled in bearing their meals; Hugh on the edge of the bed and Annie on a bedroom chair.

He was sitting up, ramrod straight, looking like a deer trapped in the headlights, which for some reason just made Annie feel angrier.

'So, how are you?' he said. 'What is wrong?'

'I just told you what is wrong!'

'I'm no good at being put on the spot, Annie. You said something was worrying you? What?'

'Our children for a start. Aren't they worrying you? Daisy's emailed me twice asking for money for a dress, but not even asking a single thing about how I am, or what Mumbai is like; and Ben has yet to come out of the grunting stage. He's grunting in his emails! Doesn't that seem odd to you?'

'Oh, Daisy asked me for the money first and I told her to go to you, but only because I thought you girls would want to chat about it,' Hugh said, relieved.

'So you think it is perfectly all right for us to keep forking out money left, right and center — in this case for a dress for one party that costs the same as it would to feed a family here for a year?'

Hugh's relief was short-lived. 'Well, we can't really expect Daisy to know what it's like over here.'

'Can't we? Why not?'

'She's only twenty-two, Annie. You didn't even know what it was like over here until you came, neither did I. It's apples and pears. It's different.'

'I knew there was poverty here — that we're lucky to come from where we come from. And maybe I feel that even more now that I've seen it firsthand. But when I was twenty-two I'd have stuck needles in my eyes before treating my mother like an ATM, before ignoring enormous changes in her life. Are you saying I should just give Daisy anything she wants, whether or not she shows any interest in or compassion for me or anybody?'

'I'm not saying anything. Annie — what has changed? I thought it made you happy to give her things.'

'Well, now I want something back! And I want a son who doesn't have to be pressured into sending me a one-word response when I try to keep in touch with him. He could be dying of starvation for all I know. Or buried under a mound of filthy laundry.'

'Ben's fine; he's on an abseiling course,' Hugh said. 'He passed his last lot of exams with flying colors, so I told him to go for it.'

Annie stared at him. 'He passed his exams? When did

he tell you that?' 'Yesterday, I think.'

'He called you?'

'He emailed.'

Hugh must have known from the look on Annie's face that this was the wrong thing to say.

'He emailed you? And you didn't think to tell me?'

'He doesn't email all the time. Twice a week, maybe. No, more like once. I, I'm sorry. I should have told you. I should have been keeping you up-to-date. I just didn't think it was—'

'Hugh!' His name blew out of her like a gust of polar wind, tears springing to her eyes. She stood up, her chair falling backwards onto the floor, and fled to the bathroom, locking the door and catching sight of her lined, anxious, tear-stained face in the mirror.

They never rowed, never, but she was so angry with him, with what her life had turned into, what they had turned into, what she had turned into: this big, beige blob desperate to be understood by someone, anyone. 'This is not me,' she wept into the hand towel. 'This is not me.'

She was pathetic, her problems were first-world, but that didn't make them not her problems.

Through the closed door she heard Hugh's phone ring, and him answer it, talking in a low voice, which she tuned out as she tried to calm her breathing, staunch the flow of tears.

She couldn't keep hiding: it was childish. That was Hugh sitting out there, the man she'd been married to for twenty-five years. Surely they could work it out somehow?

She dabbed at her face with a cold cloth to get rid of the

puffy cheeks, and ventured back into the room.

Hugh was still sitting on the side of the bed exactly as he had been before, looking as though he'd been hit by a bus. 'Annie,' he said, 'I can forward you Ben's emails from now on if that would make a difference.'

She did know him well. That was true. But after all these years, it seemed he did not know her. She was just another missing banana- picker as far as he was concerned. Never mind why she had gone missing — it was all about locating her whereabouts now, getting back on track, moving on.

'It's not just that, Hugh.' She was tired now, her anger softening into a bitter pool of disappointment. 'It's that they don't want to tell me anything. It's that they don't seem to want me in their lives, and I don't know what I have done to deserve that.'

His incomprehension was growing. 'You've done nothing,' he said. 'Nothing bad. You're great. They're just kids.'

'But can you understand how I feel, Hugh?'

'I thought perhaps a holiday here might help you . . . '

'Might help me what?'

'Cheer up, perhaps, after . . . '

'You want me to cheer up? After my mother dies, my dog disappears, my children abandon me, and you —'

She looked at him, sitting there, utterly bewildered. What had he done? He did not have a single clue what she was talking about. He did not get it. He did not get her.

'I don't know why I'm even trying to talk about this with you, Hugh.'

'Talk about what?' he pleaded. 'Annie, I'm sorry, but I

just don't understand.'

'Exactly,' she said, as his phone started to ring. 'Nobody does.'

Chapter Twenty

'Your laughing was only with the body today,' Heavenly told Annie when they finished on the beach the next day. 'Your heart not in it, eh? Come sit with me in the shade.'

Annie let the old woman take her hand and lead her to the stone benches beneath the banyan tree.

'Pinto is here?'

'Yes, he's asleep around the corner.'

'Would you like to do me a favour?'

'Of course, Heavenly,' Annie said. 'Although I don't know how much help I can be to you.'

'I need to bring something to my niece in her village outside of the city. I'm thinking if Pinto is not busy taking you somewhere else, he could take me there and you could come, too.'

'To the village?'

'Mrs Hugh Jordan, there are three things you must see to know the best of India, and these are the laughing yoga at Chowpatty Beach, the village life not in the city, and the Taj Mahal in Agra.'

'She is right,' said Priyanka, dressed today in daffodil yellow, as she plopped down beside them.

'And Jaipur,' said Kirti. 'That is another third thing.'

'And Goa,' added Malika.

'South Goa,' corrected Pooja.

'No, Kerala,' said the man with the gold teeth, whose name Annie could never remember.

'And if you are going to go to the Taj Mahal, you must

go to the abandoned city on the other side of Agra,' said Shruti. 'You know this one that they built before the water ran out?'

'Fatehpur Sikri,' said Priyanka. 'Yes, that is very beautiful.'

'And if you are going to the Taj Mahal and Fatehpur Sikri, you will be going to Delhi on the way,' said Malika, 'so you need to see Humayun's tomb and Qutub Minar, the oldest minaret in the world.'

'I do not think she will see anything in Delhi apart from the pollution and the traffic jams,' said Kamalijit, as if those two things were strangers to Mumbai.

'What about Gandhi's eternal flame at Raj Ghat?'

'Or the Jama Masjid mosque in the old city?'

'Too hot!'

'Too busy!'

'Too much!' Heavenly said. 'Mrs Hugh Jordan is here for a good time, not a long time, eh? I am talking here about the cream of a very fine crop, but cream it is. Laughing yoga, village life and the Taj Mahal. Then you will go home feeling that you know us and also yourself.'

'How far away is it, the village?' Annie asked.

'Maybe an hour. Maybe two. But it is very beautiful when you get there.'

Annie's heart was not in anything, but more particularly not in another day spent on her own at the hotel. If Pinto was game, she decided, so was she.

Pinto was game. There were only two of them, after all, so he was clearly not breaking his nice-cool-cab protocol.

By the time they hit the freeway, past the Sanjay Gandhi

National Park, the traffic started to ease, or at least seemed to all go in the same direction at a similar pace.

Annie was surprised to see so many of the three-wheeled motorised rickshaws competing with the many buses and trucks and much bigger, much faster-moving objects on the eight-lane interstate.

One particular rickshaw kept falling behind them, then catching up again. There were five people crushed in the front of the tiny buggy, and at least that many in the back. The woman sitting at the end closest to Annie had a sleeping child on her lap, and the sleeping child's fat little feet were sticking out the side of the rickshaw.

Annie couldn't see more than the beaded bracelets around her ankles, the frill of her dress, and the arm of the woman on whose lap she slumbered, which was holding onto the canopy of the rickshaw as it weaved its way north.

Was the owner of the arm not afraid that the baby's precious feet would get caught by a passing truck, or bike, or another rickshaw? Didn't she worry they might get clipped and the chubby little body flung out beneath the wheels of a bus?

From what Annie had seen, Indian parents loved their children as much as, if not more than, any other parents anywhere else in the world, yet they appeared to her so cavalier with their safety. Tiny children riding pillion on motorbikes, playing with petrol cans and matches, sleeping under cars, running at the edges of busy freeways, cuddling diseased dogs, chasing each other through rubbish dumps. These children would surely grow up without fear for their own safety and everyone needed a bit of that. Didn't they?

'Do you let your children play outside on the road, Pinto?'

'In Jammu? Yes, ma'am, all the childrens play on the road. The house is too small for them to play in there, ma'am.'

'But don't you worry about them getting run over by a truck?' 'No, ma'am, because the driver of the truck will have his childrens playing on a road somewhere, too, and he will not want them to get run over, so he will not run over anyone else's childrens.'

This was karma working as it was supposed to, Annie guessed.

'You worry about other people's children and your own children,' Heavenly said, although her eyes were closed and Annie had assumed she was sleeping. 'This is a lot of worry.'

But worry was part of being a parent. It simply had never occurred to Annie during all her years of child-rearing that terrible things would not happen to her children just because she would not do terrible things to anyone else's. Where Annie came from, one assumed the worst and worked backwards from there.

Watching those fat beaded ankles out the window of the car, she had to wonder if maybe the Indian way was better. Maybe the baby's mother never so much as dreamed that any ill would befall her darling, just left it to destiny. That way, what would be would still be, and she had just saved herself the worry of it.

Annie didn't think she had been more protective of her babies than any other mother she knew, yet Daisy — for all those withering pronouncements about other people being pathetic — had grown into a chronic germaphobe. Annie had asked their doctor about it when her daughter was only ten, because she was so insistent on not touching door knobs or escalator rails, shopping-trolley handles, other girls' hands — she would even make Annie remove the straw from a soda at McDonald's and throw it away in case it had been touched by someone else on the way to her cup.

The doctor had rolled his eyes and said it was no surprise kids were paranoid because they were taught to be at school, and sometimes, he said, looking over the top of his bifocals in a way that only a certain sort of doctor seemed to manage, at home.

Annie had hand wash in the bathrooms and by the kitchen sink, and she had not been able to watch her kids' noses run for even a second without snatching a tissue and wiping them, but she was not herself overly afraid of germs.

Daisy remained cautious on that front, and a few others. She didn't like unfamiliar food or sleeping in a bed other than her own or using public restrooms, although she was better about most things than she had been during those awful dark teenage months when Annie had feared so greatly for her survival.

Now she might use the end of her sleeve to open a door, but she could walk into a room full of strangers and charm them without even thinking about it. Germs aside, she wasn't generally afraid.

And neither was Ben, although Annie worried even more over the physical risks he took now. Maybe her over-protectiveness was why he took the risks. Maybe it was why he answered Hugh's emails but not hers. Maybe he didn't want to tell her things because he thought she would try and stop him or nag him, which she didn't think she would, though she might express her worry.

She pursed her lips to push away the thought of her son avoiding her (and abseiling), and concentrated instead on Mumbai, stretching out along the side of the freeway, one identical suburb blending into the next.

If she closed her eyes for ten minutes, she was sure when she woke up the scene outside the window would be exactly the same — exactly the same as the one on the drive in from the city the day she first arrived. Mile after mile after dusty, dirty mile.

She had forgotten on her regular route that took her from Bandra to South Mumbai that this city had twenty-four million people in it and most of them didn't live down there: they lived in these grimy high-rises stretching back into the haze, or in the patchwork of slum buildings that spread like weeds across the ground in front of them.

Annie looked over at Heavenly, who still seemed to be sleeping. She looked older in repose. Her hands were very wrinkled, and she was tiny beneath her orange tunic; her legs like little sticks almost disappearing into the grey upholstery.

Annie leaned back and thought of her mother, how frail she had become in the past few years, how that tin in the corner shop had dropped and ripped open her skin, how hard it was to see strength of spirit trumped by weakness of flesh. Awake, Heavenly Hirani had the air of a wise, mysterious warrior. Asleep, she was a little old lady. Still, that seemed comforting more than anything else, and on thinking that, Annie closed her eyes and drifted off to sleep herself.

When she woke up she had a crick in her neck and the landscape had changed.

They were no longer on the freeway but on a four-lane road filled mostly with the colorful trucks she kept seeing everywhere with their Horn Please OK (India is Great) signs painted on to them.

The high-rises were gone, as were the slums, and instead they were driving through a shonky mixture of rural and industrial wasteland. A pipe factory sat in the middle of a string of green fields, fat cows grazing nearby, then a couple of miles later, in the middle of a vast expanse of dirt, a Mercedes dealership sprouted.

Nothing quite made sense, like in a dream. It seemed reasonable to have a yard of broken-down trucks in the middle of nowhere, but not a mile down the road — with nothing in between — to have an enormous Thai restaurant, tattered prayer flags sagging in the heat, the CLOSED sign slumped against the boarded-up door like a drunken customer. Where enough people desperate for a laksa would come from to fill such a vast eatery Annie could not imagine.

As she was trying to, Pinto slowed down and turned off the main road onto a dirt track leading towards a distant mountain.

Away from the traffic, the landscape brightened. The sky ahead was blue — the hazy layer of pollution clinging to the metropolis they had left behind — and although the track was orange with dust, along the sides of it brave trees bloomed green and gutsy, their spindly trunks out of tune with their lush foliage.

The road curved and a wide clean river emerged beside them. With the sapphire sky, the distant mountains, and the serene beauty of the gently- bowed brick bridge across the glassy river, it was starting to look like the sort of travel destination that Annie had seen in the pages of glossy travel magazines: nothing short of spectacular.

'This is very good bridge,' Pinto said. 'I never come to this bridge before.'

'This is a five-star bridge,' Heavenly agreed, grinning at Annie. 'My own designation.'

As they reached the middle of it, Annie looked north, where the river widened and a smattering of fishing boats were moored on water, so still and inviting that she couldn't believe this was the same country where stagnant brown puddles grew plastic shopping bags like lily pads.

Pinto drove slowly across the bridge, then turned down another dusty road, still heading towards the mountain. Now the landscape changed again: strange flat-topped pyramid-like structures rose out of the dry mud in the bare fields beside the road.

'What are these?'

'These are bricks, ma'am,' said Pinto. 'I see bricks like these before. You see each field is big and square with trees around the outside? In the monsoons, these fields are rice paddies. But now, the peoples make bricks from the mud on the ground because when the monsoon comes, the mud is staying mud.'

'So they're stacking the bricks to dry in the sun? Will that do it?'

'No, ma'am,' Pinto slowed down at the side of one of the fields. 'See this stack close to us is uncooked brick? But behind, ma'am, is cooked brick.'

On closer scrutiny, in the same-shaped stack further away the bricks were a darker color. As Pinto explained it, the uncooked bricks were stacked around a central open fire with air gaps at regular intervals, then a final layer of cooked bricks was added around the outside, creating — to all intents and purposes — an open-topped kiln.

'You have these in your village?' Heavenly asked Pinto.

'Yes, auntie. In Jammu. I build my house with these bricks.'

As they continued down the dusty road, she soon saw how the cooked bricks were used when they passed a particularly dark woman walking along the road carrying a pile of them — on her head.

Annie wound down the window. It must have been forty degrees outside, yet the woman, in a light-green top and sari skirt, was walking with the grace of a gazelle. The muscles in her stomach would have put anyone lifting weights and sweating through spin classes in a Western gym to shame.

As they rounded the next corner, Annie saw where the woman was heading.

Right beside the road a house was being built, by hand, by what looked like one single family.

'Can we slow down, Pinto? I want to watch this,' Annie said.

As they cruised by she saw another woman, very similar — a sister perhaps — to the one they'd passed, walking around the side of the house with another stack of bricks on her head.

Annie calculated she must have been carrying twenty at least. No wonder she was so thin! Nothing more than muscle and sinew. 'The women in this village do not need yoga,' Heavenly said.

'But they do need laughing.'

On this side of the house, a third woman was standing on a rickety bamboo scaffold and, as Annie watched, the brick carrier reached up and took two bricks off her head, then passed them up to the one on the scaffold, who spread a layer of mortar from a bucket at her feet on the wall she was building, and added the two bricks, then reached for two more.

In the shade of the building, two men were asleep next to a tethered goat. Next to them, a little boy was playing with a baby, rolling a ball towards it and laughing as its fat little hands reached in front but failed to get a grip on the toy.

'Why aren't the men helping?' Annie asked.

Pinto shrugged. 'Sleeping,' he said, as if that were enough of an excuse.

Heavenly shrugged, too, but managed to get an eye-roll in with it.

'So that's their own house?' Annie asked.

Heavenly squinted to get a better look. 'I think so.'

'And if the moneys run out, they stop building it for a while. This is so, auntie?'

'This is usually so.'

'But where would they get the money from in the first place?'

Pinto shuffled in his seat. 'These peoples is not your family, auntie?'

'Not these ones,' Heavenly said.

'So I think these peoples come to Mumbai and work for the moneys and save their investments to come home and make bricks from the fields for their house.'

'Do you mean they're beggars?' Annie asked.

'I cannot know this, ma'am,' he said.

'Would they be, Heavenly?'

'I cannot know this either,' Heavenly said.

'Is a very nice house,' Pinto said.

'Maybe the men make dresses for African ladies at Dharavi?'

'Maybe,' said Heavenly.

It was hard for Annie so see how such a small square made of lumps of mud from the surrounding field could ever be seen as a 'nice house', but it became clearer when they arrived at the village proper.

At its entrance was an archway swathed with fabric in peach, dark red and white silks.

'Must be for some wedding,' Pinto said, pulling the car over to the side of the road, maneuvering it so it got as much shade as possible. 'We walk from here I think.'

The heat hit her like a ton of bricks, the ones she had just seen been baked. It was much hotter than Mumbai, and so dry she could feel her lips instantly start to crack.

She grabbed her bottle of water and followed Heavenly

through the archway into a scene of most unexpected delight.

The little squares of mud did not stay that muddy for long.

The village wasn't chocolate-box pretty in the manicured window-box way of rural England or fairy-tale Tuscany, but in terms of sheer joyful color it was the brightest neighborhood she had ever seen.

The first house on their left was small, boxy and pale blue, with an artistically rusted iron roof and an outside well at which a group of women were doing their laundry.

Opposite this was a pale green house with crazy paving on the ground in front and salmon-colored woodwork around the windows. The door was orange, as was a pile of fabric sitting beside an old treadle sewing machine, one length of the tangerine material still beneath the needle, the rest of it coiled like whipped cream on the paving.

From this house to a nearby tree was strung a rope from which two bedspreads hung; and going from the same tree to another house opposite were strings of multi-colored bunting, fluttering in what little breeze there was.

Behind the single row of houses, Annie could see another dry field that was criss-crossed with well-worn paths, and it was soon obvious why when she came to a gap from which emerged a tall, slim woman carrying a stack of two silver water urns on her head.

She was followed soon after by another, and another.

'No water for drinking in the houses,' Pinto said. 'The womens get the water from the wells outside the village.'

'But they're all coming from different directions!'

'Some different families have some different wells.'

The next house was the most brilliant shade of purple. On its front porch sat one single chartreuse chair, and from the iron awning hung a string of white shirts.

If someone had told her she was in the middle of a movie set Annie would have believed them. Despite the dusty ground, the piles of rubbish that she was becoming so accustomed to, the odd roving dog and the satellite dishes everywhere, there was no denying its beauty.

It made the suburbs of home seem impossibly dull. She might have running water and electricity around the clock, but what had she been thinking with room after room decorated in similar shades of what was basically, when it came down to it, white? Her decorator could call it Spanish Pearl or Afternoon Whisper, but compared to these colors it was lifeless.

The next part of the village was made up of bigger houses, all two-storied, and most of them painted a similar shade of pink, although one had blue and yellow window treatments, another turquoise, a third a darker shade of pink.

A fourth house had some of everything: it was painted turquoise; the front posts that supported the second story were pink and purple stripes; the windows were yellow; and the porch railings a speckled green and grey.

Spread out in front of the house on a square of plaid matting was a sea of drying red peppers currently being pecked at by a baby chicken, while Heavenly looked on and laughed.

Immediately opposite this fiesta of color was a faded

brown wooden building that looked like it had been abandoned by cowboys a hundred years before. A stable-like door swung open and out of it walked a single rooster. If he had pulled a gun out of a holster and shot her, Annie wouldn't have been surprised, but instead the rooster just stood still and watched her for a while, then stalked over to the shade of a wooden cart that appeared to have been left in the street when the bullock pulling it ran away — or died.

She looked up to see a group of women walking beneath a flame tree up ahead. There were about eight of them across three or four generations, and no two were wearing the same color.

It was an explosion, a feast, a smorgasbord of turquoise and pink and red and yellow. Annie stood in awe and watched as the women passed by, their scarves and saris fluttering silently behind them.

Heavenly said hello, but Pinto just stood in the shade, hands in his pockets, kicking the dust.

'Is this the most beautiful place you've ever been?' she asked him.

'No,' he said quietly enough for Heavenly not to hear. 'You should come to my village in Jammu. Is nicer.'

'How do you bear leaving it, Pinto?'

'I am always leaving. And I am always going back, so this is good.'

'To me this just seems ridiculously beautiful. Ridiculously. I mean look at that!' She pointed to the next house, which was grand-looking, quite Moorish in design, probably brick but rendered smooth with arches cut in above two square windows either side of a single door.

The render or paint, once a peppermint shade, had faded and was peeling, the posts in front of the house were a dreamy grey, the window frames and shutters a faded rusty red. In front of one of them was a dog the exact same color of the concrete on which he sat, sphinx-like and panting, his pointed ears sticking straight up, his gaze on a distant cat.

'It's perfect,' Annie said. 'Like a postcard.'

'My village is also like a postcard,' said Pinto, a trifle sulkily. 'We have mountains in my village.'

'Next time I come to India I will come to your village,' Annie said, although it was the first time she had considered that there might be a next time.

What a strange place it was in which there could be no running water, no dishwasher, no computer, no telephone, no supermarket, none of the things she took for granted, other than the ubiquitous TV aerial, yet the houses were painted to look like jewellery boxes and the people in them clothed themselves to look like jewels.

Heavenly had stopped outside one of the smaller houses on the far side of the village. It gleamed just as brightly as the other emeralds and sapphires, albeit with more of a ruby glow, painted as it was a dusky dark pink with a sea-green tin roof sheltering the small front porch.

There was no door on this house, just a beaded fringe tacked up above the doorframe. On the walls on either side of the doorway someone had drawn pictures of matching terracotta urns filled with spiky blue flowers.

'This is the house of my niece,' Heavenly said, leaning towards the door.

'Hello! Hello!'

A large chicken came running out as if its tail had been set on fire, and ran right between Pinto's legs, causing him to leap in the air. 'Scary chicken,' he cried. 'Scary chicken!'

Annie heard giggles from inside the house, and into the doorway emerged a plump Indian woman, short, with a tiny girl clutching her blue sari and two more women about the same age as her standing behind, with three more older ones in the background.

Heavenly introduced Annie and Pinto, who had recovered from the attack of the scary chicken, explaining that the house belonged to Nishi, the woman in blue, and that the two women of a similar vintage were her sister and sister- in-law, and the three older women their mothers and a neighbour.

Nishi asked them into the house and Annie stepped through the door.

It was basic, in every sense of the word. There were no windows and the bare brick walls were exposed, but light poured in through the gaps beneath the tin roof to reveal a spotless concrete floor.

Two bright-blue plastic outdoor chairs were the only furniture. Sitting in front of the pale brick wall in the filtered light they could have featured on the cover of Architectural Digest.

In the far corner of the room a sort of lean-to had been made out of brush and bamboo, and in front of that a saucepan was sitting on a small open fire between two bricks on the floor. Next to it sat three empty aluminum dishes and three spoons.

In the opposite corner, fixed to the brick wall, was a

metal shelving unit that held an array of pots, pans, utensils, mugs, cups, bowls, jugs all in the same aluminum. Next to that was a single bench-top held up at one end by what looked like dried straw bales, and at the other end by two pieces of four-by- two timber.

This bench was empty but for a row of tins in descending order of size.

On the wall opposite, the artist responsible for the flowers outside had painted Ganesh, the elephant-faced god, sitting on a grassy riverbank, mountains in the background. Next to this was a single table holding up a television. That was it. Four walls with a kitchen on one side and a television on the other.

It was impeccably tidy.

'I love your house,' she told Nishi. 'You must be very proud. Thank you very much for letting me visit.'

Nishi indicated that she should sit on one of the blue chairs and, as much as Annie refused, in the end she just had to sit down.

Heavenly was offered the other chair, but demurred, in Hindi, and went and lay on the floor, falling instantly asleep.

After more argument, the eldest of the old women sat down next to Annie.

From outside, she heard more giggling and, when she looked up, three girls were peering in through the door. They were wearing dark-blue school pinafores and pristine white shirts, and their shiny black hair was plaited in thick beautiful braids, although they were bare-footed. The littlest one looked about five while the tallest was maybe ten.

Annie smiled and said hello, but at this they dissolved into gales of laughter and fled.

'These are your daughters?' she asked Nishi, but Pinto translated that only the baby girl was Nishi's; these girls belonged to the sister, Divya, and the sister-in-law, Rupali.

The little girls could speak English, Pinto said, but were shy because they had never before met anyone like her.

'Are they scared of me like you are scared of the chicken?' she asked Pinto.

'No, ma'am! Chicken is scary, but ma'am is not scary. Just for these small girls, different.'

The girls went to school in the next village, Pinto explained, although it was more than an hour's walk away.

'This is very good school, though,' he translated for Nishi. 'This makes very clever girls.'

'Will the girls go to university in the city when they finish at school?'

Nishi laughed when Pinto translated this, as did the grandmothers.

'No, they stay here in the village and make some good marriages.'

'So even if they are very good at school, there is no future for them anywhere else?'

'Their future is at home, ma'am,' Pinto said, without translating the question. 'Looking after the husband and the childrens and the old peoples. They will not want to go anywhere else.'

'But what if they want to be doctors or lawyers or astronauts?'

He did translate this, and the ladies thought it was

hilarious, but Annie was serious. Why send the girls to a good school if all that lay in store for them was carrying water from the well to their parents' house?

Nishi's mother then wanted to know if Annie had children, so she told them about Ben and Daisy, how Ben was studying law and Daisy was studying (for want of a better word) marketing. She told them they were far away, doing their studying in other cities.

The ladies discussed this among themselves for a while, then Nishi asked when they would be coming home.

'To visit?'

'No, to live,' Pinto said.

'Well, they might not,' Annie said. 'They will get jobs wherever they can, and get married and settle down and have children of their own.'

Saying it out loud did not make it sound as good as she meant it to. Of course it was better for her children to be off doing their own thing than living in her pocket, no matter how much she wanted it that way. It was how her world worked.

But Nishi seemed to find this hard to believe, judging by the questions she continued to ask Pinto, and by the spirited debate that emerged between the women as a result.

'Do they talk to you on the telephone, the children?'

'Sometimes.'

'Do they write the emails?'

'Sometimes.'

'Do they cook for you when they invite you to their home?'

She could hardly outright lie. 'No,' she said. 'Actually

they usually come to my home and I have to admit they're not much good at cooking.' Or doing laundry, or helping her in the garden, or anywhere else for that matter. They didn't even make their beds. She did it: she did everything. She'd made some feeble attempts over the years to change this, because she knew she should equip them better for life after her, but she hated the ensuing arguments. And she didn't want to think about life after her.

'What are they saying?' she asked, as the women continued to debate among themselves.

'I do not know, ma'am,' said Pinto.

'What do you mean you don't know? You don't know what they're saying?'

'Yes, I do know what they are saying, but I do not know that you will want to hear it.'

She felt a flicker of irritation. 'Come on, tell me anyway.'

'Ma'am, they say for you it is very bad that your children want to move away from home and not come near you and do not make the foods for you, because this will make you sad and lonely.'

His words cut right through her, landing in the hopeful flame in her heart that had recently been fighting so hard for air and space. Of course Pinto knew what she would or wouldn't want to hear — she really ought to have picked that up by now.

'Oh.' She nodded, tears welling in her eyes, a tide of emotion building inside her. 'Well, yes, I suppose when you put it like that it does make me sad and it does make me lonely.'

Nishi's mother said something to Nishi, who repeated it

to Pinto, who then said to Annie: 'Are you moved away and not near your mum?'

Annie's chin had started to wobble. Why was it that the more you wanted to keep tears at bay, the more they insisted on pushing through? 'My mother died earlier this year,' she said, 'but she did live with us, just like Nishi's mother does, and she had done for quite a few years, so I had not moved away from her and I loved being near her, and without her . . . ' She looked around this immaculately kept one-room house and wondered what the hell was the matter with her.

'Well, "lonely" is the word,' she admitted, feeling a tear slide down her cheek. She tried to suck it back but all that encouraged was a little gasp, the sort that came just before a big torrent. 'And without the children, without my mother, our house is too big. I'm sorry to even think that when I should feel so lucky, because it's a beautiful house, but I look around your house, Nishi, and I see you all here together, and you have absolutely everything you need but nothing more, and you have this big raggle-taggle family here so you probably never even have a moment to yourself and for all I know that's what you dream about, but I have so many moments to myself, my whole life is nothing but a collection of moments to myself. And it's awful being lonely at my stage in life, because how is that ever going to change? I'm not going to make a whole new bunch of friends; I'm not going to have more children. If Ben and Daisy have children of their own, they probably won't even come to see me — at this rate they won't even tell me it's bloody well happening. And you know what? I had a dog that I loved very much, too, but he disappeared not long after my mother died and so my whole life seems completely totally empty, actually. Not just my house. My whole life. Me.'

Pinto was looking at the floor, biting his lip, looking on the verge of tears himself. The Indian women, though, were staring at her, fascinated. They hadn't a clue what she'd said, but they probably knew they were onto it with 'sad' and 'lonely'.

After an awkward silence, Nishi elbowed her sister-in-law, who blinked, then timidly tested her English.

'Dog dead?'

'I think so, yes.' Annie wiped the tears from her cheeks as they continued to spill. 'I'm so sorry. This is such a terrible way to behave.' Nishi's sister-in-law said something to the others, who all nodded, then she repeated it to Pinto.

'They say you can have their dog,' he said.

Their dog was a scabby-looking thing collapsed outside on the porch. Its ribs stuck out like garden-fork prongs, one leg was oddly angled, and if she hadn't seen its scrawny chest rise and fall she would have thought it was dead, too.

Annie's polite crying turned into big embarrassing sobs.

Nishi came over and leaned down to give her a hug, the smell of spices clinging to her like a shroud, a faint oniony flavor emanating from her smooth brown skin. Divya stood and came over, too, wrapping one arm around Annie and the other around Nishi, then Rupali joined in, as did the grandmothers, until Annie was being all but smothered in bare midriffs, swallowing mouthfuls of sari, inhaling body and cooking odors, essential oils, at least three different fragrant perfumes and, from somewhere she couldn't quite pinpoint, peppermint.

Despite the fact she could not stop crying, in that moment, in that room, with five dollars' worth of interior decorating and the sun pouring in through the cracks, she did not feel lonely. She doubted anyone in that room ever would.

By the time Heavenly woke up, Annie had been calmed with two cups of masala tea and a selection of little fried biscuits whose deliciousness defied description.

'Ay, that was some good sleep,' Heavenly said, stretching. 'Now if you will pour me a cup of that tea, I will have it and then we should be on our way back home.'

It wasn't until they were nearly back at the hotel that Annie remembered why they had gone to the village in the first place. 'You were taking something to Nishi,' she said to Heavenly. 'Did you forget to give it to her?'

'Not at all,' Heavenly replied. 'The something I was taking was you.'

Chapter Twenty-One

Preeti was gone.

There it was, in the paper when she got back to her room, on page seven; a tiny story with the same photo of her beautiful face smiling in front of the plain red background. But Preeti would never smile again. The internal damage had been worse than doctors feared and overnight she had succumbed to multiple organ failure and cardio-respiratory arrest.

Her lungs stopped functioning, a plastic surgeon at the hospital was quoted as saying. Her trachea, vocal cord, food pipe and lungs had been reduced to a terrible state. Her kidneys stopped functioning, and then gradually her heart stopped beating.

Her father and mother were inconsolable, having been at Preeti's side when she drew her last difficult breath, the paper said.

The railway police would keep looking for the attacker, but were now concluding that it was a case of mistaken identity and nothing more than a terrible tragedy. Their CCTV, it confessed, had not been working when the acid attack occurred, so there was no evidence.

Annie threw the newspaper on the floor of the hotel room. That poor woman! That poor family! Nothing more than 'a terrible tragedy'? Terrible tragedies were as bad as it got.

She felt sick with rage and sadness — even more so after two glasses of the expensive wine from the minibar.

Preeti was dead! It was too awful for words. If Daisy

died . . . Well, Annie had considered that possibility before, and no matter how spoiled rotten her daughter was, she could not contemplate it again.

Quickly calculating the time difference and working out that it was late, but not too late, she picked up the phone and dialled Daisy's mobile number.

'Who's this?' Daisy answered.

'It's Mom.' Annie said. 'In India.'

'Who?' There was a lot of noise in the background at her end. 'It's me, it's Mom,' Annie said, louder. 'Where are you? It sounds like a party!'

'Oh, Mom! Hi. No, I'm just at Freya's with a few friends. How are you doing?'

'I just wanted to hear your voice, darling. To see how you were.' 'I'm good. I'm great. Freya! Turn the music down. It's my mom.' 'How's uni?'

'Same old same old. You know. How's India?'

'Did you not get my email?'

'Oh, I haven't checked. Did you decide about the dress?' 'Goodness, sweetheart, you should probably read the email first because—'

'Mom, the party is this Saturday so I kind of need to know now.'

'It just seems so much for one dress, darling. When you see how little they live on over here, it just doesn't feel right.'

'Seriously? OK, Mom. Whatever. Don't worry about it.' 'I'm sorry, sweetie, but since I've been here—'

'Yeah, yeah. India. I get it.'

Annie heard a commotion in the background, a

champagne bottle being opened, followed by laughing and shrieking. She thought she heard a glass break. Someone called Daisy's name. Were they drunk?

'Is everything OK there?' Annie asked. 'Yes, everything's fine, don't stress, Mom.' More shrieks. More laughter.

'Are you sure?'

'Yes, it's fine, but I've got to go,' her daughter said, laughing. 'It's full-on here. Freya's sister just split up with her boyfriend, so we're having a wake. Talk to you soon, OK? Bye! Love to Dad.'

'Oh, Daisy,' Annie said into the phone. 'Daisy?' But Daisy had gone.

Although she had not hung up the call.

From the other side of the world Annie heard the phone rustling in her daughter's pocket. She knew she should put her own phone down. She knew she should stop listening.

She heard Freya ask if Daisy was getting the money for the dress.

She listened as her daughter replied that no, her mother had gone all Save the Children and that there were too many poor people in India or whatever.

'She's in India?' someone else asked. 'Wow, that's pretty awesome.'

'Yeah, but my dad had to, like, drag her there,' Daisy said. 'She'd never come up with an idea like that on her own. Borrring!' Laughter. 'Hey, Frey, can I borrow your red strapless dress for the party? The one you wore to Troy's the other night?'

There was another shriek as more champagne was

popped. More laughter. Daisy and another girl started talking about Kim Kardashian.

Annie put the phone back in the cradle.

She poured another glass of expensive wine and cried as she drank it; she cried for her own broken heart, for Preeti, for Preeti's mother, her own mother, her dog, her absent husband — all of them, ghosts to her now.

She woke when Hugh came home and slipped under the sheets, sighing far across the bed from her and falling instantly into the deep, rhythmic pattern of sleep.

This is what we've come to, she thought, her pillow soaking up more tears. Silent, distant, separate, miserable.

Hugh had become surplus to her requirements, just like her own long-lost father. He was not the real one after all.

She woke well before the sun, and lay there, turning her aching thoughts over and over, mixing them, sifting them, trying to calm them, get them in an order that didn't feel like she was running around behind them, panicked.

Daisy was right. She was boring. She'd noticed it herself. Everything about her was beige.

And it was true; she herself would never have had the idea to go to India, although that did not excuse Daisy's cruelty for saying so, for belittling her like that behind her back. Was it even cruelty if Daisy didn't know Annie had heard the belittling? Annie supposed she must have said awful things about Eleanor when she was younger, although she suspected the world had changed in that regard. She had been brought up to respect her elders. And in those days there were no cellphones that didn't get hung up, no emails going to the wrong address, no texts or sexts or tweets or posts or other ways to accidentally reveal things that were supposed to be private.

She hoped that when Daisy grew up and had children of her own, she never had to feel the pain her mother was feeling now. Even if what she said was true.

Finally, to her relief, it was time to get up and go to laughing yoga. She went through the motions, peeling her coconuts and telling off imaginary policemen, and to her surprise with every laugh something deep inside her shifted a little. For the better. On the fine sand of Chowpatty, the laughter was once more working its magic.

'Something changes for you today?' Heavenly asked as they walked across the sand after the exercises.

'Oh,' said Annie. 'What makes you say that?'

'I see it in you. Something that was not there yesterday.'

'Yes, I suppose something has changed.'

'I think so,' agreed Heavenly. 'I think the village visit was good for you?'

'Yes, it was good, but now . . .'

'Exactly,' interrupted Heavenly. 'Now this just leaves the Taj Mahal. Wonderful!'

'I don't know about that,' Annie said as they sat down in the shade.

'Of course you do not,' said Heavenly. 'You have not been there yet. But after you have been there, then you will know about it.'

'About the Taj Mahal?'

'Yes, Mrs Hugh. The Taj Mahal. Remember I told you that to know India and to know yourself that you need to come to laughing yoga, visit a small village, and go to the

Taj Mahal?'

'I remember you saying it—'

'Then what else is there but for you to go?'

'What else is there? Well, I'm not sure . . . '

She wasn't sure. Despite her earlier self-congratulation on stirring up the sediment of her deep unhappiness, in some ways she was still less sure than she had ever been.

But what was she going to do now? Go back to the hotel where she felt as far away from Hugh as she was from home? Go home, where she felt as far away from everyone else as she was in India? Where her own daughter delighted in telling everyone how boring she was?

Both options were, indeed, boring.

'What are you not sure about?' Heavenly asked. 'It's just one flight and a short drive.'

'I'm not sure about anything,' Annie said.

Heavenly took her hand and squeezed it. 'Most people are not sure about much,' she said. 'But you only really need to be sure about one thing. This is why for you the Taj Mahal is a good idea.'

'I don't know about that,' Annie said again.

'I do. Trust me.'

'I do,' Annie said, and it was true. She trusted her. 'Then go to the Taj Mahal!'

She sat there in silence, holding the old woman's hand, and a strange tiny nugget of something like anticipation wriggled in her stomach like a mustard seed frying in hot ghee, jumping and popping. Everything nice and safe was boring. Everything dangerous and risky was exciting.

Maybe she should try some excitement.

Whatever she was going to do, she knew she could not spend another night feeling lonely and sad on the desert of the king-size Taj Lands End bed.

Somewhere along the line in the past few hours, maybe the past few years, something had ended. She saw that now. So something else was about to begin.

'Maybe I will,' she said.

'There is no maybe about it,' Heavenly said.

'But it means I won't be coming back to laughing yoga.'

'Oh, we hear that a lot,' the old woman said, 'and it is very rarely the case, but if it is, we just have a good laugh.'

At that, Shruti, who had been demonstrating what looked like a complicated gymnastic maneuver to Priyanka, farted so loudly that two crows flew out of the banyan tree in fright.

Heavenly Hirani's School of Laughing Yoga erupted into raw, wonderful, real peals of infectious joy, and Annie erupted with them.

'Thank you for everything,' she said to Heavenly when it was time to go. 'You are a wise and wonderful woman.'

'No more wise and wonderful than anyone else,' Heavenly said.

'You should not forget this.'

'I won't forget anything,' Annie said, standing to leave. 'Ever.' The two embraced, and, although Heavenly was so small, it felt as though her arms were wings, and inside them Annie felt warm and safe and loved.

'Goodbye,' she said. 'And thank you, thank you, thank you.'

'This Heavenly is very good woman,' Pinto said as he

drove Annie back to the hotel. 'Do you think so?'

'Yes, Pinto, I do.'

They had stopped at a set of traffic lights near a many-pronged roundabout that was beautifully planted with lush shrubs and blooming flowerbeds.

'Oh, I stay here once,' Pinto said, looking idly out the window. 'Where?'

'In this garden, ma'am. See these bushes? Inside this is an empty space. Very nice. No mosquitoes.'

'You mean you lived in the bushes?'

'At night for some weeks before I get my new taxi job. There is a very good gardener who works there, for the city, and he is never mean to me. I see him now, sometimes, in the street but he is very old. He doesn't work there now, I think.'

'Does he remember you?'

'No, ma'am, just I remember him because he is nice.'

His tendency to casually drop into the conversation, without expecting even a smidgen of sympathy, the likes of sleeping in the middle of a roundabout staggered her.

'Your life makes mine look like a tired old hall rug,' Annie said as they pulled away with the green light.

'But, ma'am, you are only on your first life and I have had six.' In the back of his cool cab, Annie smiled.

When they reached the hotel, she pulled out the usual fare and handed it to him, his shy smile her extra reward.

'Pinto, I think I'm going to start my second life today,' she said. 'So if I were to need a ride to the airport later on, would you be able to take me?'

'You are going home, ma'am?'

'Yes, I think so. But I'm going the long way round.'

'Oh, this makes me sad because you have helped me and been so kind for me, but yes, I will take you any way you would like. Just SMS me the time. Thank you, ma'am. See you, ma'am.'

And so the decision was made. She was leaving.

It was surprisingly easy to put the wheels in motion; in fact it was energizing.

As soon as she got up to her room she rang Maya, and asked her to arrange the earliest flight she could find to Delhi and a driver from there to Agra.

Annie Jordan was going to see the Taj Mahal.

'Sure, there is a flight at midday we can get you on, and we have a tour company we use there all the time,' said Maya. 'They will send a guide as well. You are in for a real treat. Trust me — you will love it. But make sure you do not go to the Taj tonight — go first thing in the morning so it is not too hot. You cannot soak up the atmosphere if you are soaking already. Oh, and make sure you take a handkerchief — everyone cries. Or every woman, anyway!'

Annie quickly packed her bag, texted Pinto a time to pick her up, then sat down with a thick pad of the Taj's beautiful stationery to write a letter to Hugh.

Be truthful, gentle and fearless, she told herself. That was the best anyone could be.

Chapter Twenty-Two

Dear Hugh, Annie began, before crumpling up the sheet of paper and starting on a new one with *Darling Hugh.*

But 'Darling' wasn't right either. She was running away, after all. This was her, being fearless.

She tried just *Hugh* on its own, but that looked too bold, too cold. 'How can I finish this if I can't even start it?' she asked out loud. Then she thought of the way her mother had always called her 'my dear' and how she'd always loved that, how honest and kind it seemed; how it did make her feel dear to her mother. And she wanted to be dear to Hugh. She just wasn't sure if she wanted to be married to him anymore.

Talking wasn't working. Maybe this would.

My dear Hugh, she wrote.

I can't quite believe I am writing to you like this but I seem incapable, well, we both seem incapable, of talking to each other in any meaningful way at the moment, yet there is so much to be said — hence this letter.

And sorry about the 'hence'. I hate that word and it makes it seem more formal than it is, and it's not formal, but I don't want to write and re-write, I want to just get it out. This is me speaking from the heart, Hugh, because I don't think you know what's in my heart anymore.

This is not your fault. I think I am only just starting to find out what's in it myself. I think we long ago stopped talking to each other about what matters deep down inside, but I know now that I should have been saying more, sharing more, asking for more all the way along. It seems preposterous to me that I didn't, but somewhere back in the dips of those endless valleys of sleepless nights and countless nappies and school meetings and weeks, months, years spent ferrying children hither and yon, I lost my voice.

Or was it before then?

It seems pointless to backtrack quite this far, but, you know, I never actually wanted that big church wedding with the fancy reception and all the guests and the five-layered cake and the string quartet. I'm not sure I even like string quartets. And the cake wasn't even chocolate! But I honestly can't remember having much of a say. Isn't that terrible? I'm going back twenty-five years here, I know, but I guess I'm just trying to figure out for myself where the heck I went wrong.

I wanted to get married at that little church down the coast near where we went that very first weekend we spent together. Do you remember it — sitting in the middle of all that beautiful rolling green farmland with the little picket fence around it and the buckets of geraniums?

I wanted it to be just the two of us, Hugh, with a couple of bystanders plucked from the local town for witnesses. Then I imagined sipping champagne and having a crayfish picnic on the beach in front of the cottage we stayed at: the one hidden in the dunes that was decorated like a shipwreck.

I loved that place. It was so 'us'. Whereas our wedding was so 'everyone else'. Not that I didn't want to marry you, Hugh, please don't get me wrong about that. Oh, how I wanted to marry you! But even way back then I seemed to struggle to find my voice.

And now, all these years later, I have turned into this strange, silent, unhappy person.

I phoned Daisy last night and she called me boring. She

didn't know I was listening, but still, the awful thing is that she's right. I feel boring. I feel like I don't even recognize myself in the mirror. I don't know who this dull, ordinary middle-aged woman is. Worse, I didn't even notice I was her until I got to India. Being here has made me look at the world, particularly — strangely, since I am so far away from it — my world, with such fresh eyes. In many ways it has been extraordinary.

Utterly extraordinary.

I've been embraced here, Hugh, by strangers for the most part, in a way that has been nothing short of magical. But it's also revealed how un-embraced I am at home. Not by strangers, but by everyone: by you, by the children — by life in general.

When Mom was with us I didn't notice it so much, because I was busy taking care of her — something I loved doing and which I have to thank you for allowing, as I'm sure it took its toll on you, too, and you were so generous to let her encroach on our lives the way you did for so long without ever complaining.

Did it get on your nerves? I don't know, Hugh. You never said anything. You never say anything. Am I complaining that you never complain? I don't know; it just seems wrong to me that I currently know more about what my Kashmiri taxi driver thinks than I do about what you think. His name is Pinto and he's lived a hell of a life, but he seems happy — happier than you and happier than me, although you were right the other day when you said that I seemed happier here. In some ways I have been.

This happiness has come from a slightly mad group called Heavenly Hirani's School of Laughing Yoga. I've been joining them every morning for their laughing yoga sessions on Chowpatty Beach. Turns out they're seniors, so I have had the added benefit of being a youngster in their presence. I didn't tell you about it because, oh, I don't know, you were tired and busy and never asked, and then I realized we were so out of the habit of sharing what goes on in our lives that I started thinking what was the point of starting again now?

I mean, what is the point, Hugh?

I feel invisible to you half the time. I feel invisible to the children all the time. I'm so hurt that you wouldn't think to tell me about what Ben is up to, but I'm also hurt that he wouldn't tell me himself. As for Daisy, well, she's broken my heart, but that's a temporary state of affairs. Besides, it's probably my fault she is the way she is — I don't think I'll ever get over the fear of losing her. But you're right, it's unfair to compare her with other girls in the world, because Daisy is not aware of how the rest of the world lives. But that needs to change — she needs to be. We all need to be.

And Preeti died! Oh, that just kills me, Hugh, even if things like that do happen here all the time. That beautiful young life full of promise snuffed out. What a tragedy! What a waste! And no one seems to care!

Poor Preeti has undone me, Hugh. I don't know why. One loss too many, perhaps, and not even my loss, but a loss nonetheless.

She worked so hard, and her biggest worry was how her parents would pay for her medical care, and here we have Daisy wanting more and more, and

I don't think she knows what hard work even is. It makes me want to shake our girl until her teeth rattle, but it rattles me, too. It rattles me more.

She's my daughter and I love her more than anything, as I do you and Ben: we're a family and we always will be. But now that

I'm not needed to take care of any of you, now that no one seems to notice if I do or I don't, I can't work out what to do with myself.

The truth is that in recent times it felt like Bertie was the only person in my life who was ever truly happy to see me. And he's not even a person. Plus, he's gone.

I'm only forty-nine, Hugh, I have so much of my life ahead of me, so it's just too tragic for words that, without a slightly deranged terrier and a young Indian woman I don't even know, I am quite so lost.

Or, should I say, I was quite so lost.

I'm not sure why you brought me to Mumbai. You said you wanted to cheer me up, but then your work got in the way. Something always seems to get in the way. But I do have to thank you so, so, so much, because, despite the odds against it, I think I've found myself here. Yes, it's Eat Pray Love *but with a different ending (I assume — I really must read the whole book).*

I've tried to be a good wife. I've cooked and cleaned and hosted and supported and done my best to raise our children and, don't get me wrong, I don't regret that, I don't regret anything. I've done precisely what I thought I was supposed to, and it was a pleasure to try and do it well.

But now here I am at the next stage of my life, and it turns out I'm lonely, Hugh. I'm so lonely — oh God, I'm crying like a baby! It's wretched to be a grown woman and to feel hurt and lonely, but I do and I am.

The people I've met over the past two weeks have been the best thing to happen to me in I-don't- know-how-long and I've looked at what they have and how happy they are and what I have and how happy I am and it would be criminal for me to continue my life in the same way as I have been living it up until now.

I don't need a five-star hotel. I don't need a five-bedroom house. I don't need a new car every three years or a kitchen island or to have my highlights done every month.

I need laughter. I need joy. I need to be happy. And I need to be loved, Hugh — deliriously, openly, continuously loved. And I need to be UNDERSTOOD. I think — no, I KNOW — that this is what I deserve.

And I hate it when the kids SHOUT at me in texts, but I really DO know this.

I also know you really loved me once, Hugh, perhaps not wildly or openly, but in your own way, though whatever we had in those early giddy years before our children, your career, sick parents and whatever else, well, that seems to have fallen by the wayside.

I think the love is still there but, Hugh, I just don't know if that's enough.

When I ask you if you can understand how I feel, I need you to at least try, because otherwise I'm just another lost banana-picker. You'll methodically do everything you can to find me, then tick that off your list: a job well done.

But will you ever even want to know why I went missing?

Heavenly Hirani says that in India you don't need to die to be reincarnated, and I think that's what has happened to me. I'm a new person now and I'm done with the old one.

I don't know if we can go back. I don't even know if I want to.

My dear Hugh, I am going missing.

Sorry to do it like this, and I do hope you find the other banana-picker, the real one. I also hope you can try to understand why this one does not want to be looked for. I'm not on your list now. You don't need to tick me off.

I'm not sure when I will come home, but when I do I think it best if I move into Mom's apartment. The tenant left, and I was going to find a new one when I got back, so the timing is right for that.

The timing is right for leaving, Hugh.

I've tried to explain myself as best I can here, and

I hope you can see it, I hope you can see ME, and I hope you can understand. Please don't hate me.

I don't hate you. I could never hate you.

Maybe you'll be pleased, or relieved, or — how dreadful that I don't know what you'll be. That's the problem, right there in a nutshell.

I'll email the children and tell them I'm off on an adventure while you're busy at work.

Then let's regroup, you and I, at home, and work out what and how to tell them.

I'm so sorry, Hugh.

I'm not sure what else to say.

Love Annie

She read through it twice, folded it carefully into a Taj Lands End envelope and placed it on Hugh's pillowcase.

She had been truthful, gentle and fearless, and now she was going to get on a plane on her own and fly into the middle of India to see one of the world's most famous and beautiful buildings.

Chapter Twenty-Three

The lobby flowers had been changed again to a buttery shade of yellow. She loved those flowers. Annie had always imagined it would be stifling staying more than a day or two in a grand hotel, but she had absolutely adored it.

Perhaps if you plant yourself anywhere in the ground for long enough you start to take root, she thought, as she looked around the vast glossy space for the last time.

But how would you ever know that if you stayed your whole life in the same patch?

She tried to find Valren to thank him and say goodbye, but he'd gone back to Goa for a wedding, she was told. She fervently hoped his auntie wasn't talking him back into the priesthood, bade farewell to Mahendra and the rest of the smiling Taj staff, then stepped through the revolving door and out to the burning forecourt where Pinto was waiting.

'I take your bag, ma'am,' he said, and put it in the boot of his taxi next to his barbells.

A string of red chillies and a fresh lime hung from the rear bumper in a little posy that matched one at the front of the taxi. In fact, Annie had seen the same combination in many places; hanging from rear-vision mirrors, strung up in shop doorways, at the entrance to some of the houses in the village.

'What are the chillies for?' she asked as she climbed into the car, keen to talk about anything that would keep her mind off that fat envelope sitting on Hugh's pillow up in Room 1802.

'Is maybe seem old-fashion to you, ma'am,' Pinto said,

'but this is what we call nazar battu. We use this to protect from bad spirits, from evil eye. My boss with this taxi, he believe very much in evil eye, so he believe very much also in nazar battu.'

'What sort of bad spirits? You mean madam drivers?'

'No, no!' Pinto laughed, as if the idea of being able to ward off a madam driver was the silliest thing he'd ever heard. 'No, you know, ma'am, I tell you that Mumbai is all about the moneys, and that some people have a lot and some people have not much, and the ones that have not much can be very jealous of the people that have more, even not much more.'

He spoke with such feeling. Annie remembered how he had talked about the people in his own village up in Jammu being jealous of his hard-won earnings.

'So the nazar battu wards off those jealous people?'

'Those bad feelings from those jealous people, ma'am. It takes those bad feelings and stops them coming into my taxi. This is what my boss he says.'

'And you agree with him.'

'Yes, ma'am. It is good to agree with the boss.'

'Is he a good boss? Better than the banana-truck man?'

'Every boss is better than this banana-truck man. My taxi boss he takes five hundred rupees every day for me to drive his car, but he is my good friend.'

'What about on the days you don't make five hundred rupees?'

'Then I don't give to him and he is still my friend, just not so good.'

Beneath the nazar battu, glued to the dashboard, was

the elephant-faced god, Ganesh.

'OK, so what does Ganesh do for you?' Annie asked.

'Ma'am, you know in Mumbai there are one hundred thousand taxis?'

'Yes, I do know that,' Annie agreed. 'I think we've been in a traffic jam with just about every one of them.'

Pinto laughed. He particularly liked her Mumbai traffic jokes. 'We have a saying here that to be a taxi driver, you need six things: good honk, good brakes, good eyes, good luck, patience and Ganesh.' He patted Ganesh on his elephant head.

'And passengers,' Annie added.

'Ma'am, you are still a taxi driver, even if you have no passengers. You are just empty.'

Annie turned and looked out the window. There was something about the way Pinto spoke — Heavenly, too — that made ordinary conversations take a turn for the enlightened.

Before, she'd thought she was a lost banana-picker. Now she was an empty taxi. 'Pinto, you're amazing, do you know that?'

'Thank you, ma'am,' Pinto said. 'Another madam tells me this one time also.'

Madams of the world unite, Annie thought. Madams of the world unite.

'You are coming back to Mumbai this time after your plane, ma'am?'

'I don't think so, Pinto.' She'd rung the airline and changed her flight to go home from Delhi instead.

'And the sir, he is not going with you?'

'No, Pinto, the sir is not.'

Pinto looked at her in the rear-vision mirror.

'You have liked Mumbai?'

'I have loved it, Pinto. Thank you for being such a good taxi driver.'

'But now you are sad.'

'Not sad. A lot has happened here. To do with me. To do with my family. And then Preeti — have you been reading about her? The young woman at Bandra Terminus who had acid thrown at her?'

'Yes, ma'am, I am very ashamed about this.'

'She died, did you know that?'

'Yes, ma'am, this is very bad and I am very sorry you know this.'

'I am sorry I know it, too. But it doesn't mean it didn't happen.'

'Bad things happen, but good things happen, too, ma'am. Sometimes you must make yourself know about the good things. Especially in India. This Preeti is very bad thing, but happy yoga and the Gandhi house and the dabbawallahs is very good thing.'

There he was again, coming at her with his Indian-taxi-driver wisdom.

When Annie paid him at the airport, standing at the curb, he looked so crestfallen she almost gave him a hug.

'It's been a pleasure to know you, Pinto,' she said. 'You are a good man. You take care of your family and take care of yourself.'

'Yes, ma'am,' he said, looking at his feet. 'You have been good for me and you have helped me and I will not forget you.'

'So that's the good thing we need to know about, right?'

He nodded, but kept looking at his feet as the taxis honked, the planes took off overhead, the crowds swarmed around them.

'Goodbye, my friend,' she said and, clutching her suitcase, turned to swarm with them.

When she got to the door into the departure hall she turned to see Pinto still in the same spot, head bowed.

'Jack, come back!' Annie called over the growing cloud of black heads between them.

He lifted his head and managed a smile.

'Jack, come back!' he said. 'Jack, come back!' Even inside the terminal, she could still hear him. 'Jack, come back! Jack, come back!'

Chapter Twenty-Four

A smooth-skinned Michael Jackson-lookalike in wrap-around shades was waiting for Annie at New Delhi Airport: the sign bearing her name festooned with smiley-faced emoticons.

'Welcome to the beautiful city of New Delhi, most respected madam,' he said, grabbing her bags and pulling them through the crowd. 'My name is Sanjay. New Delhi is the capital of India with a population of twenty-two million people, and some say a reputation for corruption and dirty politics but also many parks and trees.'

His enthusiastic non-stop chit-chat was exactly what Annie needed to keep her own troubled thoughts at bay. The bravado that had enveloped her as she departed Mumbai had disappeared into the clouds as she flew to Delhi, leaving her aghast at the reality of what she was doing and, worse, uncertain of what that even was.

She had felt so clear when she wrote the letter to Hugh. She needed space from him and their marriage and her life — she needed to find out who she was and what she wanted — but, at twenty thousand feet above who-knew- where in India, being a misunderstood wife and a taken-for-granted mother suddenly didn't seem so bad.

She felt as though she was doing something that only another sort of woman would do. Yet, she wanted to be another sort of woman, which was why she was doing it. She had just expected to feel better about it.

'I noticed from the air how much green there was,' she said to Sanjay as they headed across the parking lot, although in truth she had only noticed the large pockets of parkland because the rest of the sprawling city was so brown.

'This is Deepak, our driver for the next two days,' Sanjay said as they approached the inevitable white 4WD.

Deepak came up to about Annie's elbow and had a cheeky grin that he flashed at her before opening the door so she could climb inside.

'Respected madam,' Sanjay said, twisting in the front seat to face her once they got going, 'the trip to Agra is two hours on the most beautiful freeway, but the trip to the freeway is two hours in the most horrendous traffic. Given that we will be stuck in it, should you like to see some pleasant sights on the way?'

'That's lovely, thank you, Sanjay, but I would rather just get to Agra.'

'Of course, respected madam, whatever you would wish. So you will not be wanting to stop and perhaps buy a finest pashmina? Top quality? Handmade in India?'

'That's right, thank you, Sanjay. I would not.'

But he hadn't really been asking her, as it turned out, because on the way to the horrendous traffic they managed to drive past the India Gate ('Much taller than Mumbai's small Gateway of India, respected madam'), and took a detour up the grand Champs- Élysees-like avenue to the gracious government buildings ('full of crooked politicians and thieves and vagabonds, respected madam').

'Speaking of this vagabonds,' Sanjay said, 'I know respected madam will feel sad and sorry for children tapping on her window, but these children are gypsies from other countries and are giving New Delhi a bad name which it does not deserve — for those reasons anyway. Please do not give these children money or speak to them or even look at them.'

But at a roundabout heading away from the government buildings, Annie heard scratching at her window and turned to see a little girl of about seven dressed in a purple sari, knocking and making feeding motions with one hand.

'Oh no, poor little thing,' she said, but, before she could even fully feel the tug at her heartstrings, the little girl lost interest and ran back over to the middle of the roundabout to join the half-dozen other boys and girls playing there.

Like the baby she had seen in Mumbai who was ultimately just a baby, these children were still just children. When it came down to it, a game of marbles trumped squeezing a white woman for a handful of rupees. It made them seem less sad, or it made her feel less sad for them. You had to make yourself know about the good things, Pinto had said. A game of marbles would be a good thing.

Deepak put his foot down to fit in with the traffic, which, while frightening compared to home, in the wide New Delhi avenues felt slightly more civilised than Mumbai. At one stage, Annie even let go of the door handle.

After half an hour crawling through the choked-up city, Deepak pulled up outside a finest pashmina shop.

'Sanjay, I really don't want a pashmina,' Annie said, but, like others she'd met in recent weeks, his smile was so magnetic she could not resist giving in to it. He had an orchestrated smoothness that made Annie feel more of a rich tourist than she ever had with Pinto, but still, she liked the guy. His enthusiasm was infectious.

'All right, I'll go in, but I can't spend money on a pashmina when you won't let me give any to a poor little beggar girl on the street.'

'The poor little beggar girl on the street will give the money to her boss for investments,' said Sanjay. 'She will not see a single rupee. Her destiny is set, respected madam, and the tourists find this difficult to digest, but we do not. These finest pashminas come from the hills near Kashmir where entire families make them by hand and the money goes to these families and stays with them in their village.'

'How do I know they're not made by children working in Dharavi slum?'

Sanjay looked hurt. 'Respected madam, you have just met me so you cannot know that I would not cheat you, but I would not cheat you.'

'But your friends in the store here will take a healthy cut of my pashmina?'

'So, you are going to buy a pashmina!'

Annie laughed, shook her head, and followed him inside, where he managed to vanish almost at once, leaving her in the hands of a perky salesman who trailed her, carrying an enormous calculator and tapping out conversions every time she so much as looked at anything.

To her great annoyance, a most beautiful cashmere shawl did take her fancy. It was very fine, almost transparent, in a pale, checked pattern of different seagreens.

'You have a very good eye for quality workmanship,' the salesman said, adjusting the pashmina over her shoulder. 'This suits your coloring and will be a reminder of all the beauty India holds right here in the palm of her hand.'

Annie looked at herself in the mirror and was surprised to see the same old her there. So much had happened in this one day. It didn't seem feasible that she hadn't changed on the outside.

'Madam, allow me,' the salesman said, holding his hands out to receive the shawl back. 'I would like to show you just how fine this beautiful shawl really is.'

She slipped it off her shoulders and handed it to him.

'Madam, if you please.' He was pointing at her rings.

She looked down at her hand. She hadn't even thought about her rings.

One was a single diamond in a very plain setting on a platinum band — this was the ring with which Hugh had proposed. He'd chosen it himself, and at the time she could not believe that he had known her so well, as he'd gone for the simplest, subtlest, loveliest thing she could ever have imagined.

Later, when Ben was born, he'd suggested getting it remade with a bigger diamond, and perhaps some smaller ones set into the band, but she loved that ring so much the way it was, she would not hear of it.

Was it then, so long ago, twenty-one years, that they'd started falling out of step — Hugh wanting something smarter; she happy with what she had? She felt so detached from the past that it was hard to believe it was even hers to begin with.

'Madam, your ring?'

Annie pulled off her wedding band. That they'd bought together, the week before the wedding with the fancy reception and the string quartet. It was the only thing the two of them were left to do on their own, and they'd made an event of it, choosing matching plain gold rings at a local jeweler and then going for a long lazy lunch at a little French bistro nearby.

She handed the ring to the salesman, who held it aloft with one hand, then with dramatic aplomb fed the shawl through the center of it with the other.

It was quite a feat.

'So fine, so delicate, so beautiful,' he said, handing her back the ring.

She looked at it, lying in the palm of her hand. A ring only really came alive when it was on a finger. This one was a symbol of union, of a marriage, of a never-ending relationship and, as hers was currently in tatters, she was not sure she should be wearing it.

But her hand did not look hers without it, and she had no pocket to put it in, and so she slipped it back on.

'I'll take it,' she said, nodding at the pashmina. That way the family in Kashmir would get some money, and her neck would get an adornment to remind her of this day, to remind her that she could be truthful, gentle and fearless.

'If the little beggar girl was not a gypsy from another country, would I be able to give her money?' she asked Sanjay, as they headed back into the snarl of afternoon traffic.

'If the little beggar girl was not a gypsy from another country, she would not be here,' he said, still smiling, and that was that.

The freeway, when they reached it, was indeed beautiful, in as much as a freeway could be. But after the chaos and honking of the inner-city traffic, when they hit the six-lane toll road to find barely another vehicle on it, it seemed like road heaven.

'Relax and enjoy,' Sanjay said. 'Relax and enjoy.'

There was something of the guru about him, as there had been about Pinto and Heavenly. They should get together and start producing bumper stickers.

'Have you ever been out of India, Sanjay?'

He laughed. 'No, madam. I have been to Delhi and I have been to Agra. But there is a lot to be seen in Delhi and Agra.'

Annie turned and watched the foggy turrets of the city slide into the distance as vast fields appeared on either side of her, quaint round haystacks popping up at odd intervals like abandoned Frisbees, as tall smoke stacks — a different way of baking bricks — rose out of the land between them.

The light was silvery and vague, dream-like. Annie found she could lean back into her headrest and just watch this world slide by without thinking of much, just taking it in, mile after mindless mile, almost like sleeping, almost numb.

They arrived on the outskirts of Agra a couple of hours later, leaving the modern, empty freeway and entering a slightly grubby, chaotic but nonetheless charming rustic scene.

Brightly colored ramshackle shops crowded the sides of the narrow street down which they were driving, one selling pieces of pipe, the next bicycle parts, the next stacks of rope.

A dusty no-color shack seemed to be selling children, there were so many of them sitting in the dust whorls in front of it. A handful of them were plonked one behind the other in ascending order of size, like Russian dolls, the baby at the front the only one not getting the joke.

Annie smiled as they laughed — it was impossible not to.

Tractors motored down either side of the uneven road, many of them bearing four or five people — and one, a newborn calf — and she was just starting to warm to this more laid-back rural atmosphere when they turned a corner and everything changed.

'Agra,' Sanjay said, in a depressed tone she hadn't heard before.

They were approaching a bridge over a wide, murky-looking river.

'Yamuna River, ma'am,' Deepak told her as they joined the throng of traffic trying to get to the other side. 'We cross this, too, in Delhi.'

'There used to be a lot more of it,' Sanjay said, reverting to his more jaunty self. 'It comes all the way from the Himalayas and meets the sacred Ganges in Triveni Sangam, in Allahabad. You might have seen pictures? This is where the peoples every twelve years go for peaceful bathing. This year one hundred million peoples.'

Deepak had something to say in Hindi about this, and he and Sanjay seemed to argue quite spiritedly, although it ended with Deepak laughing — a delightfully wicked little boy's laugh.

'What did he say?' Annie wanted to know.

'He say do not drink the water.'

She laughed. 'After the one hundred million people have bathed in it? That seems reasonable.'

'No, ma'am, before the one hundred million people have bathed in it. After Delhi he say do not drink the water.'

They were stuck now on the bridge off-ramp in a traffic jam the likes of which Annie had never seen, even on a bad day in Mumbai. On her right, the oncoming traffic was at a total standstill, on her left, on the road below, with which they were attempting to merge, two oxen were being swarmed by motorbikes and rickshaws, each one stuffed with more people than the last.

Cars were trying to barge their way through, even a cow was jammed between an old truck piled high with broken chairs, a tractor, two 4WDs and a fleet of scooters.

'The Taj Mahal is near here?' she asked. It seemed most unlikely that anything of beauty would reside nearby.

'Yes, madam. Just a few miles further along the river.' He and Deepak enjoyed another heated exchange, then Sanjay turned to look at her in the back seat.

'There are a lot of weddings in Agra today so the traffic is very bad,' he said. 'In this case, I will tell you now the story of the Taj Mahal so that when we go there in the morning, you will be prepared.'

'Good idea,' Annie said. It wasn't as though she was rushing to anything, or anyone. A wave of anxiety rippled through her. She'd had a few since leaving Lands End, but what had surprised her was that they were only ripples. They came, and they went.

'So, Shah Jahan was a very good king in the Mughul reign, very popular with the peoples,' Sanjay said. 'His father was Jahangir and his grandfather Akbar. You might have heard of Akbar, Akbar the Great? He also too was very popular with the peoples. But this Jahangir he gives the Mughuls a bad name with his loving for wine and women and opium.'

'Really? In that order?'

'Yes, most respected madam, really in that order. He drinks twenty-four bottles of wine a day, but when Akbar says to him, "Please my son, do not drink so much," he replies, "God gave me two lips, Father, one for tasting wine and one for tasting women!"'

'So he wasn't inclined to give either up then?'

'No Betty Ford Centers here, respected madam!'

'But Jahangir's son, Shah Jahan, was a good guy.'

'He was a very good guy, madam. He chooses one wife, Big Wife, and another wife, Simple Wife, and he is good to them but they cannot give him childrens, so one day he goes to the Tricky Bazaar to get another wife.'

'The Tricky Bazaar?'

'Yes, madam, this is when all the most beautiful girls in the world are put together in a line and Shah Jahan gets to choose one. So he goes to the Tricky Bazaar with Big Wife, and Simple Wife, and they stand behind him as he looks at all the beautiful girls in the line.'

Sanjay did a lively impersonation of a king scrutinizing the potential at a tricky bazaar.

'And then he sees the most beautiful girl of them all. She is the daughter of a lowly Persian peasant, madam, but once he sees her he can see nothing else, and like this he just breathes the word "Mumtaz", and from then on, this is her name.'

'Mumtaz?'

'Not just Mumtaz. Muummmtaaaazzz!' 'Muuummmmmt-aaaazzz!'

'Yes, respected madam. Very good. "Mum" for beautiful and "taz" for royal.'

Annie jumped as a passing elbow bumped her window. It belonged to a girl in a flowing sari sitting on the back of a motorbike. As she and the man on the front of the bike squeezed through a gap in front of them, Annie saw she was holding a baby in her arms.

They were nestled so close, the three of them, such a tight little unit in that whirl of frightening traffic. The girl rested her head on the man's back, her eyes closed, the baby sleeping squashed up between them.

Annie felt another ripple.

Had she ever trusted Hugh like that? Would she ever have ridden past two bullocks and a combine harvester with Daisy or Ben squashed between them? Could Hugh even ride a motorbike?

Sanjay had been momentarily distracted by the traffic himself, but was now ready to continue his story. 'So, Shah Jahan and Mumtaz have a very happy marriage, a very good marriage, a very long marriage and, better still, most respected madam, Mumtaz gives Shah Jahan fourteen childrens.'

'So she was a good choice.'

'She was an excellent choice, madam. Only in giving

birth to her fourteenth child at the age of thirty-nine, she feels very unwell and she knows that her time is come, so she sends for Shah Jahan and he comes very quickly to her bedside.'

'Oh dear.'

'Yes. Oh dear. Mumtaz tells Shah Jahan he must grant her three wishes before she dies. One, he must build a monument to prove his love to her. Two, he must never remarry because that would not be proving his love to her. And three, he must take care of their fourteen children.'

'That's quite sneaky, the not remarrying one.'

'Yes, ma'am, but understand that this marriage between Shah Jahan and Mumtaz it was not a political marriage, it was not an arranged marriage, it was a love marriage. And this is why the Taj Mahal is called the Palace of Love and Agra is called the city of love.'

Annie looked out the window. 'It should be called the city of traffic jams.'

'Yes, but why are there traffic jams? Because so many peoples are getting married. And why are they getting married? Because they are in love!'

'What if the marriages are arranged?'

'Of course. Most of the marriages are arranged.'

'Then where does the love come into it?'

'There is love in arranged marriages, most respected madam. Of course there is love. The difference is that the marriage comes first, and the love comes after. But this is OK. This is good.'

'Are you married, Sanjay?'

'Yes, madam. I have a Mumtaz!'

'And was your marriage arranged?'

'Yes, madam. And when we first married, we were like this.' He held his hands far apart. 'But after eight years we are now like this.' He clasped one hand over the other closed fist. 'She is a very good wife and I am a very lucky man, and we have two children. My six- year-old son and a tiny baby who is one year old and quite loud in the night.'

How odd, Annie thought, that Sanjay's arranged marriage had headed in the opposite direction to her own love marriage, to many love marriages.

Pinto had said pretty much the same thing. The Western world might just have it wrong when it came to love, she decided, flinching as another white 4WD came perilously close to clipping them.

The charm of India's explosion of lively color was wearing decidedly thin by the time Deepak pulled up outside Annie's hotel. It was five hours since they had picked her up at the airport in Delhi, and she was hot, sticky, tired and gasping for a cold drink and a shower.

'What do you two do now?' she asked as she got out of the car, her bags snatched instantly away by a tall handsome man in a turban.

'Don't think of us, most respected madam,' Sanjay said. 'We have a very nice guesthouse for the night and my tiny baby will not be waking me up, so I am very happy and so is Deepak.'

They both did look happy actually. Annie smiled. 'Thank you, Sanjay, and Deepak. It's been very nice to meet you.'

'See you very early tomorrow, ma'am. At five-thirty,

OK? This way we see the Taj Mahal in all her glory and no crowds and also not too hot.'

Chapter Twenty-Five

By the time Annie was checked in, refreshed and showered, it was nearly nine o'clock.

She had no desire to eat at any of the hotel's restaurants, which were just as dull as the rest of the place, so she opened a half- bottle of Indian wine from the minibar, snapped open a packet of potato crisps and climbed into bed.

Only then did she turn her phone on — her heart thumping — to see if there was anything from Hugh.

There wasn't.

It was possible, she supposed, that if he was still running around the place trying to find his banana-picker he would not yet have received the letter.

Possible, just not probable, given that she'd not been in touch with him all day.

Would he not at least have called the hotel looking for her? She'd said goodbye to Mahendra, but hadn't told him where she was going.

Would Hugh splutter in disbelief and beg for details, or put the phone down and go about his day?

What had she expected? Actually, she hadn't thought at all about what sort of a response she wanted from him. Indeed, until now she hadn't known she wanted any sort of response at all, but she did. One way or the other, she wanted him to bloody well give a damn!

She gulped back the rest of her glass of wine and went to find the business center, although part of her was already furious that Hugh might have responded to her by email.

He hadn't.

There was a series of reminders from stores at home that they were having sales, one request from a Nigerian prince that she launder some money, and another that she make a donation to a program trying to stop live involuntary organ donations in China.

There was nothing from Ben or Daisy, of course, nothing even from Rhona (she would no doubt have her hands full) — and there was nothing from her husband of twenty-five years. A whole lot of nothing.

She went back to her room and poured a second glass of wine. It wasn't bad, actually. And who knew there was even such a thing as Indian wine?

She checked her phone again. It was past ten now. There were no messages, no missed calls. She turned it off. It was too late now.

The Bollywood movie playing on TV seemed to be telling the same story as the one she had watched in Mumbai, and it held her attention for a while, but as soon as she felt her eyes beginning to slide closed, she sank back into the pillows, stretched out across the crisp sheets of the big empty bed and escaped into a deep, uninterrupted sleep.

When the alarm went off at quarter to five the next morning, she woke with a start, confused about where she was and why.

Her husband's name fluttered and died on her lips as the events of the previous day fully dawned on her.

I've really done it, she thought as another ripple passed through her. I've really done it. Yet she felt less churned up than she had been the night before. She felt tired, with a tinge of anxiety: a common enough cocktail, and one she knew she could handle.

Should it be this manageable? Leaving? Perhaps she was in shock. Or denial. Or so numbed by the events of the past months that nothing more could shake her.

Perhaps there would be a day of reckoning down the track, wherever that was leading, or a week or a month or a year of reckoning.

Right now it just felt . . . inevitable. And unalterable. She couldn't have changed her mind even if she wanted to. She'd fled, and there was no fleeing back. That would be worse than continuing to do nothing, than living with the status quo.

Be truthful, gentle and fearless. The words floated back into her consciousness as though on fluttering muslin in front of an open window.

Gandhi probably had not been thinking of semi-neurotic twenty-first-century housewives when he conjured up his motto, but, nonetheless, as far as a guideline for living went, she felt it. She really felt it.

And she had been truthful — probably more so than gentle — and she was trying to be fearless by leaping like this into the great beyond: beyond marriage, beyond motherhood, beyond whatever was making her so sad and lonely and dull.

'I'm going to the Taj Mahal today,' she said out loud. 'I'm going to the TAJ MAHAL today.'

She turned her phone on — still nothing.

'I'M GOING TO THE TAJ MAHAL TODAY,' she repeated, and kept repeating until it was time to leave the room.

Sanjay and Deepak were waiting for her outside the hotel. It was still dark, with just a hint of sunrise in the distance.

'Are you ready, respected madam?' Sanjay asked. 'Are you ready for the most famous monument in all of India?'

'I'm ready,' she said climbing into the back. 'Come on, what are we waiting for?'

Agra was still far from beautiful, but as the sun rose it glowed with a luminescence it had lacked the evening before. Also, the roads were empty. Even the cows and oxen were still asleep — they passed dozens of them, slumbering in between piles of litter and gangs of mangy dogs.

As they drove through an outer gate into the Taj grounds and entered a massive, dusty car park, a ribby goat wandered across their path. The ground was pot-holed and sprouted sporadic desiccated tree stumps: it was not much of a calling card to the most famous monument in all of India.

The ticket office was certainly ramshackle, and smelly. Sanjay bought her ticket and handed her a bottle of water, though she didn't want to drink it. The guide saw this and Annie felt ashamed, but it was the man in the ticket office whose filthy hands she didn't trust. He kept wiping his nose with one of them.

She opened the bottle regardless and took a long, thirsty glug. If she died of diphtheria, it would at least be a polite death.

'Come, we get the official battery bus now to the main entrance,' Sanjay said.

The official battery bus had no air-conditioning, and springs poked out of its plastic seats like jack-in-the-boxes. Luckily, it set off as soon as they got on it, so they didn't have to wait in the heat. Luckily for them anyway: as it pulled away Annie saw an elderly man being berated by a flock of women in saris for not telling them to get on in time.

They drove out of the car park and down an avenue with souvenir shops on each side, a couple of barely awake cows mooching in front of them, rickshaw cyclists snoozing on their empty rigs.

'No petrol or diesel near the Taj,' Sanjay said. 'Only battery bus. And since UNESCO say, no factories in Agra either. One time there have been more than twenty business chimneys, but the smoke is making the Taj black so then the businesses are told to go away.' That certainly explained the seen- better-times impression the city outside the Taj managed to present. Even the avenue they were on, leading directly to the favoured monument, needed a jolly good tidy-up, Annie thought.

The bus stopped and its occupants piled out at a plain red-brick entrance, the outer shell of the Taj Mahal fort.

'One queue for womens,' Sanjay said, pointing her in the right direction. 'One queue for mans. I will meet you on the other side.' The gate opened as Annie joined the back of the women's queue and she was quickly deposited on the other side once her bag was searched.

'The Taj is open from sunrise to sunset,' Sanjay said, as they walked down a long path between two emerald-green lawns, 'but early morning is best time to come because the light is changing with every minute.'

They turned right to face the northern outer gate that led into the Taj proper.

This gate itself was stunning: it looked almost like a one-dimensional church, with large domed towers on either side at the top, eleven small domes in between.

The red brick was inlaid in places with the most intricate patterns of red and green on white marble tiles. It looked like a Moorish fairy-tale castle.

In the center was a small opening through which Annie could only just make out, in the early sunrise, a blur of silvery white.

She felt excitement flaring in her belly.

Sanjay, with dramatic aplomb, was not about to let her just barrel in, however. He stopped her, a very serious look on his face.

'Most respected madam,' he said. 'I have told you the story of Shah Jahan and Mumtaz, so you know this great love between these two peoples is why we now four hundred years later still have this monument, this reminder of all that is the most wonderful between two peoples, a man and a woman.'

'Yes, Sanjay, you have told me that.'

'And do you believe in love, madam?'

Annie gulped. What a question. What a time to be asked that question.

'I am sorry, respected madam, this is perhaps not my place to ask you this. I am very sorry. Please, let me ask you something else, because even though I tell you that the Taj Mahal is the Palace of Love, it is actually something else, it is something more, something that is in the air that you cannot see or touch, like love.'

You can't see or touch love either, she wanted to say, but he so desperately wanted to please her, she could not stand in his way.

'Taj Mahal, more than anything else, respected madam, is the Palace of Symmetry. Because Shah Jahan believed in symmetry.'

She nodded. Math, she could do.

'You will notice here, even at the gate,' Sanjay said, 'that this is perfectly symmetrical, and you will notice when you get inside that everything in there is also perfectly symmetrical. Ah, almost everything. I will see if you can find the one thing that is not. But the buildings, the gardens, the mausoleum itself — everything is exactly similar on one side as the other.'

'So what is the meaning of all this symmetry?'

'Well, you see, respected madam, Shah Jahan felt great love for Mumtaz, this we know, and love, it is a wonderful thing. Love, it is all you need, it is making the world go round, is that not so?'

Annie bit her lip and nodded.

'But love is not marriage. We are talking about this before, madam. Sometimes love comes first and marriage second, and sometimes it is the other way around, and sometimes the two never meet at all. Either way, this is a balancing act, respected madam, and Shah Jahan knew this. He knew that love, that life, is about balance and that it is getting the balance right that counts, more than anything else. Sometimes from one angle love looks very good, sometimes from another angle, very terrible. This is natural;

this is what happens in life. We are only human. But when it came to building this beautiful monument to his wife, Shah Jahan made sure that at least this was the same from every angle, so that it was in perfect symmetry, always, to forever honor the balance of love and life. For me this is the most profound beauty of the Taj Mahal.'

His eyes were glistening with tears.

'How many times have you been here, Sanjay?'

'More than some hundreds,' he said. 'And for me I am struck by this every time I am here. So, shall we go?'

He indicated Annie should walk in front of him, and, as she got closer and closer to the arched opening, the blur of silvery white on the other side started to come into focus.

She stepped through and there it was, just as she had seen it in pictures, only a thousand times more magnificent: a glorious white-domed palace perched at the end of a long lake like a crown, small yews lining the lawn all the way, throwing their reflections into the pale green water to form a necklace at the throat of this astonishing monument.

The sun was just starting to hit the top of the large central dome, catching the two slender eastern minarets on its way through.

Annie opened her mouth to say something but the words just weren't there.

Instead, she cried.

It was so beautiful, so perfect, so unbelievably special, and she was there, in the flesh, looking at it, for real. She, Annie Jordan, boring old suburban housewife, was there at the Palace of Love, the Taj Mahal, in Agra. In India!

Despite everything else that was going on, she felt

blessed.

'I'm sorry,' she said to Sanjay, embarrassed, as the tears continued to flow. 'I'm so sorry.'

Sanjay tried to rein back his delight. 'Most respected madam, all my favorite peoples cry when they see the Taj Mahal. It is quite magnificent.'

'It is quite magnificent,' Annie agreed, wiping away tears that were instantly replaced with more, wishing she had believed Maya and brought a handkerchief. 'But why does it make people cry?'

'I think because this Shah Jahan loves this lady, Mumtaz, so much that he would spend twenty-two years building her a monument so spectacular just for her to rest in peace, madam. It is not a palace for living. It is only a reminder of that great love. And he builds it to last forever. Or one thousand years, which is like forever but shorter.' Annie started to follow him down beside the lake, the white marble of the Taj changing color with every step.

'This is the other best thing about coming at sunrise,' Sanjay said. 'When we go into the mausoleum, ma'am, you must not wear your shoes. You must wear shoe covers, like hats for your feet, but if the marble is not too hot, which right now it is not, you can wear just your feet.'

Annie slipped her sandals off and put them in her bag as they reached the stairs leading up to the parapet in front of the tomb. The marble felt delicious against the hard skin of her feet, warm and smooth. She thought of all the feet that had crossed into the entrance of this magical place in the past four hundred years and again was flooded with gratitude that two of them were hers.

They stopped just before the entrance into the mausoleum so that Sanjay could show her up close the intricate inlay work. 'Parchin kari we call it,' he said. 'This is where the colored stones are laid into the marble, like these arabesques here, and these blooms and flowers here. There would have been precious jewels here once, too. Those Persian workmen — like Mumtaz's peasant father, madam — they could do very wonderful things, and you can imagine how much time this work would take. Agra still has the best carvers in all the world.'

Up close, the marble was flecked with more grey than Annie could see from a distance. That was what no doubt gave the building such a dreamy appeal. It wasn't bright white; it was a vague, mysterious, almost-silver.

She stepped inside where the internal walls of the octagonal space were again decorated with the most beautiful inlay work: this with garnets and lapis lazuli, which glowed when Sanjay shone his torch on them.

'Can you imagine this in the moonlight?' he asked. 'Like a lantern. A beautiful, wonderful lantern.'

In the middle of the mausoleum, marble lattice screens — themselves works of art — shielded two marble caskets.

'There are two of them?' Annie asked.

'Yes, madam. Shah Jahan is here, too. But these are not the real tombs. Because for Muslims, the body is always below. But this is exactly how you would find them downstairs.'

'They're so small,' Annie said.

'Yes, madam. Peoples have got much bigger. We have McDonald's in Agra, did you see this?'

'No, and I don't want to,' Annie answered, still looking through the marble lattice at the tombs.

'Anything else you notice about them, madam?'

There was, but she couldn't put her finger on it. One was smaller, near the center, that was obviously Mumtaz, and closer to one of the screens was a bigger one, Shah Jahan.

'It's not symmetrical!'

'Most respected madam, all my favorite peoples spot that this is not symmetrical.'

She felt ridiculously pleased to be one of his favorite peoples. 'What happened?'

'Remember I tell you that Shah Jahan has fourteen childrens? One of them, a son, he kills the other sons so that he can be the king. He is bad, this one, and because Shah Jahan is not happy with him he throws Shah Jahan in the prison, across the river. Madam, this is very hard for Shah Jahan because he has only one small window and do you know what he can see out of this one small window?'

'Please don't tell me it's the Taj Mahal.'

'Most respected madam, I must tell you that it is the Taj Mahal, and Shah Jahan is in his tower for eight years looking out at it, then one day he looks for one last time through this very small window and cries "Muummmtaaaaaz", and then he is died.'

'Oh, that's so sad.'

'Yes, madam, and although this son is bad he still honours his father's wish to be buried with Mumtaz, but because he is not a good person he does not honour the symmetry of the Taj Mahal.'

'So he just threw Shah Jahan's tomb in, willy-nilly.'

'Yes, madam. Willy-nilly.'

'So what happened to this bad son?'

'He was very unpopular and his death after a long and ruinous reign was celebrated, but India was left the worser for wear.'

They had emerged back out of the palace now, onto the vast marble expanse between the two minarets that overlooked the Yamuna River.

'Do you see across the river that there is a shape between the trees?' Sanjay said. 'A large square and behind it a long stretch of flat empty land? That is where legend states that Shah Jahan planned to build the black Taj, a mirror image of this one.'

'Doesn't sound like you believe the legend.'

'Most respected madam, I do not. Scholars say Shah Jahan wanted to be buried there, but I do not believe he wanted to be separate from Mumtaz in death as he was in life.'

'No, I don't believe it either.'

Sanjay looked over the side of the parapet back across the long reflective lake in the direction of the red gate where they had first entered.

'Madam, you must come with me now. Something very good is happening.'

Annie slipped her sandals back on and followed him down the stairs to the narrow Taj-end of the lake, where Sanjay indicated that she should sit on a stone bench.

'In all my time I have never seen this seat empty,' said Sanjay. 'Most respected madam, please give me your camera for a photograph. This is where we make the famous photo just like Princess Diana. Do you remember this photo? Of Princess Diana?'

Of course she did, who would not?

The photo of a sad Princess Diana on her own in front of the Taj Mahal had captured the hearts of the entire world when it flew out on wire services in the early 'nineties and Annie's heart was no exception. At the time she had just thought it terribly sad that Diana was there alone, but now she realized that the princess would have heard the same story as she had: the tale of a besotted ruler falling madly in love with his wife and dying, crying out her name, after showing the world how much he loved her.

Princess Diana would have sat on this bench and known then that Prince Charles might have picked her out of a tricky bazaar but his heart belonged to another Mumtaz. Her heart must have been so broken. No wonder the poor woman looked bereft. No wonder the marriage ended soon after.

'Smile,' Sanjay insisted, and she tried, but with the smile came a fresh flood of tears.

Annie had been at home with newborn Daisy when that photo came out, wrapped in the cotton-wool world where her baby was bringing her the most joy she had ever experienced and her husband was crazy about the both of them.

She could remember seeing that photo of Diana and thinking how lucky she was, how loved, how safe and wanted. And now here she was sitting in the exact same spot.

'I'm sorry, Sanjay,' she said, weeping again. 'I'm so sorry.' Sanjay put down the camera and came towards her.

'It is I who am sorry,' he said, putting a hand on her shoulder.

'Please. I think you do believe in love and the Taj is making you realize this.'

'I don't know what I am realizing!' Annie said.

A blonde woman in hippy sandals and harem pants had come down the steps and around the corner and was now agitating to get on the bench so her boyfriend could take a photo, but Sanjay shooed them away.

'Take your time, most respected madam,' he said to Annie. 'Take all of your time.'

His kindness calmed her tears. She took a few moments to regain her composure, then twisted around to look at the Taj behind her in all its glory, hoping to dredge up a little of the gratitude, the blessedness, she had felt earlier. To her surprise it was lurking near the top of whatever else stewed in her, and she was able to grab on to it and keep hold.

She looked back at the reflective lake, the watery image of the monument wavering in it, just as magnificent moving and wobbly as it was in perfect straight lines.

And just like that, her own wobbly life seemed to settle and still. She was lonely, true, but unlike poor Princess Diana she was not bereft. Given how blurred and horrible her world had so recently become, she should have been. But she wasn't. Deep down where the real bits of her operated on their own, regardless of external interruptions, she just wasn't.

Her Shah Jahan did not have another Mumtaz; he had

just grown so used to the one that he had chosen that he had stopped calling out her name.

Hugh loved her. She knew that. Sitting on Princess Diana's sad bench she knew that with all her heart. She was loved. Maybe not wildly or openly, but deeply. So deeply that it wasn't always obvious, but deeply nonetheless.

She had said in her letter that being a wife was not enough, meaning that maybe Hugh was not enough, but actually if she knew he loved her, if she could feel it in this place, right now, where that famous sadness lingered, then it was enough. She didn't need a passenger to be a taxi driver. She was one regardless, just empty — but only until the passenger came back. Situations could change. Hugh could change. She could change. Everything could change.

The bumper-sticker Indians were right: love was all there was. And she had it, even if it wasn't displayed the way she wanted it to be.

In coming here, she might have been truthful and had tried to be gentle, but to be fearless was so much harder. The fearless thing to do was not to run away and leave Hugh behind: it was to face him, head on, and try to resurrect what they had — try to fix it, no matter how difficult and painful that was. Because he did love her. And she loved him. Heavenly had said you only need to be sure about one thing. This was it. They just needed to get the balance back again.

With all life's disappointments and complications stripped away in this far- flung most romantic of places, that much was obvious to her now. The one time in her life she'd been brave enough to do something dramatic and impulsive in the belief that she was truly following her heart — she'd found out her heart belonged right where she'd started.

So what if his headstone read if Annie wanted it, he approved? Why had she thought that such a terrible thing?

'Oh, Sanjay,' she said, looking up. 'I've got it all so wrong.'

But then, as in a dream, she saw it was no longer her Michael Jackson- lookalike guide standing in front of her.

It was Hugh.

Chapter Twenty-Six

At first she thought she really was dreaming.

For a start, the Hugh standing in front of her looked wild-eyed and rumpled. His shirt buttons were open at the top, dried sweat patches formed dark lakes under his arms, and he had trainers on, which he would never wear with his suit pants in real life.

'Annie!' he said, and it was Hugh's own voice, but not for long, as no sooner had he said her name than he fell to his knees in front of her, hiding his face in his hands, an awful raw, tortured sound erupting from behind his familiar fingers.

Annie had never seen her husband cry before. Even when the children were born he'd remained his usual solid, silent self. Proud, clearly, and happy, she assumed, but anything more explosive he kept locked up.

Nothing was locked up now, and his crying was unhinging her more than the general bewilderment of seeing him there in the first place. Her hopelessly buttoned-up, solid, serious Hugh, here, at the Taj Mahal, tormented and weeping, just when she couldn't have hoped for anything more than to see him?

She couldn't believe it was really happening, let alone that she deserved it. 'Hugh,' she said, in little more than a whisper.

'Please don't leave me,' he said, his hands dropping to his side, his face twisted almost beyond recognition. 'Please, please, please don't leave me.'

This is fearless, she thought. Hugh, coming here, acting

like this, when he had spent his whole life trying to be the opposite.

'I love you,' he wept, gripping her legs, forcing himself to look in her eyes, his own red-rimmed, brimming, dark with pain. 'I can't say it enough. I can't say it ever. But I love you, Annie. Please, please don't leave me.'

The woman in the harem pants had appeared again, but was now dragging her boyfriend back away from them, and Sanjay, too, had melted into the shade of a nearby tree.

I do believe in love, Annie thought. I do believe in love, and this is it. It hurt. Oh, how it hurt. And it was hard, indescribably hard. But she was so sure of it.

She took Hugh's hands and pulled him to her, his tears soaking through her thin shirt, his cheek hot on her chest, his broad shoulders shaking beneath her arms.

'I'd rather die than make you unhappy,' Hugh said, his voice breaking. 'Although that's what I've done and it makes me sick, but I don't know how to fix it, Annie. All I know is that if you leave me I'm finished.'

Who knew anything when it came to love? Other than Shah Jahan — and look at the sticky ending he came to.

Annie kissed the top of her husband's head, closing her eyes and squeezing him even tighter. They might be in the middle of something sticky but it wasn't an ending. It wasn't the leaving Hugh that had been inevitable, it was the getting it out, how she felt, how he felt. There would be no living with the status quo now. The status quo was gone. Even their marriage was being reincarnated.

India really was the most extraordinary place.

'Shhh, Hugh, darling, it's all right,' she said.

'It's not,' he said into her shoulder. 'You're the most precious thing in my life and I've hurt you by, by just being me. I can't bear it.'

She knew then, as her husband shed his stoic outer shell in the unlikely setting of the rising Uttar Pradesh sun, that they really were going to be OK.

'Hugh, honestly, please. Look at me.' She felt him steel himself, then, slowly, he sat back on his heels and looked at her, his eyes still wild, his hair all over the place.

She took his handsome, creased, worried face in her hands. 'I don't know how to say this, so I'm just going to blurt it out,' she said. 'I'm un-leaving you. I made a mistake. I was wrong.'

She watched as this sank in, felt the muscles in his face relax beneath her fingers, the tension slide out of his shoulders, the fear retreat, to be replaced by the familiar look of bewilderment in his eyes.

'I meant everything I said, in the letter,' she said. 'When I wrote it, I did. But then I came here.' She nodded at the Taj Mahal behind her. 'And it suddenly didn't seem so bad. We're in trouble, Hugh, but I think we can get out of it.'

'I haven't done it openly, but I have loved you continuously,' Hugh said. 'I have. And I'm so sorry that you couldn't tell that. I'm no good at delirious, or wild.'

Annie laughed, a lovely light laughter that bubbled up inside her from the best bits of everything they'd ever shared together. 'You turned up unannounced at the Taj Mahal and declared your undying devotion,' Annie said. 'That's pretty wild!'

'It is, isn't it?' He tried a smile. 'Maybe I'm not such a

lost cause after all.'

She leaned forward then and kissed him; a deep, long kiss, the sort she could not remember giving him in a long, long time.

'Come on,' she said, standing and pulling him to his feet. 'Let's go and sit in the shade. We need to vacate the sad Diana bench and let the other lovebirds get their shots.'

'This is the sad Diana bench?'

'You know what I'm talking about?'

'Daisy was a baby.' His voice was gluey with tears, but he kept talking. 'You were upset on her behalf and I never like to see you upset. I'm just no good at saying these things, Annie. It feels . . . '

'It feels what, Hugh?'

'It feels like being naked, you know, like . . . like in the dream where your high-school friends turn up and you've forgotten to get dressed.'

'There's nothing wrong with being vulnerable, Hugh. It's how people know who you really are.'

'But I'm a husband, Annie, a father. I'm the provider — I don't want you to see me vulnerable. I want to be strong.'

'You can't be strong all the time, Hugh. No one can.'

'I should have paid you more attention. You were right. It was a terrible way to treat you and I'm sorry.'

This is so not how I thought this day would turn out, Annie thought, as they walked hand in hand towards the trees. 'And I am sorry for saying what I had to say in a letter, instead of to your face, but I meant it when I said we seemed to have lost the art of actually speaking to each other.'

He squeezed her hand. 'Yes. I was never much good at

it, and I just got worse and worse.'

'But you're here, Hugh! You're here talking to me now. How did you even know where I was?' she asked, as they sat in the shade of a large cyprus in the middle of one of the symmetrical gardens, away from the reflective lake, from the growing crowd of other tourists.

Hugh got a handkerchief out of his pocket and wiped his face and neck. 'Heavenly Hirani,' he said.

'You spoke to Heavenly Hirani?'

'After I Googled her, yes.'

'She's Google-able?'

'Laughing Yoga is the number three thing to do in Mumbai on TripAdvisor.'

'Oh my god, you're kidding me!'

'No, she has a website and a mobile number.'

'And she told you where I was?'

'No, she told me what she tells everybody, apparently: that I shouldn't leave India without going to the Taj Mahal.'

'But what made you think I would do that, on my own, without telling anyone?'

'After reading your letter, I figured you could probably do anything.'

'It was that easy?'

'Yes, it was that easy.' He shook his head. 'And also I knew that if this Heavenly told you to go to the Taj Mahal, you would. You do that sort of thing. You went to stitch 'n' bitch because of Rhona. You went to zamba or whatever it's called because of Daisy. You tried rock-climbing because of Ben. And you came to Mumbai because of me, although I hadn't really thought that through. It's always busy when

I'm here, but on this trip the problems just got bigger and bigger and . . . '

He looked down at his hands.

'I should have tried to be more understanding,' Annie said. 'I was carrying too much baggage.'

'Annie, I do see you, I do, it's just . . . It didn't fall by the wayside, what we had. I just get . . . stuck. I have always been stuck, but in the past few years it's been worse. I can't explain it. I closed down and I didn't know how to open up again.'

'Hugh . . . '

'I thought you were having an affair,' he said. 'I thought I had lost you, here in India, to someone else.'

'What?'

'When you were leaving early in the morning, sliding off, I thought you were going to meet someone.'

'But, Hugh, I would never do anything like that!'

'And I couldn't blame you,' he said, blundering on, 'but I couldn't think what to do either: it was like grabbing sand and watching it slide through my fingers, like a nightmare.'

'Why would you even think that?'

'I found Bertie!' he said, the words exploding out of him like cannon shot. 'The day after he went missing. He'd been run over and I found him, but I couldn't tell you because I knew what he meant, that he was your favorite thing and I just didn't want to be the one to . . . ' He was weeping again.

'Oh, Hugh!'

'I'm so sorry.'

Annie wept then, too, but they were, strangely, tears of relief more than anything. Bertie's little dog soul might indeed be in an Indian chicken now, or a Princeton undergraduate, or just another wily terrier. She need not worry about where he was or what had become of him. His time had passed. It was all right. 'I understand,' she said, wiping her eyes. And she did. She would not have wanted to tell her either. She had not really wanted to know until now.

'What did you do with him?'

'I took him to that park behind the dunes at the beach where we used to go with the children and I buried him. I couldn't think what else to do. And then it got worse when you kept coming up with ways he might still be alive and the longer it went on the worse it was that I hadn't told you.'

'Oh, Hugh, I'm so sorry.'

'No. I'm sorry. It's me who—'

'Shhh,' she said. 'It's OK. It's going to be OK.'

'I wanted that little church, too,' he said. 'To get married there. I wanted the picnic and the lobster.'

But now Annie could not believe she had even dredged up that little nugget of disappointment from the past. Most of what she and Hugh had was a good thing: and it was those that mattered.

He took her in his arms then, arms that she had missed for so long, and she felt safe, and loved, and hopeful for the future, even though she was still grieving the loss of that silly old dog.

Chapter Twenty-Seven

They talked all the way back to Delhi. Driving along the beautiful freeway from Agra, it was as though a cork had been popped and he could not stop the flow of everything he wanted to say.

He said he'd known when Ben was still a toddler that he was starting to clam up more than usual, but he'd felt unable to do anything about it.

'You know you said in your email that it felt pathetic to be grown- up and lonely? The thing is, I know that feeling. I had that feeling when the children were little, and that just seemed so . . . weak. I wouldn't have wanted to tell you that even if I could have, but I still felt that way. Then I got used to feeling that way, but I stopped remembering why, so that it was just there, all the time. You three together and me slightly distant. And after we lost the baby . . . ' His eyes filled with tears. 'I didn't know what to say, Annie, so I didn't say anything. I just wanted you to feel better.'

Annie wiped away her own tears. 'We survived it, Hugh.'

'You were so brave. I wanted to tell you, to talk about it but . . . but I wanted to be strong. I'd do it so differently now, I'm sure I would.'

'Well, you've been doing something right, because our son doesn't even answer my emails and our daughter only wants me for my money.'

'I was wrong not to tell you about Ben, it was thoughtless of me; and I'm so sorry you felt ignored, because he asks about you in every email, wants to know how you're doing, if you're still so sad about Eleanor and Bertie. I should have told him to ask you. I don't know why I didn't. That's my fault. And there's no excuse.'

'And Daisy?'

'She asked me about the dress and I did tell her to ask you. But what's all this about saying you were boring? What happened? Did you two argue?'

'No, I called her and she didn't hang up her phone. She told her friends I was too boring to ever have gone to India on my own.'

'Oh god, really? I always think of you two as being thick as thieves. I'm sure she didn't mean it; she was probably just acting up in front of her friends. But it must have hurt.'

'It's true, though, Hugh. One thing I've realized after going to laughing yoga is that I don't have enough fun. I am boring.'

'You are not!'

'I am. I was. But I don't want to be anymore. I want to take Bollywood dancing lessons and learn to paint and speak French.'

'Good for you. I'll come to the French lessons if you want me to, but I think I'll sit out the dancing.'

'Do you worry about Daisy, Hugh?'

'Honestly? I suppose I do. I wasn't sure if you felt that way or not, but sometimes I think she seems to lack . . . well, not maturity, exactly. But something like it.'

'I think perhaps I have mollycoddled her too much and it's not going to do her any favors in the long run.'

'You've had your reasons,' Hugh said softly. 'We both have. They are good reasons.'

'But how long should that last? I think it's more a habit now than anything else. She's doing well enough at university and she seems healthy and happy and all but grown-up, yet we're still paying for everything.'

'We would probably help her more by slowly weaning her off the drip-feed.'

'Yes, I think you're right. We can't expect her to sort herself out overnight. But she has to make a start or she'll never be independent.'

Annie looked out the window as her heart skipped a jump; the happy kind.

'How long is it, Hugh, since we talked about the children? Since we talked about anything?'

'A long time,' he said. He reached for her hand. 'You did the right thing, with the letter, with the Taj,' he said. 'The thought of my life without you in it . . . it was so shocking to me, Annie. And I mean shocking, as in — electric. It fired me up somehow in a way I didn't know . . . Well, anyway, that's terror for you, I suppose. I will never let you feel that way about me again, I promise.'

'I'm not perfect,' Annie said. 'I know that. Your life got busy with work and you got used to pulling away, and I filled my life up with the children and got used to biting my tongue. That's how we derailed.'

'Never again,' Hugh said, squeezing her hand. 'I promise, never again.'

He barely let her hand drop all the way back to Mumbai, and when they fell back into their bed at the Taj, exhausted, he held her so tight she truly felt he would never let her go.

When she woke up the next morning, she was half convinced the whole escapade had been a dream, except that when Hugh's eyes opened they stayed on hers, and he smiled, then pulled her close.

The love was still there, and so was the desire, the desperate need for her to lose herself in his familiar scent, against his bare skin, as they moved together, as close as any two people can be, once more on the same track.

Hugh had more or less finished his work in Mumbai, he said, and wanted to spend the day with her. He now knew where the machine-that-shall-not-be-mentioned was, and he was delegating responsibility for its safe return to someone else.

He marveled at his wife as she wolfed down a stuffed dhosa and three cups of masala tea for breakfast, as Adesh fussed over her.

'They all but dust and polish me,' she told her husband. 'I love it.'

'OK, I'm all yours,' he said, after they had finished, as they sat looking out at the Arabian Sea, which was able to scrape up a sparkle this morning despite its natural murk. 'What would you like to do?'

Annie knew exactly, and had already organized it.

She was going to show her husband some of the jewels of the city she had discovered while he had been otherwise occupied.

Pinto was waiting for them outside the hotel at ten, grinning from ear to ear.

'Sir, please, sir,' he said. 'A very warm pleasure to greet you.'

Their first stop was the Mahalaxmi railway bridge to watch the dhobi wallahs beating, rinsing and drying the city's laundry and themselves.

'This is where your work shirts have been coming,' Annie said, as she pointed out a never-ending coil of brilliant blue fabric twisting around the crooked posts on one of the laundry rooftops.

'It's a miracle they ever came back white,' Hugh said. 'How do they do it?'

'Good old-fashioned elbow grease,' Annie said. 'And here's me complaining about my washing machine needing updating. I won't do that again in a hurry.'

Hugh loved the dabbawallahs even more, stopping one of the more elderly of the tiffin coordinators — the proud owner of the splendid white walrus moustache — to ask him how long he had been working outside Churchgate station.

'Since before I am remembering, sir,' he said. 'Some long time.' His job was taking tiffins from the younger men, he explained, through Pinto, who carried them from the train on their heads so he could disperse them to the other younger men who delivered them by foot or bicycle.

At the Gandhi house Annie showed Hugh the puppet room and the letter to Hitler.

She paused in front of her favorite framed relic of wisdom: Be truthful, gentle and fearless, and Hugh stopped behind her and read it over her shoulder, but she didn't tell him what it meant to her. It meant so many things after all. She'd left him on that premise, and run back into his arms on it, too.

Next Pinto took them to the Sassoon Docks to watch the fishermen who worked on the brightly colored boats that she had admired bobbing in the harbor, tied loosely now to the battered jetties.

'No photos here,' Pinto said. 'No tourist peoples.'

They didn't have to ask why. The catch of the day was more often than not poured from bins onto the bare ground and then picked over by dozens of bare hands as dogs and children wandered between the piles of slapping butterfish and pomfret.

The health authorities at home would have a conniption, thought Annie, but the docks bristled with the rainbow of people going about their jobs unsullied by hygiene regulations.

As they walked back to the taxi, stepping delicately over rivulets of water and fish innards, they passed two elderly men sitting on the deck of a shabby- looking boat threading little sea creatures onto long strings that criss-crossed the vessel from bow to stern like Christmas tinsel.

'For the dried fishes paste,' Pinto said. 'Some other peoples like this.' From the look on his face he was not one of them.

After leaving the docks, he took them through the streets of the colonial East Indian tea buildings — 'I call it Little London,' he said.

'Although I never go to Big London.'

Then they drove slowly down a single, cluttered, impoverished strip where 'the Bangladeshis' lived.

'These are the poor peoples in Mumbai,' he said. 'No papers. No investments. No nothing.'

Their homes were made out of bits of wood and cardboard and colored plastic, roped or stuck together, clinging haphazardly to the fencing behind. It was obvious that Pinto was right — these people had nothing. A toddler was going to the toilet on the side of the street as his father lay asleep next to a pile of rags beside him and his mother scratched at some rice from a pot lid.

There were animals, there was rubbish, there was a broken- down handcart, a half-burned mattress, and yet the constant movement, the clash of vibrant colors — it was brilliant and busy and bizarre.

'It feels like we should be seeing this in black and white, don't you think?' Annie asked Hugh.

'I'm not sure what it is,' said Hugh. 'I've never seen anything like it.'

'I wonder if you would ever see everything there is to see in this place,' Annie wondered. 'Pinto, what can we do about this? How can we help?'

He shrugged. 'These peoples belong in Bangladesh,' he said. 'You help by coming to Mumbai and being in my taxi. Or coming to Jammu and staying on my cousin's boat.'

He then gave Hugh the run-down on just how superior his village in Jammu was to Mumbai and everywhere else in India — in every way imaginable. It certainly sounded like paradise the way he described it: lakes, mountains, rivers, greenery, and the best ghee in all the universe.

At her behest Pinto stopped on a busy corner, and she and Hugh queued up at a street cart to buy two of Mumbai's famous masala grilled cheese sandwiches, stuffed with spiced potato, chili sauce, tomato, pepper and layers of grated mozzarella.

'Look at you,' Hugh said, wiping a bit of sauce from the corner of her mouth as she finished her last mouthful. 'I can't believe it.'

'Believe it,' she said, giving him a chili-fuelled kiss.

Before they headed back up towards the Sea Link and their hotel, Pinto took them to the Gateway of India, parking in the shade of a tree half a block away and waving them off without him.

Annie and her husband went through their separate security checks and met on the other side.

'I can't believe I've never been down here,' he said.

Annie watched as he moved through the crowd, a head taller than anyone around him, framed in the basalt curve of the Gateway, the colors of portside Mumbai swirling around him.

A turquoise scarf floated past her in the welcome breeze, fluttering from the neck of a teenager dressed in cerise. A gaggle of children ran helter-skelter behind her, shrieking with laughter.

An elderly man swathed in white walked by with two huge balloon-like collections of bright-pink fairy floss in cellophane bags as Annie smiled but waved away a plump woman thrusting a fistful of peacock feather fans at her.

She looked through the elegant arch of the Gateway to the silvery mother- of-pearl waters beyond, alive with the bright ferries and faded fishing boats that crisscrossed perilously from one side of the harbor to the other, and to Elephanta Island in the distance.

Hugh stopped, turned, saw she hadn't followed in his

footsteps and reached out his hand for her.

What Daisy said was true. India was a country she'd never hankered to see: indeed, quite the opposite, she had particularly not wanted to see it. But come here she had and in less than two weeks she'd fallen head over heels.

Of all the things Annie had expected to find in the air here, love — in all its hot, messy splendor — had come as the biggest surprise of all.

Chapter Twenty-Eight

That evening, Hugh said it was his turn to show Annie something. He wanted to take her to the Mexican restaurant in Bandra, he said, not too far away from the hotel. He knew it was odd to eat Mexican in India, but still he'd heard it had great food and good margaritas and he wanted to try it.

Annie agreed without a moment's hesitation and, to his astonishment, eschewed the forecourt taxi and instead took his hand and led him down to the sea face where the auto rickshaws were lined up like mosquitoes, honking and jiggling on the spot.

'Are you serious?' Hugh asked. Despite his repeated trips to the city he had not yet been in one himself.

But Annie was serious. She wanted to take this city in all its craziness and wring every last drop out of it before they went home. And if that meant dancing with death in the heat and dust and intensity of north Mumbai's crazy night-time traffic in nothing more than a glorified lawn mower on the way to sample Indian tequila cocktails, so be it.

They clambered in the back, and off they sped, barely missing a three- legged dog straight off the mark as a group of teenagers crossed in front of them, another rickshaw came behind them, a bus rumbled towards them and a motorbike zipped somewhere in the middle.

Annie closed her eyes, breathed in the salty, smoky air, the muggy warmth, the noise, the clutter, the mayhem, felt Hugh's hand strong and safe in hers . . . and she laughed.

She let go of the loneliness, the pain, the resentment, the fear, the past, the disappointments, the worry about the children, the future, the car accidents, and she just laughed.

Because everyone needs to laugh.

What was done was done, what was lost was lost, but there was still a lot to be found.

'This is crazy,' Hugh cried, over the honking and squeaking and shrieking. 'Completely crazy!'

'I know,' she shouted back. 'Crazy and amazing!'

In the din of a sultry Mumbai night the cries of two happy foreigners were little more than a whisper, but their laughter was still ringing in Annie's ears when the sun rose the next morning.

She let her husband sleep and slipped out for one last trip to the sands of Chowpatty Beach.

'I am please to see you happy, ma'am,' Pinto said, when she slid into the back seat of his taxi. 'I am feeling like Jack frozen in the water when you leave Mumbai before.'

'Thank you, my friend,' she said.

'I am your friend,' he agreed.

'Yes, well, on that subject,' she said, as they made their way along the esplanade by the sea face. 'I have been talking to Mr Hugh about you, Pinto, and we would like to do something for you.'

'Yes, ma'am. What is this?'

'We'd like to buy a own taxi, no strings attached, because but you have been such a good friend, and because we can manage it. I want to make a difference to someone here in India, to say how grateful I am for everything India has given me, and I think it should be you.'

Pinto kept his eyes fixed on the road ahead, reaching out to touch the head of his Ganesh hood ornament. 'Ma'am, this is very kind, but I cannot accept this,' he said. 'For sure I cannot.'

'Oh! May I ask why?'

'Ma'am, remember I tell you about the bad man who stole my taxi license money and then I save for two years and get another one?'

'Yes, of course I remember.'

'This time, I have a good friend and his father helps me with the license. I tell this man that he is like a father to me and I am like a son to him and this man he changes my life. This man and his son, my good friend, they own this taxi, they own two taxis, but then this man is sick and before he dies I promise this man that I will work with his son — we are in it together for always. His son is my boss, but he is a good boss and I make a good promise.'

'That is a very fine story, Pinto.'

'Yes.'

'You're a good friend to others, too.'

'Yes, ma'am.'

'And you're happy? You earn enough money?'

'Ma'am, I send ten thousand rupees to my father this week because of you. If I am good to the madams and the sirs and take them good places in my taxi, then this is good for me. In my village, I have already buy land and one day, in four years or five years, I will move back there and open a shop, with things for children and rice and groceries.'

'Wow, Pinto, you have a plan.'

'Yes, ma'am, I have a plan. Now I just have a space, but soon I will have some walls, then a roof, then my shop.'

He certainly knew how to surprise her. 'Well, if you're

sure you're happy, Pinto — then I'm happy, too.'

'Ma'am, if you should still like to make another persons happy, I think this hospital in Colaba where Preeti Rathi was going to be a nurse, they could like some money for another person to go there in her place. This would help you think a good thing about Mumbai.'

'I think a lot of good things about Mumbai,' Annie said. 'And that could be second on the list, but you, Pinto, are at the top of it.' He did not take his eyes off the road, but she could see him smiling.

'Thank you. No other madam ever tells me this.'

'Jack, come back,' she said.

'Jack, come back,' he replied.

They fell into a companionable silence as Annie watched the sun rise behind Mumbai's skyscrapers for the last time.

'Happy yoga,' Pinto said, reclining his seat before Annie could even get out of the car to cross the warm sand and join Heavenly Hirani.

'Ha ha ha, he he he.' The group clapped and smiled at her as she approached.

'Ha ha ha, he he he.'

She slid into her place between Shruti and Priyanka, and gave them each a nudge.

Heavenly stepped away from the center of the circle and glided, as was her way, towards her.

'Reach to the heavens,' Heavenly told the group, 'Reach to the stars and bend, bend, bend. To the left. The left. The left, Pooja. The other left.'

She came up to Annie and looked her in the eye as they bent. 'To the right, the right, the right,' she sang, never dropping her gaze. 'So, Annie, you made it to the Taj Mahal and back,' she said, as they straightened. 'Did it change you?'

'It changed everything.'

Heavenly smiled in the saintly way she had that made it seem like every good idea in the universe had possibly been hers to begin with. 'I told you it would.' She turned back to the group. 'Now everyone, come in, come in, come in. Link arms behind the person next to you. No, not like that . . . link arms behind Kamalijit. Are you trying to give her a sexy time? This is not that sort of yoga. Come in, come in, come in. Tight as you can. Come in. Now, everyone lean back as far as you can, further, further, further, lean back, close your eyes and keep leaning, no one will let you fall. Lean, lean, lean, there is safety in numbers, although Pooja, watch out — you know how Suraj can drop people. Now open your eyes and notice what you see. Really notice it.'

Annie opened her eyes and saw the vague outline of puffy clouds, building up for the pending monsoon. She saw the apartments below the hanging gardens of Malabar Hill and the Mumbai crows flying this way and that on their way to steal food out of the mouths of stupid tourists. She saw the leaning tops of city skyscrapers, the jetstream of a plane flying high above. And all the while she felt the hands and arms of Heavenly Hirani's School of Laughing Yoga linking, holding her up, helping her, and she felt beyond blessed.

When she leaned forwards and stood straight again, as bid by Heavenly, the yoga teacher was waiting for her, smiling.

'I just realized you called me Annie,' said Annie.

'This is because I finally see who you really are,' said Heavenly. 'And you are very well, wonderful and beautiful.'

After the class, Annie meandered back to the banyan tree, holding Heavenly's hand, relishing that soft warmth, sitting next to her in the shade.

'Hugh tells me you have a website,' she said.

'Yes,' Heavenly nodded. 'My son-in-law gave me a computer and set up my email and what-not years ago now.'

'You have a daughter?'

'I have a son and a daughter just like you do. He is in IT in New York and she is an art dealer in London. They have each given me two beautiful grandchildren and I now have five great- grandchildren. My family is getting very big.'

'But they live so far away — don't you miss them?'

'No, not really. I visit and they visit. And I have a business exporting Indian linens to Europe, so that, and laughing yoga six mornings a week, keep me pretty busy.'

Annie's face betrayed her astonishment.

'You thought I was a super-dooper yoga yogi?' Heavenly said. 'The sort who can put her ankles behind her ears but does not believe in material possessions?'

Annie shrugged.

'I am an ordinary woman, Annie, just like you, but older. I cannot even put my ankles behind my ears. I never could. The only secrets I know are that if you keep your body moving and you know what is in your heart, your life will be better for it. It is not rocket science.'

'Then why do so many of us find it so difficult?'

'I think for you, Annie, you needed your mother for longer than you had her. This happens to some. I had my mother till I was seventy-two, so I had all the time I needed to learn from her. Yours was taken too early. But you are wiser now, I think.'

'Thanks to you.'

'I am not a super-dooper yogi but it is not the first time I have played a surrogate mum. It is why I am here and it is probably why I do not miss my own children so much. It is not magic, Annie. It is just noticing.'

But it was magic, really.

'You say big goodbye to auntie,' Pinto said when Annie finally wrenched herself away from the shade and goodwill and cheery goodbyes beneath the banyan tree.

'Yes, Pinto. She really is quite an amazing woman.'

'And she lives in very amazing house up on Malabar Hill.'

'She does? How do you know that?'

'Sometimes I take her there in my taxi.'

'Since when?'

'Since a long time.'

'You knew her already, before I came to laughing yoga?'

'Yes, ma'am. She is another one who is kind to me, like this gardener I tell you about. After I am in the hospital for the stitches, from the insane person who is not the Beer Man, she sees me sleeping on the street one night and she is good to me. I stay in her house for some time, then I go to the guesthouse.'

'So, Valren at the Lands End hotel got you specially to take me to laughing yoga that first time?'

'This is the young boy from Goa?'

'Yes.'

'Ma'am, he tell to auntie and auntie tell to me to take you to Chowpatty. I know auntie, but I do not know about laughing yoga. I just know after not-the- Beer-Man that she is a good person. This is a problem for you?'

'Oh, no, not at all, Pinto. I just thought all these wonderful things had happened by some divine sort of mystic accident, but in fact it all makes perfect sense.'

'Perfect sense is better, ma'am.'

'It's a joy,' she agreed.

'And we like some joy.'

'We do indeed.'

What's more, Annie knew in her heart that she had much, much more of it to come.

The following day, from Pinto:

U r always be happey. God blasé u. Have a nice joriney and u r in my eyes and my heart. I allwayes pear far u. God give u long life. U happey me. Thunk u. Pinto.

The following week, from Pinto:

Hi how r. U be happey always all day I m talking about u. U always in heart thunks 1000 time u take care about me. Pinto.

The following month, from Pinto:

Hi. How r u! Its ok I don't want money, I rember u evry day. Pinto.

The following Year, from Pinto:

U r happey? U stay in my heart and mine alyws in you. Come back jack. Pinto.

Thanks

I often berate the good fairies for not visiting my computer while I'm asleep and writing my books for me, but in fact the little darlings more or less did work their magic on *Heavenly Hirani's School of Laughing Yoga*.

Like Annie, I had no intention of ever going to India, let alone writing a book set there. Indeed, a good friend of mine, after reading my novels about Irish cheese, French wine and Italian cookies said, 'I think it's fair to predict you'll never be writing a book set in the slums of India, Sarah-Kate!' Ha! Little did he know that one Easter my lovely ginger husband would get a phone call from American production designer Barry Robison asking whether he could come to Mumbai to work on a Disney film called Million Dollar Arm, starring John Hamm from Mad Men. The Ginger did not know who John Hamm was, but I most certainly did, and I told Barry — who several films previously I had stolen off the Ginger for best-friend purposes — that yes, of course he would come.

And as travel editor of *Woman's Day*, New Zealand's biggest-selling weekly magazine, it seemed churlish that I would not go with him.

Also like Annie, I had my reservations: the poverty, the smells, the beggars, the danger. But these were all blown away before I even got out of the airport, when it turned out that not getting a visa before I arrived was not my best decision ever.

The ten or so people I dealt with in sorting out this snafu were all so charming and helpful and friendly that I just knew that, whatever India smelt like, I was going to love it.

And love it I did.

I started writing *Heavenly Hirani's School of Laughing Yoga* the next day from my hotel room, Room 1802, at the Taj Lands End. I had read about laughing yoga in Fiona Caulfield's wonderful guidebook, *Love Mumbai*, and eventually found my way to Chowpatty Beach to join Kishore Kuvavala and his smiling gang of welcoming laughers for their early morning sessions.

Kishore wasn't quite the inspiration that Heavenly is (on my last day he told me I owed him a thousand rupees per visit, which somewhat wiped the smile off my face), but I could see how India makes you look for gurus. Of course, whether you find them or not is entirely up to you.

I left this amazing, mad city a month later with thirty thousand words under my belt. I didn't know whether it was going to be a novel and I didn't care. I just wanted to write about the color, the energy, the craziness, the possibility, the allure of Mumbai.

And I wanted to explore the empty-nest syndrome which was afflicting a few of the people around me at the time, and delve a little into the crisis a woman faces when she hasn't thought about life for a while because she's been too busy living it, and then, all of a sudden, she has time. Nothing but time.

Heavenly Hirani's School of Laughing Yoga is the result. It is something of a bonus book, so I hope you like it — but even if you don't, it was a joy to write, so I'm happy!

I did see John Hamm, by the way. In fact, I lay beside him at the Taj Lands End swimming pool while he talked to some film producers about the loss of Angelina's bosoms. (He talked about them very empathetically, as it happens.) I was too shy to introduce myself, as I had on a very old worn swimming suit and did not look my best, which is a warning to you all that you must keep your bathing attire in top-notch condition at all times in case a movie star hoves into view.

But mostly what I did in Mumbai were the things Annie does. I went exploring with the real Pinto, a taxi driver who spotted us mooching in Colaba one day and made sure he was there when we needed a ride back to the hotel. A lot of what Pinto says and does in the book is made up, but the rest of him is real, and if you are ever going to Mumbai, please email me and I will give you his number, because I think he is the best taxi driver in the world.

I still get a text from him every now and then when he hooks onto a free international system. I felt very lucky when I was in Mumbai to have found someone like Pinto, who was so happy to share his view of that world with me. Taxi drivers in other places can be more interested in the *sshole making a U- turn in front of them or the gum-mint, but there was no question I could ask that Pinto didn't want to answer, and his enthusiasm for India was infectious.

I had some other stellar, more official, guides during my stay as well. Suresh showed me the Mumbai transport system (which is where you have to watch out for the full-body massages) and also took me on the tour of Dharavi slum (www.realitytoursandtravel.com).

If you are interested in how this incredible mini-world operates, Kevin McCloud of *Grand Designs* fame made a two-part documentary about it. It has to be seen to be believed.

And then there is the Taj Mahal. Despite never wanting to go to India, the Taj Mahal was on my bucket list, so I'm not sure how that was going to work. But even though Mumbai is on the west coast, and Agra — where the Taj is — isn't, I vowed to make my way there. As it happened, some of *Million Dollar Arm* was filming nearby, so I made my way separately but met up with the

Ginger at sunrise, before he went to work, so we could visit this iconic monument together.

Here I have to thank the real Sanjay, who really did have the same flair for drama as Annie's Taj guide in the book. I was so keyed up about this giant marble love-letter to a lost wife that I burst into tears the moment I saw it and didn't stop.

It is more beautiful in real life than in the pictures — and beyond romantic. I still cry when I think about it, because I don't truly think I ever expected to get there, and I am just so enormously blessed that I did.

Back in Mumbai, I did not have a pedicure, but instead enjoyed a wonderful lunch with Nikhila Palat, the Taj Palace Hotel's director of PR, who gave me even more insight into the Mumbaikar way of life.

And back across the Sea Link in Room 1802 at the Taj Lands End, I must thank Ashok, our housekeeper, who every morning came in and tidied up my desk, while I worked at it. I loved that man, even more so when he knocked on my door one afternoon and, having seen a card the Ginger had made out of a photo of the two of us for my birthday, produced a frame, put the photo in, placed it carefully on the desk, smiled, and departed.

Not everybody has my kind of experience in India, but I'm not everybody, I'm just me; and this book is my love-letter to a place on the planet and a space in time that put a smile on my face and a warmth in my heart that will never go away.

Until we meet again, I remain... Yours
Sarah-Kate

About the Author

Sarah-Kate Lynch lives in New Zealand and is one of the country's most successful novelists and a much-loved magazine columnist. Reading 'Date with Sarah-Kate' in NZ WOMAN'S DAY is like catching up with her every week for a coffee — something it can be hard to do in real life*, given that she's also the magazine's travel editor. This means she's often abandoning the dog and her husband, film production designer Mark Robins, and fleeing solo to foreign parts. In the case of *Heavenly Hirani's School of Laughing Yoga*, however, it was Mark who did the fleeing — although Sarah-Kate refused to be abandoned, so she went too. The dog was not so lucky. Follow Sarah-Kate on Facebook, Twitter and Instagram, or visit her website: sarah-katelynch.com.

* It's particularly hard if you're not in New Zealand!

Also by Sarah-Kate Lynch

FINDING TOM CONNOR

A jilted bride escapes New Zealand and follows a wild-goose chase to the twisted Irish town of Ballymahoe, where what's she's looking for and what she finds turn out to be two very different prospects.

BLESSED ARE/THE CHEESEMAKERS

Two ageing Irish cheese-makers try to matchmake a new generation of dairy producers, to continue their magical farm where cows are milked to The Sound of Music by pregnant unmarried vegetarians.

BY BREAD ALONE

A heartbroken baker living in a fairy-tale tower on the English coast hankers after the one she left behind — a saucy boulanger with whom she rolled in the flour in happier times.

EATING WITH THE ANGELS

A New York food critic finds a spanner in her works when she wakes up without a sense of taste and has to rediscover all the delicious things in life from scratch.

HOUSE OF DAUGHTERS

Three estranged sisters inherit a crumbling Champagne house, and have to bottle their differences to protect the precious family elixir for future generations.

ON TOP OF EVERYTHING
A distracted wife believes bad things usually happen in threes until she gets six of them in a row — but it's written in the tea leaves that good things can come in clusters as well.

DOLCI DI LOVE
A workaholic Manhattanite discovers her husband has a secret family in Tuscany and goes to find them, but instead gets caught up in a web of interfering widowed Italian matchmakers.

THE WEDDING BEES
A mysterious southerner arrives in New York with nothing but a hive of bees and an insistence on good manners, and sets about improving the lives of everyone in her orbit.

SCREW YOU DOLORES
Sarah-Kate's Wicked Approach to Happiness is about knowing when to do what someone tells you and when to stick it up their jacksie. It's also about shoe-shopping in Paris, friendship, dogs and milestones.